TO TELL YOUR LOVE

MARY STOLZ

Cover by James Woodend
Illustrated by Artur Marokvia

SBS SCHOLASTIC BOOK SERVICES
New York • London • Richmond Hill, Ontario

TO MY MOTHER

CHAPTER ONE

At six o'clock on a summer morning, the milkman halted his truck before the Armacost house on Fannell Street. He shoved three bottles of milk, one half pint of cream, one dozen eggs into his wire basket and walked to the side door. The bottles rattled glassily, their wet sides already softening the cardboard of the egg carton as he put them on the porch. Then he climbed back in the truck and drove it along down the street.

The Armacost house looked very like any other house on the milkman's route. It sat back the proper distance from the street, its two small pages of lawn correctly clipped, its six rooms and bath modestly contained.

Within, the morning light, now well advanced, fell on rooms serenely clean. The furniture was old: old cherry wood, smooth and lustrous. The chintz was crisp, but not new either. "Thank heaven," Mrs. Armacost would say, "for slip covers." She had two sets, to hide the weathered chairs and couch forever—cheaper than new furniture. "Anyway, the old things are fine. Better than we'd get nowadays," Mrs. Armacost occasionally assured her family. "Okay, Mom, nobody minds," her son Johnny would reply absently, not particularly concerned with furniture so long as there was something to sit on, but always with an answer for his mother.

In the early stillness, the tick-tock of the grandfather clock throbbed in every corner of the house. With the ascendancy of age and grace it waved away the voice of the red electric clock that hummed to itself on the kitchen wall.

The great striped cat in the living room rose and

1

hooped her back, spread her claws, settled again, paws tucked in. Her eyes fixed on the stairs as she awaited the descent of a breakfast-giver.

When Theo wakened, she lay a while, eying her sister Anne asleep in the other bed. Flat on her stomach, one arm hanging over the edge of the bed, Anne's fingers curled lightly, almost touching the floor. The tangle of her thick brown hair sprayed over the pillow, and the soundless breath came and went through her delicate, highly enviable nose.

Theo's contemplating eyes were vaguely troubled. Oh dear, she thought, how very little use we are to each other: Anne, so lately frothy and lighthearted, now so sad, so anxious not to show it.

She pushed her own pumpkin-colored, bristly hair, sighed, and looked at the clock. Six-ten. Well, get up now or bolt another breakfast. Your choice. But still she lay, eyes circling the room, enjoying again the new wallpaper, spriggy green leaves with small flowers on a white background. Fondly she contemplated the big hooked rug, rose and yellow, with a trace of gray. Eyes closed, she listened to the trees murmuring:

> When I see birches bend to left and right
> Across the lines of straighter darker trees
> I like to think some boy's been swinging them. . . .

Great oaks, so moving in their massiveness, radiant dappled birches, wide languid willows. The trees, restless scatterbrains, rock-rooted. Theo listened to the warm wind in the talking leaves.

Cautiously she took a book from the night table. Reading before breakfast, she thought, riffling pages, is a pernicious habit. Worse than smoking. However . . .

   . . . climb black branches up a snow-white trunk
Toward heaven, till the tree could bear no more,
But dipped its top and set me down again.
That would be good both going and coming back.
One could do worse than be a swinger of birches.

She closed the book thoughtfully. Robert Frost is forever writing of trees, she mused. That's understandable. I wonder why more of them don't.

Abruptly, she threw back the sheet, pulled on a cherry-colored robe that shrieked at the nearness of her red hair, and padded off to the bathroom.

When she came from the shower, the odor of coffee spiced the air. Mother gets up so early, Theo thought, impatiently beating at her head with the hairbrush. She dressed quickly, stopping as she drew on a stocking to crook her leg in the graceful pose Anne assumed at this task. It simply doesn't work, Theo realized. The angle is the same, but the effect is wrong. Anne, with her sort of stagy attitudes, looks so dreamy, quite unconscious of the tilted chin, the rapt expression. I seem to be looking over my shoulder to see who's watching. She dragged on the other stocking, took a fresh uniform from the closet, her nurse's cap from the drawer. At the door, she turned. Anne, cautiously opening an eye, encountered the full gaze of her sister.

"You look like a snowman," Anne murmured, reshutting the eye, then with an easy motion rolled to her back, clasping her hands under the mass of sepia hair. "When are you through with this early day stint?"

"Tomorrow. I have to run." Theo closed the door, reopened it immediately. "Go to sleep," she commanded, and left.

Mrs. Armacost was squeezing oranges in her kitchen. The garden was always Dad's, the kitchen, Mrs. Armacost's. Johnny said the bathroom was Anne's, only by courtesy available to the rest of them. And Anne, frequently relaxing in a warm tub redolent of some spicy oil, or foaming airily with bottled bubbles, more or less agreed. People who take showers, she would think, wriggling her pink-enameled toes through the froth, have no respect for ritual. Anne's bathing ritual occupied a dreamy hour of every day, when, with Hebe-like curls, terry robe, and raspberry scuffs, she disappeared into "her" bathroom, there to stand, one finger tapping the famous nose, in pleasant uncertainty before her shelf of colored bottles. Then Anne in the tub would think of Cleopatra, and murmur softly, sighing, "Oh, Serpent of the Nile." Not the remotest chance that anyone would ever call her this, although Johnny, exasperated over some trifle, was very apt to call her a snake in the grass.

The trouble, Anne saw clearly, was that no one exaggerated in the grand manner any more. "Understatements all around us," she admitted sadly. She considered her father, a teacher of English at the high school. Her father was steeped in the magnificent syntax of the past, but his everyday speech was rather devoid of flavor. Deliberately, Anne was convinced. At her own efforts to heighten the value of conversation, he was apt to wince.

"How in the world," she once said to him, "your love of the great works of literature has ever been transmuted to us, I cannot fathom."

" 'mitted," her father replied.

"What?"

"Transmitted, not 'muted."

Anne, looking up "transmuted" in the dictionary, giggled. You could hardly call father base metal and the rest of them gold. Because, though Theo knew poetry, Johnny kept a journal (secret), and Anne languished over nineteenth-century novels, it had to be admitted that father knew a good deal more than all of them together.

"Still, it's a pity it doesn't show," Anne concluded.

4

"What doesn't?" her father inquired from behind the sports page.

"Your vast store of knowledge. I mean . . ."

"It does. But modestly, modestly."

Theo entered the kitchen. It wavered in sunlight, gleaming refrigerator towering like an iceberg, waxed red linoleum reflected in the red of the curtains, the rim of the wall clock.

"Good morning, darling," her mother said, handing her a glass of orange juice.

"Morning, Mom." Theo wandered to the window, walked to the stove where an egg was simmering. "I guess there's no point in repeating that I could get my own breakfast."

"None," her mother agreed cheerfully. "I like it early in the morning." She scooped out the egg.

Theo sat at the white-topped table, eying the toaster suspiciously. With commendable promptness, it rang a small bell, bobbed up a piece of toast. "What's the matter with this thing?" Theo wondered aloud. "It hasn't burnt a piece of toast in four days. Don't tell me Johnny actually fixed it."

Mrs. Armacost hesitated. "Well, he did something with it. And then I took it downtown and had Mr. Powers tinker a bit more."

"I don't think that's such a good idea. Now Johnny will think he's an engineer, and heaven knows what he'll decide to fix next."

Mrs. Armacost sat down with a cup of coffee. "I rather think John's in on my secret. Tacitly." She added firmly, "It's a matter of face-saving. Johnny's ambitions must be faced patiently. And with dignity."

Theo nodded. "And with frequency." Looking at the clock, she grimaced and dove at her breakfast. Then, minutes later, ran for the bus, a light coat pulled over the uniform, her cap carefully carried in a paper bag.

Johnny, slowly struggling toward wakefulness, lost his expression of tension. Carefully his daytime mask of poise edged into place, settling more firmly as he blinked his eyes, blew a breath toward the ceiling, and finally admitted that morning was here and he awake to face it. He sat up, scratched the fuzz on his head, tossed an arm around to scratch his back, conscious of a hot summer day when it would be fine to swim, but who can face the day with little between it and him but bones?

He bounded to the floor, his fourteen years all knobbly bones and slender muscles slung in blue pajamas, glanced at the door securely closed, began his exercises, furtively at first, as though concealing it from himself, then with increased pleasure. Sort of fun, he conceded, lunging toward the floor, arching into the air. He sat down to row a boat, his movements flowing in and out of each other like the water he pretended to skim. Anne had once mentioned that Johnny was very graceful. His response had been anything but gracious.

"Oh, for Pete's sake," he bellowed, stalking from the room.

Anne blinked after him. "Now what in the world is his trouble?"

"At this stage, I don't think Johnny relishes a quality like grace," Mr. Armacost suggested.

"Why not?"

Pinching his ear lobe reflectively, her father answered, "He's interested in more—hm—manly attributes. That's quite natural. He'll have grace when he gets around to it. At the moment, he'd probably rather be so muscle-bound that he couldn't pick up a book without hitting himself in the jaw."

6

Anne choked, causing her father to add, "I trust your kindness would keep you from . . ."

"Oh, of course I'd never say anything to him," Anne protested. "I was laughing at you, not him."

Mr. Armacost nodded, reassured.

When the boat-rowing was finished, Johnny coiled back on his shoulders and, with an easy lift of his legs, bicycled in the air. Pumping with piston precision, he scowled resentfully at his legs—bare, brown, thin as nutshells. With painful deliberation, he watched his knees advancing and receding. "Radiator caps," he gloomed, transferring his gaze to the ceiling. He thought perhaps he'd go out for baseball next year. With a baseball uniform, you could wear about six pairs of socks, maybe. Oh, what the heck . . .

He dressed hurriedly, started out, turned back to his closet. From the top shelf, under a mess of yearbooks, comic books, textbooks, he took the Journal, a green ledger. He opened it quickly to a fresh page. Writing the date, he scribbled angrily:

"It is now two weeks since I sent for that course. I've practically cemented myself to the mailman, who thinks I'm crazy. Anne makes dopey remarks about being in love, which is just like her. Or at least," he wrote more slowly, "she *was* making them which *was* just like her. Pretty soon, if they don't send it by at least the end of the month, I'm going to write and tell them I'll figure out some other way. By tonight I'll know whether I went swimming today."

He closed the book, craftily stowed it away in the heap of camouflage, ran downstairs.

"Hi, Mom," he yowled, bursting into the kitchen. He lifted his head, sniffed voluptuously, and smiled. "Muffins!" Sighing hugely, he dropped to a chair at the table, where he sat beaming impartially at the oven and his mother.

7

Mrs. Armacost handed him his orange juice, rubbed the palm of her hand lightly on the round brush of his head, admitted that the muffins were laced with dates and nuts (but did not confess that they'd been made from Muffo-Mix).

July, the tiger cat, rubbed lingeringly against his leg, leaped to his lap, and thrust her blunt face into his. Her dynamo purr roared ecstatically as his fingers massaged her ears.

"Johnny. Now really, Johnny. Put that cat away from the table." Mrs. Armacost frowned at them.

"Ah, she's got to say good morning. Okay. Down she goes," he added quickly. Deposited on the floor, July glanced up in brief despair, drifted away.

"How's the toaster going? Poor Theo didn't get any muffins, did she? Where's Dad?" Johnny dropped two eggs in a skillet, sprinkled them lavishly with salt and pepper, opened the oven door a crack, and announced, "They're done."

Mrs. Armacost ignored most of this, but as she pulled the muffin tins out, murmured, "The toaster's going fine, just fine, Johnny."

Her son glanced at her sideways. His mouth quivered in a smile as he turned his attention back to the eggs. "All I asked was how is it going," he said. "Honest, Mom, just curious."

"Well, now you know." His mother laughed as their eyes met.

"Seriously, Mom," Johnny argued, "being an engineer is a pretty good profession. I think I'd better give it some thought."

"I think so too, John," his mother agreed. "It's only . . ."

"Only what?"

"That you think of so many things to be, darling. You hardly have time to examine one before you're off to another."

Johnny waved a reassuring hand. "Got a lot of ground to cover. I'm going to settle down next year."

Mrs. Armacost's eyes widened. "Settle down?"

"Yup. To my career, you know. I'll be a sophomore this fall, and I'd like to have things lined up by then." He peered out the window. "Dad in the garden?"

"Yes," his mother replied rather weakly.

"Think I'll get him. He'll want some of these muffins." Johnny strode to the kitchen door and out.

Now, at a little after seven o'clock, the garden gleamed in spatters of dew. To the right, at the side of the garage, a little vegetable garden lay in trim array. Great crimson tomatoes, streaked with gold, hung heavily on the vines, leaning their heads toward crawling vines on which cucumbers, like little crocodiles, clung fiercely. A stand of corn spiked up greenly with hugging tasseled ears. Pea plants blossomed palely, and a patch of pole beans mounted firmly, as though to bear Jack to the Giant. Johnny liked his father's gardens, the vegetable and the flower.

The flower garden was bigger. Flamboyantly it sprawled away from the house to a row of cherry and apple trees more than a hundred feet back. Water-crystaled roses, red and white, budded in reckless confusion. Closer to the ground, poppies, sweet peas, petunias thrust their rainbow cups and tangles through the wet earth to open on the sunny air. The vivid, the pastel, the ivory petals, mauve-veined, smudged with yellow pollen, curved round the delirious honeybees.

Johnny sniffed at the volatile incensed air with the same respect he'd given the muffins. Then, spying his father, Johnny turned his head a little, smiling.

Mr. Armacost crouched among his blossoms, absolutely motionless, with a poppy in his hand. He was trying to lure a hummingbird. Ever since Johnny could remember, his father had loved hummingbirds. Whenever one of the little shiny things streaked into sight, Mr. Armacost would seize the nearest flower, then sit incredibly still, trying to look like a trellis, waiting for the bird to take a sip from his flower.

Johnny remained on the steps, fearful of disturbing the delicate balance between his father and nature's shyest, fleetest creature. Presently, Mr. Armacost rose, dusting earth from his knees. He carried the flaming poppy carefully as he came to the house.

"Morning, John," he smiled.

"Muffins, Dad. Come on in. No luck with the humming-bird?"

"No. Not today." Mr. Armacost took a slim bud vase from the kitchen cabinet and arranged his poppy. Then he placed it on the white-topped table. "There. Well, it all looks awfully good," he approved, sitting down and selecting a muffin.

As always, at the mention of her baking, Mrs. Armacost's eyes dropped with an appearance of demure pleasure that masked her nervous knowledge of a larder stocked with Kwickie-Kakes, Kwickie-Kookies, Muffo-Mix, and Fasto-Krust—a larder secretly resorted to, never referred to, but often considered in apprehensive silence. What had started as an experiment now practically amounted to fraud. But the moment of confession seemed to recede with every new package of ready-mixed dainties, the praise was as sweet as if she'd deserved it, and the deception went on.

"What are you planning for today, Johnny?" she asked, to reroute the discussion.

Johnny paused. "Oh, nothing much. Cooper Maloney is coming over, then we'll decide." He grabbed another muffin and hoped no one would mention swimming.

CHAPTER TWO

WHEN THEO closed the door the second time, Anne lay motionless, for Theo might think of something further. But the light footsteps ran downstairs. When they were out of sound, Anne allowed her face the luxury of crumpling before the misery that pressed within her. She tried, during the day, never to let her family know that any Anne existed save the one who, as they said, "Would never die of a broken heart."

Well, no doubt she wouldn't die—or not for love. But in her innocence of heartache, she felt surprise that it actually did ache, that it felt swollen, bruised. She was aware of it all the time, beating painfully, pitifully rebellious that it must bear the entire burden of Doug's desertion. It *was* desertion, wasn't it? Nearly a week since they'd last been out together, since he'd called, since the sound of his old car rolling up the gravel drive had caused her heart to race eagerly while she went through the motions of indifference or surprise.

Her mind unhelpfully protested, "But he *couldn't*, he simply can't. What of all the things he said? What of the dancing, the drifting over the lake? What of all the *things* he said?" But the sad heart flopped and questioned wearily, "Well, where? Why not? He's here in town. There are telephones, you know. The telephone rings many times, but is it ever Doug lounging at the other end? Ever Doug saying, as he used to say, 'Come along, lamb chop, climb out of the dictionary and let's go dancing.'" Anne squeezed her eyes shut. I do not think I can stand this.

Anne had known Doug for a long time, but it was in the past December, during the Christmas holidays, that he had first noticed her. She was a senior in high school, Doug a freshman in college. She hadn't seen him for months.

On a snowy morning just after Christmas, she and her mother were in the kitchen having breakfast. As her mother turned from the stove with a pot of coffee, Anne had laughed aloud, with the sheer pleasure of morning, of the compact, bouncy freshness of Mrs. Armacost.

"Mom?"

"Anne, my love?"

"I sometimes wonder how . . . I mean, sometimes I think . . . that I'm going to explode. Not for any reason . . . just because everything . . . it's all so absolutely marvelous, don't you think? Truly, don't you?" Anne, the voluble, forever tried to put in words the wordless, mysterious emotions that tossed her this way and that.

Her mother smiled. "I can remember. . . . Well, yes, this morning I do, anyway."

Anne was satisfied. She ate enormously, then tilted back in her chair, piling her long hair to the top of her head with narrow fingers. "I think I'll go for a walk."

Mrs. Armacost glanced at the window. Thick snowflakes swirled behind the pane, drifting straight down, then twisting back up again, rolling around. A snowball, thrown by Johnny, who was shoveling the walk, hit the glass. It clung, all spattered, then slid down slowly.

"That would be fun, to walk in the snow."

"You come along," Anne invited.

Mrs. Armacost shook her head. "Snow may be the prettiest nuisance there is," she said, "but a nuisance, nevertheless."

Anne stood up, stretching her arms high in the air, spreading her fingers. "Not to me it isn't." She went up to change. Old black ski pants, big woolly red sweater, a

12

helmet of red wool over her hair. A Joan of Arc clad in woolen mail, she clattered downstairs in her scuffed ski shoes.

"'By, Mom," she called, and shot out to the snowy morning, expecting . . . what? Not anything. But eager for it, ready for it.

Johnny's arms scooped and lifted easily, tossing the powdery snow aside. Behind him, the huge flakes idled down, whitening the gray walk as his shovel left it. Up and down the street familiar houses took on a strange, lacy beauty as the snow drifted gently up clapboard sides, traced the curves of porch façades, piled soft caps atop the mailboxes. Anne leaned against the white air, lifting her face. For what? For the little melting drops that sprayed on her lashes and outstretched tongue?

She walked around to the front, crunching snow Johnny hadn't reached. The little blue spruce on the lawn was mountained whitely, its branches drooped, and the slim dark needles showed only on the under sides. Anne stepped into the deep drifts and reached her mittened hand over to shake the small tree free of its burden. The branches sprang up gratefully, showering drifts as they tossed into position.

"Be kind to trees week?" someone said close to her.

Anne turned, and sighed.

Here was what she'd been waiting for. Not something —someone. Here, as so often in the daydreams, Douglas Eamons was talking to her. Doug . . . in college now, emptying the vast high school when he left, leaving the crowded corridors, the wide classrooms empty, taking the flicker of promise from lunch hours, when she might see him, stripping the crisp, vivid pageant of football to nothing but bands, color, battle, and hundreds of people . . . to nothing, without Douglas Eamons tossing his body in the cold autumn air to snare a flying football on the wing. Douglas Eamons . . . standing right in front of her, shaping his words for her answer, snow nestling on his yellow hair, his amazing shoulders.

"Oh, I do that for my sister," she answered carelessly. "She's a dryad."

"What's a dryad?"

"Someone who lives in a tree."

"She must get pretty cold these nights."

Anne laughed, but she couldn't answer. She couldn't talk about Theo. Who was Theo? Who was anyone, when everyone stood right here with her, laughing in the snow?

"You weren't by any chance going for a walk," Doug inquired hopefully.

"I was. That's why I came out."

"That's marvelous. I couldn't find anyone who wanted to." They took a few steps, side by side, then grinned, walking faster, filling their lungs with bright air. "What's the matter with everyone any more, won't walk in the snow!" Doug scooped a handful of snow, rolling and packing it carefully.

"I know, isn't it terrible? I'm the only one I know who does," Anne responded, with the barest silent apology to Theo, who worked in the hospital and walked in the snow when she could.

Doug studied his snowball. Then, leaning back on his right leg, he lifted the left high in the air, brought his right arm back, curved forward in a long pitch. The snowball hit a tree. Anne smiled up at him with candid delight, looked quickly away. She was a girl well used to charming and captivating boys. But this time, she told herself, I must be very careful. This time it's very, very important.

They went a long way, saying little, rolling snowballs till pellets of ice clung to their mittens. Doug walked swingingly, kicking fountains of snow before him. Anne raced along beside, sometimes falling back, then running to catch up. The air felt cold now. It splintered icily on

14

her cheeks. But she'd have walked across the steppes of Asia rather than mention it.

I'm glad I'm me, she thought. I'm glad I'm my age, walking where I am. I'm glad, and I can't believe it. I can look at him, and there he is. Talk to him, and he'll answer. Glad, glad . . .

Doug glanced down at her. "Are you always this frisky?"

"Oh, no. Not always. It's . . . the snow. I get this way in the snow."

"Well, whatever it is, it's nice."

Anne didn't answer. She wished she could ask him to say it again. But he *had* said it. She repeated the words in her mind. Doug took her hand lightly, swung it a moment, let it go.

Am I so much in love, she wondered. For three years she'd watched and dreamed of and thought of Douglas Eamons. No matter whom she was with, she remembered Doug. But this much? Her heart cried, "I love him," and she listened. Her mind, tugging at her sleeve, said, "Here, take it easy!" and she wondered. . . .

They reached the limits of town, the end of Park Street. No snow falling now. A pale winter sun wheeled like a lemon in the high noon sky. The fields, stretching away to low-mounded hills, were untrodden, save for the flying tracks of a rabbit; unbroken, except for gaunt berry bushes that thrust skinnily, blackly, upward. They stood listening to the wind roaring through the high stripped branches of the trees.

"This is beautiful," Doug said softly. Anne nodded, not speaking. With Doug, words shied away from her. Because she might say the wrong thing? Because her whole being was absorbed with the wonder of walking beside him?

At the end of Park Street stood the Wellman place, derelict last house of town. Massively enclosed by grounds, ringed round with ancient regal trees, it stood aloof. The nearest dwelling was a full quarter-mile away.

Anne and Doug stopped in the road.

"I guess we better go back," the boy said.

"All right."

But they didn't move. They gazed, a little sadly, at the tottering structure across the road, at all its cupolas, juttings, unreasonable small windows. On the roof a Captain's Walk tilted brokenly away from the Widow's Watch. No glass remained in the many windows, sightless sockets with here and there a rag of curtain shredding down. This hulk, once a pearl, had submitted without grace to the affronts of time and neglect. Through the chemistry of changing styles, its elegance became ugliness. This was the town's haunted house, awesome treasure of small boys, who dared each other to race through its dark, decaying rooms.

"Ever been in it?" Doug asked.

"Once, in my salad days."

"In your what?" he laughed.

"When I was young."

"Want to go in now?" he asked suddenly, then seemed surprised at the words.

Anne hesitated. It was cold and a long way home. But time spent with Doug was not to be taken, or rejected, lightly. And there was the lure of the house itself, the mighty fallen, the dark echo of years.

They walked slowly toward it. A low iron fence, its gate fallen flat and clasped by frozen ivy, ran round the grounds, rustily enclosing a great garden of tangled grass, twisted trees, and, here and there, a broken stone statue. One giant oak towered to the height of the house, spreading its snow-rimmed branches toward the roof.

"What a pretty tree that is, in the summer," Anne recalled.

Doug glanced up at its imperial tallness. His eyes

16

strayed to the porch. "We'd better not go in that way," he decided. "A leaf would send it tumbling to the ground." They walked through the deep snow toward the back of the house where, in its shadow, the snow sloped away in weird mounds and planes. A cellar door, long since pried open, slanted up from the ground. The lock, broken and turned back, had rusted into the wood, and clung imbedded when Doug threw back one panel of the door.

Staring into the black pit of the cellar, they felt the clammy atmosphere rise up when the door was opened. Doug glanced at her doubtfully, then tested the stairway with his foot. "Seems okay. I'll go down first." Anne shivered, following. They waited a moment, adjusting their eyes to the darkness. A pole of pallid sunlight from the open door fell on the huge old furnace, picking in detail at its fuzzy blanket of packed dust. The cellar was divided into many small rooms, but Anne looked where she knew the stairs would be and walked to them.

Above, the icy stillness of the air was even more penetrating. Gloom sifted through the lofty rooms, and the unstirred dust lay thickly over the floors.

"No little boys been haunt-hunting lately," Doug suggested.

"At this time of year? They'd be crazy."

Doug studied her with amusement. "And we?" he asked.

Anne considered that they were crazy too. But, she added to herself, there's a method in *my* madness. She brightened, thinking perhaps there was in Doug's too. In a curious manner the old Wellman place, scene of so many children's fascinated brushes with the supernatural, seemed to fix a mutual past for them so that their shyness fell away, and they glanced at each other sidelong, remembering together the delicious terrors of the past.

Two rooms, leading off the wide hallway, were identical, each with slim high windows facing the porch, each

17

with a marble fireplace and mantel, the marble cracked with dirt-clogged fissures. In the room on the right, a pair of broken brass andirons leaned drunkenly from the hearth.

The room, an enormous rectangle, stretched to the back of the house. Once-rich raspberry wallpaper, printed with deep red harps, peeled away from the crumbling plaster where cobwebs swung heavily, laden with insects trapped and wrapped in the meshes. As they moved back to the hall dust swirled over the random board floors.

"It must have been quite a place in its day," Doug said, shivering.

"Yes," she answered slowly. "It must have had . . . style."

In the cavernous hall, their words of tribute seemed to rise up the stairwell, seemed to take on shape, as though they would endure, little frosty forms, clinging to the high walls.

"Let's get out of here," Doug said abruptly.

They walked back toward town quickly, running sometimes, filling their lungs gratefully with the clear air. So, in a little while, the intolerable sense of the vulnerable past left them. The Wellman place was a child's bogey, easily forgotten.

"Do you like college?" Anne asked.

"Oh, sure."

"We certainly missed you last football season."

Doug, taking this as his due, frowned thoughtfully over something else. "You were there all the time, weren't you?" he said at last.

"Where?" Knowing perfectly well where.

"Over at the high school."

"Oh, yes, I was there," she answered demurely.

"I can't understand it."

"What?" Knowing perfectly well what.

"What I was looking at all the time. Why didn't you trip me up or something?"

"You were too busy looking at Dody Colman. Besides," in an offhand manner, "I wasn't wasting my time."

Doug scowled. They walked along in silence for a while.

Then, "This your last year?" he demanded.

"Mmm. I'm going to college in the fall."

"Anywhere near me?"

"Well, yes. It's a girl's school. It's quite near yours."

He nodded. Anne smiled to herself at his silence. Oh, there was plenty of time—to be tantalized, to be sure, to wonder. To drift apart, so as to hurry back. Only this time she knew it was important. The fulfilled promised of the morning welled deliriously within her. "I love him," cried her heart. Her mind made no answer.

". . . miss him, you know," Doug seemed to be saying.

"Miss who? I'm sorry . . ."

"Sam Chapin. He was supposed to go up with me, and then all this getting married business, so he had to cut over to City College. Can't even play football." Doug shook his head gloomily.

"But, my goodness," Anne protested. "I'm sure he'd rather have Nora than play football. After all, he asked her."

"Still, it's tough," Doug assented in a flat voice.

"His wife is a friend of mine. Nora."

"Doesn't it sound funny . . . his *wife?*" Doug, indeed, said the word in a way that made it sound appalling. Anne didn't think it funny . . . rather breathtaking and very touching. But she'd hardly reached a point with Doug where it would be wise to argue, or make any difference in his opinion. She was on the verge of mentioning that Sam and Nora were now the parents of a son, but refrained. After all, if Sam hadn't told him, she saw no reason for her to be the bearer of what he would obviously consider calamitous news. Sam and Nora, nineteen and eighteen, with a son. And with three more years of Sam's school confronting them. She sighed deeply. It was a little young, and yet . . .

At her house, Doug said he couldn't come in for hot chocolate. "I have to get along home now," he explained. He looked down at her, a prolonged, intent gaze. "I . . . you look pretty in that red hood." He started off, turned back. "I'll . . . call you, Anne. All right?"

"All right," said Anne, thinking how little words say or mean. Just "all right," while within her a voice cried, "Come back to me, Doug. . . . Don't forget."

Somehow the rest of the day passed. Anne baked a cake that might have been good, if she'd remembered the salt. She wandered around the house with a duster clutched in her hand.

"What are you going to do with that duster?" Johnny asked, meeting her in the hall.

"What?" Anne stared at her hand. "Here, you take it."

"I don't want it," Johnny protested.

"You don't? Oh well, in that case . . ." She drifted off. Johnny stared after her suspiciously.

She sat through dinner, eating everything with dreamy absorption. Her father studied her closely. "Anne," he said finally, "is there anything wrong with you?"

"Why, no. What could possibly be wrong?" Mr. Armacost shook his head. Mrs. Armacost gazed at the tablecloth and thought, Well, well . . . the imperturbable Anne. . . .

After dinner Anne announced that she planned to take a bath and go to bed. "That long walk in the snow," she explained. "It must have tired me."

"It unhinged you, if you ask me," Johnny snorted.

Anne smiled at him affectionately. Stung to further protest, Johnny snapped, "You might leave a cupful of hot water tonight, in case anyone wants to wash their hands."

"Of course, darling. I shall be most frugal," she assured him. Johnny bowed to a superior tactic and fell silent.

In the tub, drifting in fragrant waves of Quelques Fleurs, Anne went once again for her walk in the snow. Lingering here, there, repeating the beautiful words, moving through and around the unspoken words. Looking back. Drifting ahead . . . to what? She closed her eyes and sighed. To something mysterious, wonderful, and, as they say, inevitable. Douglas Eamons, after all these years.

She wondered, will he call tomorrow? Tomorrow, she thought, I have a date with Peter Crosland. If Doug calls, should I break it? No, that's out. Unethical and unwise. But will he call tomorrow?

Quelques Fleurs. Some flowers. How much prettier it sounds in French. Perhaps I should major in French at college. So much more sophisticated than English, or Social Studies. *Je suis une majeure du Français. Je vous aime. Je t'aime.* Douglas.

Now, on a summer morning, she lay in bed and tried not to remember. Somebody said that the unhappy times hurt most when you recall the happy ones. Well, that was true. Everywhere her thoughts turned, some recollection of Doug rose up to wound. Nearly a week now, and no word at all from him. I'm tired, she thought. Tired from wondering and hurting. Tired, too, from the long daily struggle to keep herself from phoning him. She *could* call. A gay question, "What *have* you been doing, Doug?" Casual, as if nothing but friendly curiosity. . . . The blood rose to her face, a wave of absolute nausea.

At the window the snowy curtains bellied in, pressed back against the screen. Down the street someone mowed his lawn. The sweet spinning whir of the mower harped

21

through chitter of birds, stopped, started again. A child called something to his mother, then ran down a gravel path. A screen door banged.

Anne squeezed her eyes tight, then with sudden submission let the tears come.

CHAPTER THREE

Six hours before the milkman halted his truck at the Armacost house, six hours and ten minutes before Theo furtively read her pre-breakfast poetry, six and a half hours before Anne wept for something she must have lost, Nora Harrison Chapin, in a one-and-a-half room apartment in New York City, heard a church bell strike twelve.

Midnight.

But to Nora, turning her head on the hot pillow, it was no time of night. Just some part of the nights . . . this night, last night, two weeks from tonight. Part of what the nights were now . . . tension, with the nerves tremblingly alert for the cry, anxiously treading the surface of sleep so there wouldn't be so far to rise, when the cry came.

There must be a moon tonight, she thought. I can't see it through this window, but there's a pearliness in the sky so the moon is somewhere. If I were home I could walk to the other side of the house, to look out the window. I could walk outdoors, looking for the moon. But here, to see the moon, I should have to walk down four flights of stairs and stand on the sidewalk, looking up. Or I could walk across the hall and knock on the apartment door there. I could say to perfect strangers, "Do you mind if I walk through your rooms at midnight? I wish to look at the moon."

Nora moved restlessly, turning a phrase in her mind. If I were home. But what did that mean now? Wasn't this home? She shivered a little in the hot room. Oh, no, not this, not home. But home, in the little town thirty miles away? It wasn't, not any more. A place to go, but rarely, a room she used to know, with a few things still there. Things belonging to another life, another girl. Her mother certainly didn't consider it Nora's home. She had been, Nora recalled bleakly, rather wispy and confused about having her and the baby even for a little while. Nora's explanation that the landlord wouldn't let them stay with the baby any longer had disposed of her mother's arguments but not of the strain between them.

"It seems to me, Nora," she heard her mother's voice saying, "that you and Sam could find some place. After all, you can hardly expect to stay here forever." A note of alarm had crept into her voice. "How long *do* you intend to stay?" she'd inquired suspiciously.

"Oh, Mother, I don't know," Nora had almost cried. "We'll find a place. I should think," she said hesitantly, "I thought perhaps . . . you might be pleased."

Her mother clacked over the phone, a sound of exasperation, and shame too, Nora thought. Nevertheless, "Nora, I told you, I *told* you . . ." She paused. "Oh well, of course, stay here as long as you like. But I *must* ask you not to make a lot of racket, especially with the baby. My boarder is a very quiet woman. Oh dear," she said fretfully, "what a mess you've made of everything."

Nora closed her eyes in the dark, opened them again, stared at the pale square of the window. A mess is right, she thought. Sometimes, even now after a year of marriage, she would wake in the night, shuddering with despair and disbelief. "What have I done, what have I done?" she would cry silently in the silence. Sometimes, to her own incredulous surprise, she would cry, "Mother!" And if she had been in another mood it would have struck her as humorous. There must have been a time, Nora thought, when I could call her that way, and she would come, to comfort me, talk to me. I don't remember when. There was a time, not so very long ago, when I could have called to Sam, and he would have come. If I still had Sam, I'd be all right. But where is he? And who is this, lying beside me? Who is this, who looks like Sam, who gets up early to work in a garage, who comes home quickly, goes out again to school? Who is he?

The easy, accustomed tears, the hot tears that sprang and flowed at night, every night, rolled down her cheeks.

She thought she was prepared for the cry. But now, when it came, her nerves sprang trembling with shock. For a second, she tightened convulsively, then carefully edged from the bed. Not, she thought, that *he'd* wake up. Concentrated hate welled in her, and as quickly ebbed as she eyed his still bulk in the bed. It isn't really fair, she realized. He should be a college boy. But he's a father, a working man, a night-school student. He's nineteen years old, and tired.

She turned on a dim light so that the part of the room near the kitchen in a closet took shape, but the corners edged further into darkness. Moving to the bassinet, she stood looking down at the baby, her eyes heavy. She leaned over, picked the baby up, gazed uncertainly around. Then she opened the kitchen-closet door, holding the baby under one arm, took a formula from the icebox, put it in a pan of water to heat. The baby still cried, so she took it back to the bassinet and changed its diaper. Skinny little legs, faintly mauve-colored, with long feet, waved in the air, and the thin arms jerked nervously. Its tin-like cry went on and on. She left it, got the bottle, which she put on a table next to the armchair. Then, awkwardly, she settled the baby. It gulped hungrily, eyes turned up to her. She stared across the room, shifting her arm a little now and then, not looking down.

I don't feel like a mother, she thought. I feel like a stone. Not for the first time she wondered what she'd be doing now if she'd answered differently that night in the canoe on Price's Lake when Sam had asked her to marry him. If she'd said no, would he still be her Sam, writing letters, asking her to college weekends, waiting for the times he could see her? He wouldn't be at a college in the city, and he wouldn't be working in a garage. He wouldn't be a father. Would he still be hers?

I'd be in college myself, she thought, and Anne Armacost would be coming up this fall. That would have been fun. Anne . . . I wish I were like Anne. Poised, pretty, so very level-headed. Anne wouldn't lose her mind on a lake and wind up here.

She remembered how her mother had stared, shuddered, weakly wept when Sam and Nora said they were going to be married. Mother, with her sick headaches, her endless tangly problems of what to have for dinner, what to say to the boarders, what "your father would have said if he were alive." It was due to her father, and the miracle of a scholarship, that she'd been planning to go to college at all—the small educational policy he'd left for her. But Sam had said, "Marry me, Nora," and she'd thrown away college without a thought. "Will you be sorry to give up school?" Sam asked, and she laughed. "School?" she said, "I'd give up the world for you, Sam."

Well, she thought wearily, I just about have.

But last year she'd been sure, without a flicker of hesitation, that Sam was what she wanted, she was what he wanted, and nothing could ever be anything but beautiful if they could only stay together. Almost, she smiled a little, sitting in the dim light that filtered through the parchment shade, remembering their honeymoon . . . Brides, she had heard, feel frightened. A little, or a lot, but some. Bridegrooms feel a bit resentful (as a man would who had chased a butterfly, only to have the

25

quarry turn and pop the net over him). She and Sam hadn't been like that. They took a train, they went to a hotel, not minding at all that people could tell they were newlyweds. They even went to Niagara Falls. Sam looked down at her, she looked up at him, and the other people swam in and out of vision like fish. Then when they got to their room and the bellhop was tipped, Sam closed the door and stood looking at her. Nervous? She'd been almost gloating. Here he was, her Sam, and nobody could separate them. Sam lifted his chin a little, a signal for her to come to him. Without saying a word, he asked her to come, and without a word she went across the room into his arms. . . .

The baby stirred restlessly. She looked down at it blankly, realized that the bottle was empty. The baby was trying to push it away. She put the bottle on the table, lifted the now quiet infant to her shoulder, patting its back gently. One small fist connected with her hair, closed on a few strands. In a little while the baby burped. She waited a few moments more, then replaced it in the bassinet, turned out the light. She slipped wearily back in the bed. Briefly, her husband stirred, snored, sank into the deepness again.

We have nothing to say to each other any more, Sam and I. What did we say last summer, when we were so in love? The same things, over and over again?

"Nora, I love you. You're beautiful. Marry me, Nora."

"I'll marry you. I'll love you all my life."

So we talked, dancing to the bubbly, bright jukebox at Price's, sliding over the dark lake water . . . slap of water as the canoe rocked gently, phosphorescence gleaming as the paddle dipped and lifted.

"Nora, you're sure? You're giving up so much. What will your mother say?"

She kissed away his questions. She didn't want to go to school. She'd learned all she needed to learn, that she loved him and he loved her. But she kissed away more than college that summer.

So they came to New York, to this disheveled apartment, and they didn't notice the dinginess because they shared it. Her mother took the insurance money, kept half. "After all," she complained, "you aren't using it for college. I don't know what your father would have said." Nora almost remarked that her father wouldn't have gotten a chance to say anything; he never had. But the half her mother gave them, and it *was* generous of her, had disappeared by now, payment for the birth of their baby.

Nora had taken a job when they were first married, as a stenographer. But the typing and shorthand she'd had in high school hadn't taken very well. She lost that job in a week and found another, selling neckwear in a department store. It didn't matter. Anything, just to make some money, so Sam could finish college.

Then she got pregnant and didn't tell Sam. So that's when she knew that something was wrong. Because she didn't want to tell him. She didn't want to have a baby. She felt horrible. Neckwear nauseated, cooking made her dizzy. She hardly ever cleaned the small apartment any more.

Sam took a mop one night, ran it under the daybed that became, at night, a double bed, pulled it out drifted with gray dust.

"I wouldn't ask my worst enemy to go under that bed," he said sourly, shaking the dust into the alley.

Nora shrugged. "That's the way I feel about the dust mop," she said indifferently. They had a quarrel, and the next morning she was too sick to go to work. Sam was very apologetic, but didn't guess why she was ill.

A few nights later she was at the kitchen part of the room, trying to broil some hamburger, wishing they could just have ginger ale for dinner and go to bed, when Sam came in. He stood a moment, eying the rumpled, unmade

27

daybed where she'd been lying off and on since noon. She'd quit her job because it was quite impossible to stand for eight hours and longer.

"Has that been unmade all day?" Sam asked. He put his books on the table, running his finger over the light surface of dust, then turned to her, waiting for an answer.

Nora just stook blinking at him, breathing through her mouth. "Oh, sure," she said finally. "Not clean, but everything in its dirty place."

Sam stared at her steadily. "You're getting to be just like your mother," he said slowly.

Nora nodded. "The highest possible accolade." She knew he was annoyed about the daybed, the dust. Only not just that. He was as baffled, as frightened, as lonely as she was. He didn't know what had happened, and neither did she. They only knew that something had, that they didn't know how to stop. So they fought over any trifle, perhaps to fool themselves that there was something to fight. To say, "We're angry with daybeds and dust," not, "We thought we were in love, we got what we wanted, and now there's nothing left."

The meat was burning, so he yanked it out, slammed it down on the stove, started away. Sam caught her by the arm. "I may not have a clean house to come home to," he said, very quiet now, very polite. "But may I ask if I'm going to have any dinner?"

"I don't know what you're going to have," Nora replied coldly, "but I'm going to have a baby."

Sam looked as though she'd slapped him. His shoulders drooped, but he put his arms around her. "Poor Nora," he said against her hair, "poor Nora. I haven't been very bright, have I?"

After that he was very nice to her. He had to leave school eventually. He got a job in a garage and arranged to go to school at night.

Lying beside him now, Nora wondered if they would

ever know each other again. He was pleasant, the little time he was home. He even helped, when he could, with the housework. Now and then he played a bit with the baby. But he was usually too exhausted. Nora's eyes grew heavy. I suppose, she thought through slumbrous vapors, that things will be better when he gets out of school. I don't see what else I can think.

The sleepy languor crept through her body, swam into her head. It seemed she never got enough sleep any more. But surely now the baby would sleep, and she could . . . She burrowed into the pillow. Beside her, the clock ticked racingly, its little nervous voice chattered into her numbness, growing fainter and fainter. She slept, but lightly, treading the surface.

CHAPTER FOUR

THEO PUSHED a couple of bobby pins through her hair, clamping her cap firmly to the springy curls, glanced at her reflection in the mirror merely to see that the cap was properly set, and left the Nurses' Room. The long hand of the third-floor corridor clock snapped to seven as she stepped out of the elevator.

At the nurses' station, Judy Tracy, floor supervisor, was filling a hypodermic syringe.

" 'Lo, Theo," Judy said, squinting at the fluid.

"Good morning. Why don't you ever get here on time?" Theo picked up the report of the night nurse.

Judy laughed. "I've only been here five minutes." She spiked a bit of cotton over the needle, laid the syringe on a small tray, waited as Theo read the report.

"Any new patients?" Theo asked.

"No. They weren't very busy last night. Snap duty."

"They can have it. Mr. Warren on regular insulin now, eh?"

"Yes. But check with Dr. Dolan first."

"All right. Well, shall I start in the ward?"

"No. That is, we aren't too busy, so would you mind . . . taking another letter for Mr. Coombes?" She seemed a little embarrassed at the strangeness of the request.

"Before breakfast?"

"Yes. Before breakfast. He's setting a high example of industry for the rest of us."

Theo nodded. "Splendid. Only he shouldn't use nurses to do his correspondence. I could be laying my cool fingers on someone's fevered brow, you know, instead of . . ."

"He owns practically every brick in this hospital," Judy interrupted. "And you can be sure that if he owns the bricks, he owns the nurses."

"Well, he should have kept his specials." Theo shrugged. "Not that I should complain. There are lots harder jobs than taking letters."

"He said the specials cluttered him. Go along, Theo, will you? He seems to think you're the only one who can figure out what he's talking about."

"He's wrong. He talks too fast. I didn't get half what he said written down last time."

Judy picked up the tray. "Who's this Dr. Johnson he's always talking about?"

"An English writer, eighteenth century."

Judy gaped. "Oh, for heaven's sake, I thought he meant a *doctor*! Do you know what I said to him?"

"I'm afraid to think."

"I told him if he ever hoped to get well he'd better stick to one doctor at a time."

Theo laughed, because Judy expected her to and because she was really a little amused. But what a pity, she was thinking, all the beautiful books . . . She thought of her father, gently proffering his treasure, more often than not finding it discarded at his feet when school was over.

"Go in and calm him down," Judy was saying. "I think I raised his temperature four degrees." Judy went off down the hall on her comfortable white shoes, leaving Theo rather uneasy in hers. Mr. Coombes was not an easy man to deal with. Sighing, she extracted the Coombes chart from the rack, examined it, thrust it back. She moved slowly toward room 314, rapped lightly on the door.

"What do you want?" an irritable voice demanded.

Theo opened the door and thrust her head in. "Did you want me, Mr. Coombes?" she questioned softly, though nothing could shame his voice to modulation.

"Oh, it's you. Come in, come in. Close the door. Can't stand watching the hobbledehoys parading past."

In the bed, trapped by a formidable array of plaster, wire, hoists, and boards, lay an elderly man. His brown eyes snapped brightly, his body was held rigidly helpless, but his tongue waved with frantic energy.

"Where's my breakfast?" he demanded, eyebrows surging toward each other.

"The trays haven't come up yet, Mr. Coombes," Theo explained.

"Get a man up at five in the morning and then make him wait half the day for his food," he grumbled.

"It's only a little after seven," Theo pointed out. She popped a thermometer in his open mouth, seized his wrist, watched his angry respiration. This was the only time anyone had the old man at a disadvantage, and Theo waited longer than was necessary to remove the thermometer.

"Did I get it up to normal?" he inquired.

Theo smiled at him imperturbably.

With the sudden inattention of a sick person, Mr. Coombes stared out the window. Theo picked up a pad in which she'd scribbled the last letter he'd dictated. She had no knowledge of shorthand, so she simply got down as much as possible, not convinced that it mattered anyway. Mr. Coombes had a good deal of discomfort and a very bad temper. Theo judged these letters were escape literature, which would go no further than the pages in her hand.

"Didn't you want to send this last letter, Mr. Coombes?" she inquired, willing to play her part.

"Eh? Is it still in there?" he queried in great surprise, craning his neck in a useless effort to see the pad. Theo held it before him. "Well," he murmured perplexedly, "had we finished it?"

She turned a page. "I'm not sure. I guess we hadn't. At least, there's nothing to say whether we did or didn't."

"All right," announced the old gentleman, "we'll go on from there. What was the last part?"

She read, "Life, though it be not long, is surely tedious, since we are forced to call in the assistance of so many trifles to help rid us of our time. . . ."

Mr. Coombes lowered his eyelids. "You read that nicely," he said in a thoughtful way. "Well, well, to get on with it . . . Since the great Dr. Johnson wrote this in one of his letters to Baretti, I doubt . . ."

Theo's fingers flew, and quickly cramped from the attempt to keep up with his rolling voice.

". . . in my youth, I myself was considered something of a scamp, but am able to say that in all instances refrained from excess and took care that no vestige of outrage or injustice should result, albeit certain . . ."

Some scamp, Theo thought silently, wondering if she could learn to write with her left hand, since at this rate the right wouldn't hold out long. His sonorous voice, which seemed almost trained, so rich it was, so able to shade and highlight the complicated structure of his speech, fell pleasantly on her ears. She wrote, skipping

32

parts, but never stopping. She knew he never asked to see the notebook, his self-devised therapy.

". . . you, my esteemed nephew, observe no such refinements, nor, to speak truly, any refinements at all. I learn with regret that despite many examples of probity . . ."

He must be very fond of his nephew, Theo was thinking. Every letter, except the one to the *Times* demanding a thorough investigation (of what, he hadn't specified; Theo suspected he would want a complete inquiry into everything), had been directed at this nephew. Theo, discounting a good many adjectives, was beginning to feel irritated, too, with this . . . boy, was it? Or man? His neglect of what was, after all, a sick and sad old man seemed cruel.

". . . I deem it futile to reason further in this matter, so must solicit your attention to . . ."

Theo sighed. *What* a lot of words. I don't really think he knows what he intends to say at all. He's so busy sounding like Dr. Johnson that he forgets anything except getting the words right. Carried away by his sentence structure, that's it.

The voice stopped abruptly. Looking up in surprise, Theo found the old man beetling at her through the plaster pillars of his arm and leg. "What did you say, young lady?" the full voice demanded.

"Say? Did I say something? Oh, I'm sure I didn't say anything, Mr. Coombes." Theo found herself stammering. No matter how you fixed him in your mind as a garrulous, old bore, Mr. Coombes could be vastly formidable in anger.

"You said something about sentence structure. In what particular do you find my sentence structure faulty?"

"Oh, not at all. I was talking about Dr. Johnson," she substituted unwisely.

The thick brows lifted. "Do you mean to say that you have the temerity to criticize the stately syntax of the master? You astonish and confound me, young lady. I find myself without words to . . ."

"No, no," Theo interrupted. "I wasn't criticizing. I said his sentence structure carried me away. At least, that's what I should have said. Or, I mean, what I would have said, if I'd said anything." She sighed, recognized a flaw, hurried on, "and of course I said something or you never would have said I said . . . I guess I was so inspired I spoke without thinking. . . ." Hopeless to go on, she thought. It's getting worse and worse.

But oddly enough he seemed mollified, and contented himself with remarking that to speak without thinking didn't as a rule require inspiration.

A timid knock at the door was followed by the wary face of an aide. "Breakfast is coming, Mr. Coombes," she squeaked. "What would you like?"

"Irish Cream Ale," said Mr. Coombes loudly. At the aide's confused nod, he added, "And no toast."

Theo got up. "Come now," she said brightly, in her mock-nurse voice, which appalled her now and then by appearing quite spontaneously, "we must be sensible about our meals." Mr. Coombes glared at her. "Mr. Coombes will have his regular breakfast," she told the aide, who backed quickly out.

"Why do they ask me, then?" he demanded triumphantly.

"You probably told them to," Theo guessed.

"Pah."

Theo fingered the pad. "Do you want to go on with this a little later?"

"What's that?" he looked at her absently. With one of his abrupt changes, he seemed to shrink within his skin, the lusty vigor that filled his body quite gone. "No," he replied indifferently, "let it pass. I just thought," he murmured to himself, "that I'd write him a letter." He exhaled a huge breath. "He hasn't come to see me at all."

"You've only been here a few days, Mr. Coombes," Theo offered for solace.

His gaze wandered to the window. He forgot her. Theo moved a flowered screen, stood helplessly a minute. "Would you feed him?" she asked as the aide came in with the tray.

The aide looked dubious.

"Mr. Coombes?" Theo questioned.

He turned his head. "Yes, Miss, uh, Armacost?"

"You *will* eat your breakfast, won't you? Mrs. Kramer is here to help you."

He regarded them both blankly. "Oh, yes," he answered finally, "I'll eat."

The aide seemed reassured by his docile mood. Theo, walking down the corridor, was sickened by it. Stupid oaf, she thought, her mind on the nephew. It would take so little . . . a visit, a card now and then, to an old man who obviously loves him. Old man, with broken limbs and a certain broken bravery, his only refuge bluster and verbosity. She wondered, not for the last time, why she had chosen to be a nurse, took Mr. Coombes' chart, and scribbled in it. Then she sat back, brooding. Anne would love him, she thought. If she'd come up here now and then, she could take his letters. She'd adore his determined revival of the speech archaic.

I think, she decided, getting up, that I'll ask her about it. She drummed her fingers thoughtfully on the desk. I wonder what's become of our butterfly . . . who stunned her? Anne, so free with her words, so close with her feelings. That Doug Eamons, Theo pondered . . . It was so hard to tell what Anne, screened behind her mesh of chatter, was thinking. Probably there'd be no point asking her to come here. Right now she's not interested in anything but her own troubles. She might make him feel worse instead of better.

"Oh dear," sighed Theo. She picked up the medication sheet.

Dr. Dolan, resident, strode toward her. "Top of a dear bright morning to you, Miss Armacost," he greeted.

"If it's all the same to you, doctor, I'll stay here at the bottom."

Concern appeared on Dr. Dolan's smooth features. "Now what would be troubling you?"

Dr. Dolan was comfortable. Sometimes he took Theo to a movie or a dance. She had had a fair portion of attention from men, and if her response was something less than eager, she felt sure the trouble lay within herself. "I," she had once told her father, "should never have had red hair." "No? Why?" he asked curiously. "Because red hair requires high spirits, flair, you know. I'm about as dashing as an egg white." Her father smiled. "I think, Theo, that you haven't yet seen anything you'd dash for." Theo wasn't convinced. There's something about me that's completely negative. It looks to other people like serenity, but *I* know. It's the still, sweet calm of a vacuum.

"Nothing's wrong, really," she answered Dr. Dolan. "I just hate to get up early."

"Well, that's a normal enough symptom," he observed, relieved that she hadn't produced a more complicated answer. Dr. Dolan preferred organic to emotional problems. "How's Mrs. Bacon this morning?" he asked.

"I haven't been in the ward yet. She'll be glad to see you, I know."

"A broth of a woman, Mrs. Bacon. Her blind admiration is the sauce of life to me."

"You're a very lucky man, Dr. Dolan."

"That I am, that I am. Well, I'll be trotting in to see the old girl. I feel in need of my daily shot of ego."

Theo smiled at his retreating back. He might make light of it, but old Mrs. Bacon's firm conviction that he represented the apex of human production and medical genius was very soothing to him. Dr. Dolan was the sort of man who drinks praise, grows dry, and must drink again, over and over.

Judy Tracy popped her head out of the women's ward just as Dr. Dolan left it. "Help me get Mrs. Bacon into her walking frame, will you?" she asked.

Mrs. Bacon, mountainous and jovial, lay waiting in her bed. The ward was a babel of voices, spinning of fine lint in the air, bathing, bed-changing, flapping of linen. Theo recollected the voice of a teacher she'd had in training, a woman austerely consecrated to Nightingale. "A good nurse," this teacher had said threateningly, "a good nurse *never* flaps." Among the ballooning sheets Theo sensed a disapproving ghost.

"Morning, dearie," Mrs. Bacon boomed cheerfully.

"How are you, Mrs. Bacon?"

"Oh, I can't complain. Dr. Dolan was just here. He says I'm coming along fine, just fine." Her voice was reverent.

"Of course you are."

"He's a wonderful man, and a fine doctor," Mrs. Bacon asserted, as though at a fresh discovery. She eyed Theo sharply. "It's too bad some people can't see a diamond when it's dangling right in front of their noses."

Theo had no intention of discussing the peerless doctor with his most ardent champion, so she asked Mrs. Bacon whether she'd been bathed yet.

"I'm practically peeled."

"Well, good, let's get you started, then."

Judy pulled the walking frame forward, a large wooden square with a bench in it. She and Theo leaned over the bed so that Mrs. Bacon could put an arm around each. They straightened, pulling her to a sitting position. As Theo held Mrs. Bacon's back, Judy swung the fat legs around to dangle at the bedside, put slippers on the puffy feet. They put on her old cotton bathrobe. Then, breathing heavily, leaning heavily, Mrs. Bacon was helped to the floor where she stood trembling a second. Supported by Theo and Judy, she took three uncertain steps into the frame, turned laboriously, subsided to the bench.

"I made up my mind a long time ago," Mrs. Bacon puffed, "that I'm a burden, so there's no point worrying about it."

"Well, Mrs. Burden, suppose you stand up and start walking," Judy invited.

"Just a second, catch my breath . . ."

"Come on, come on," Theo coaxed. "You plan to get back for lunch, don't you?"

"Well, if I don't, send it down to the solarium. That's where I'll be, stranded in this contraption."

"This contraption will have you walking alone, and then you'll be sorry you talked about it that way."

Mrs. Bacon smiled faintly. "Will it?" she asked in a soft voice.

Theo found no answer. Always, with the old chronic cases like Mrs. Bacon, after the surface of joking, or whining, was scratched, this unanswerable sadness lay exposed. Watching the round old face, whose every wrinkle seemed pleasantly knowing, grow pensive, Theo felt her own face twist with sympathy—with something more than sympathy. A passionate desire to know . . . Why? When Mrs. Bacon left here, she would, if fortunate, go to an old ladies' home. If not, the County Farm. But why? There was a time, Theo thought, of big houses. They don't build big houses any more, like that crumbling ruin at the edge of town, the kind that were made for all the generations of a family. Two, three, sometimes even four. People in the old days kept their old as well as their young. They kept even their mad ones, guarded against the world and themselves. Now the old people say proudly, "I'll never be dependent," and go away to molder alone on annuities, in old folks' homes, on poor farms. And once in a while the young ones come by to bestow an automobile ride, a two-pound box of chocolates. "How sweet," a tottering woman murmurs, clawing at the candy, "how good your Mamie is to you." "Oh, nothing's too good for me! Last month it was a basket of fruit, remember?" They nod, tossing the frail ball back and forth. What loving remembrance! How fortunate!

Mrs. Bacon looked up, suddenly smiled wryly. "There now," she said, "that wasn't very nice of me. And anyway, I'm not at all sure I want to get better, because then I'd have to leave you girls. Now help me up again, and I'll get started."

Gripping the sides of the frame, she moved her immense body forward, small dragging steps halting after each two or three feet had been covered. She turned to nod approvingly at the two nurses.

"Doing very well today," she announced briskly. Theo watched her labored progress, smiled encouragement, turned to make the rumpled bed.

"Eyes I dare not meet in dreams, in death's dream kingdom, these do not appear. . . ."

"What's that?" Judy asked, spinning around.

Theo shook her head. "I don't know, Judy. I don't know what anything is." Funny, she thought, sometimes I say things aloud when I'm sure they're just in my mind. Judy looks annoyed, and no wonder.

At a little past nine o'clock, Theo walked down the hall with a tray of medications. A tall man hurtled around a corner, almost colliding with her.

"Whoops!" he exclaimed. "I'm sorry."

Theo retained a rattling grip on the tray, steadied herself, and smiled slightly. "That's all right. You startled me."

"Well, I should think so. Barging around like that. I am terribly sorry," he repeated.

Theo smiled again and started off.

"Say . . . ," he called after her, "could you tell me where

room 314 is? I can't find anything but kitchens and closets."

"Four doors down on the right," Theo told him, adding quickly, "but you can't see any patient now. Visiting hours for private rooms start at lunchtime." This is the nephew, she was thinking. He doesn't look like someone who'd get letters regretting his behavior, certainly not like a man who'd neglect a sick old uncle. He looks very . . . kind. His lean face flew his uncle's flaring brows above the same clear green eyes. His nose rose narrowly to a broad brow, his lips were finely modeled. Theo flushed, realizing that she'd been simply staring at him. He was looking back at her in an amused way, as though he expected some comment to follow her study of his face.

"I'm sorry," she repeated firmly.

"Oh look, I just found out my uncle was here, and . . ."

"Seems funny you wouldn't have heard before," Theo blurted. She shook her head and with an effort resumed the expression of nurse talking to visitor. How odd, she thought, to feel so easy with a man you've literally just bumped into.

He didn't appear to notice anything untoward in her manner, but went on rapidly stating his case. "I didn't know," he insisted. "I was away and my mother didn't want to spoil my vacation by telling me." He sounded a little irritated. "She meant well, but I know he'd want to see me."

Theo still looked dubious.

"It's true," he said earnestly. "I've been fishing in the Adirondacks. It would have been hard to get me anyway, but they didn't try." He seemed very anxious to have her believe him.

"I know he wants to see you, but . . ."

"How did you know?"

Theo didn't feel that Mr. Coombes would want the letters mentioned. "I . . . he's spoken of you," she said, "but really, this is no hour for it."

"For a minute," he pleaded. "Just to let him know I hadn't heard about his falling off the ladder till I got home last night."

"Ladder?" Theo burst out. "What was he doing on a ladder?"

"In his library. He fell off the ladder trying to reach Boswell."

"How like him," Theo murmured.

He cocked his head. "You seem to know a lot about him."

Theo hedged. "We all do," she said vaguely. "Well, you may go in for a minute, but do your visiting later, please."

"Thanks, that's very nice of you." With a wave of his hand, he strode off. Theo stared after him, went on with her tray of medications.

In room 320 was Lydia Colman, a succulent young woman mentally dubbed by Theo "the blond assassin," whose sole purpose seemed to be the skillful laying of man-traps . . . even in a hospital. She distributed her snares with the assiduity of a man whose livelihood depends on fox pelts, making her rounds of inspection frequently and carefully. Having found some helpless prisoner, she popped him in her sack, prepared the trap for further use. Her need was never-ending. Like the fur trapper, so long as the fox remained ignorant of her plot, she was indifferent to the knowing eyes of others. She was, at present, busily plotting the capture of Dr. Dolan. Theo thought it a pity.

When Theo entered, Miss Colman was at the window, anxiously trying to see the top of her head in a pocket mirror. She thrust the mirror hastily out of sight when the door opened, produced it again immediately.

I guess she knows a nonentity when she sees one, Theo thought with amusement. "Your pills," she said.

41

Miss Colman, who paid scant attention to nurses, surprised her by saying, "Come over here, will you?"

Theo shrugged slightly, moved toward the window.

"How does my hair look?"

Theo lifted an eyebrow. "Look?" she repeated. "Very nice."

"No, no. I mean, is there any dark showing in the part?" She dipped her head, trying again to see in the little mirror by the light of the window. "I've been in this horrible place so long, it must be growing out. I simply have to get out of here. . . ." She twisted a curl around her finger, frowning irritably.

Theo leaned over and studied the part in the bronze hair. Unquestionably, there was a thin dark line on either side. She said as much.

"Oh, for the love of heaven," Lydia snapped. "What a lot of nonsense." She got up and paced around the room.

"Your medicine," Theo reminded her.

"What? Oh, I'll take it later."

"Now, please," said Theo firmly.

Miss Colman studied her minutely, then walked to the bedstand and gulped the pills. "I don't know how anyone can be a nurse," she said sullenly.

Theo walked to the door. "It's difficult, sometimes," she agreed. "Of course, some times more than others." She stepped into the hall, drawing the door closed.

Judy Tracy was folding blankets, piling them with precision in the linen closet. Silently Theo assisted. It was hot. The antiseptic, feverish odor of the hospital seemed more pungent than usual. Judy sighed heavily.

"Make out all right with Mr. Coombes?" she inquired.

"Mmm." Theo started to mention the nephew, changed her mind. Down the hall, Dr. Dolan emerged from the men's ward. He spotted Theo, brightened, started for her.

"Oh, Dr. *Dolan*!" Lydia Colman called, wide-eyed with flattering delight. "How *nice* to see you. . . ." Ravishing in a white robe, a scarf of strawberry-tinted silk poised like a butterfly on her hair, Miss Colman burst beautifully on the scene. Theo noted the scarf with interest. Must annoy her to cover the hair that's still yellow, she thought unkindly. Then, in self-defense, explained to herself that, after all, you don't like to have a man who's practically yours, whether you want him or not, simply scooped up before your eyes. Miss Colman, the gleam of the seasoned trapper in her eye, drifted up to her prey, rested a feather-like hand on its arm, glowed up at it with unconcealed pleasure.

"Oh, hello, Lydia, you look nice," Dr. Dolan commented, unaware of his fate. He turned again toward Theo. But Lydia was receiving his remark with an air of recognizing undertones not for the public ear. She smiled shyly, her gentle detaining hand on his sleeve.

"I . . . oh, this is going to sound so silly," she laughed softly, catching her underlip with undeniably fine teeth. She hesitated. Then, with pure candor, "May I speak to you . . . just for a moment? I have a problem, and there isn't anyone for me to turn to. My family?" She lifted her shoulders, delicately disowning her family. "But you . . . I know you would . . ." She stopped, turned with a half-shy glance at him, and went toward the solarium.

Dr. Dolan was touched. He flapped after her, to be presented with the bait.

"Well, I'll be darned," Theo muttered, greatly impressed.

"Why don't you do something about it?" Judy demanded.

"What? Hurl myself bodily between them?" Theo shook her head. "I'd get scratched."

"Well, you can't expect a man to climb out of all that syrup without a little help."

Theo shoved the last blanket in place. "I expect nothing," she said truthfully.

"You just have no spunk," Judy snapped, less irritated with Theo than outraged by Lydia Colman.

"You're wrong," Theo answered mildly. "I have no interest. He just isn't someone I'd dash for," she added, then fled as Mrs. Bacon, inching through the solarium door, darted a speculative glance from Theo to Dr. Dolan and his captor.

CHAPTER FIVE

ANNE TOOK a book and went through the flower garden to the little patch of fruit trees. Here she wouldn't know whether the telephone rang or not, and perhaps, when she went back, someone would say, "Oh, by the way, Doug called." The familiar pain pinched her heart, but still the small hope bubbled up. Every time she left the house, the nervous expectation rose again. Perhaps this time . . .

In the beginning, during the first few days, she'd lingered in the house all the time, afraid to go out for fear the phone would ring and no one would be there, or for fear whoever answered would forget to tell her. Now she stayed out as much as possible. Like July, she thought, walking away from a mouse hole, pretending not to care. But July remembers the mouse hole, and I remember the telephone. And it isn't as if this hadn't happened before, she told herself. It happened once at the beginning of the summer. . . .

It had been the first truly warm day of June. Swallows over the garden set a brilliant pace of flight. After them, the ruddy robins seemed clumsy, the sparrows unutterably drab. Anne, picking rhubarb, sat back on her heels to sniff the leafy heat. The afternoon vibrated in melting light. The sounds of the day . . . far off Good Humor bell, lawn mowers, young baseball players . . . were muted in the new summer haze. Anne, turning the purple satin stalks in her hands, absorbed, bemused, the odors and the sounds. She was already, in her thoughts, past the afternoon, past dinner. She was dancing with Douglas at Price's Beach. But how to make the afternoon pass? Two o'clock now. Six hours till eight. What to do to pass six hours, till Doug came?

She thrust the rhubarb in a basket.

"Doug, Doug," she whispered, wondering what she'd ever thought of, before Doug. Since the day they'd walked in the snow, he had never left her thoughts. Oh, sometimes he seemed to recede and other things came forward, but always he was there. They had written to each other when he went back to college: Doug's letters brief, frequent, casual; Anne's less frequent, longer, equally casual. There's lots of time, she told herself.

When he came home for spring vacation, they'd gone out together often. Twice Doug took Dody Colman out. Anne still saw Peter Crosland, a few others. But they were straw people. It was difficult to talk to them, they got in the way of her thinking about Doug. Taking Dody Colman's measure, Anne decided uncertainly that she enjoyed the slight barbs of jealousy Dody gave her. This is all part of falling in love, she told herself. Because she had certainly fallen in love. So had Doug. She knew that. He didn't say anything, but she knew. Didn't she?

She picked some pansies, arranging them artfully, so their bright faces sprang through the slim rhubarb stalks. Then she took the basket in to her mother.

"That's pretty," Mrs. Armacost told her. "I rather hate to disturb it."

Anne smiled at the basket, then plucked out the pansies. She put them in a shallow bowl of water where they floated, brilliant immobile butterflies.

Mrs. Armacost was ironing. She whipped open a rolled dampened shirt, spread it on the ironing board. The collar smoothed out stiff and white beneath the swift strokes of her iron. Then in turn the sleeves flattened out and lost their wrinkles, the front and back panels submitted, and the shirt was hung, still warm, over a chair back.

Anne watched with admiration. "I simply never could manage it that way," she approved, eying the snowy folds.

"You know," her mother confessed, reaching for another shirt, "this sounds ridiculous, but I like to iron."

"Order out of chaos, I presume," was Anne's analysis. "I don't ever seem to produce anything but smooth wrinkles."

"That's because you don't dampen properly. That's the secret of good ironing. And to move fast."

Anne meditated. "Here," she offered, "let me do that. You go away and rest somewhere."

Mrs. Armacost felt doubtful.

"Oh, come on, Mom," Anne persisted, taken with the notion of helping her mother and at the same time beguiling the long hours. "You have it all dampened properly, and that's the secret of good ironing, you know. And to move fast. I'm an expert at fast moving."

"I know," laughed her mother, "but it isn't generally in the direction of work."

"Now that's not so. I do my part. . . ."

"Of course you do, darling. But you don't usually ask to do someone else's part. Anyway," she went on, "I'm not sure. . . . Not that it isn't perfectly lovely of you to offer, but . . ."

Anne pushed her mother away from the ironing board. "You go out on the glider and read a book," she ordered. "I'll make out fine."

"Well . . ." Mrs. Armacost yielded. She went as bidden to the glider with a book which she didn't read. Her daughter's chirpy uncertain voice came through the still house singing snatches of popular songs.

Mrs. Armacost sighed. Anne, though she moved behind a shield, was in love with Douglas Eamons, that was obvious. *Doug seems like a nice boy. I just hope . . .* She picked up the book, tried to read. *I just hope she doesn't get hurt.*

A couple of hours later, the ironing was finished, sorted, piled on various beds for each person to deal with himself. Anne, feeling happily domestic, folded the ironing board, started to set the table. The dining room was cool, shaded from the afternoon sun. In the center of the table, her bowl of pansies glowed vividly. The grandfather clock struck one vibrant note. Four-thirty.

Johnny, like a rocket, burst on the shadowed stillness, waving a shirt in his hand. "What is this supposed to be?" he shouted, thrusting the shirt in Anne's face.

"Isn't that yours?" his sister asked innocently. "I tried to sort them out properly. Isn't yours the fourteen and a half?"

"What I want to know is, what were you doing with them before you sorted them?"

Anne's eyes widened. "Why, ironing them, of course."

"What did you iron them with? A rolling pin?"

Anne sniffed. "I'll never learn to iron if I don't get any practice."

"Why don't you practice on the dish towels?"

"Don't be a cretin. Dish towels don't get ironed."

"Neither do shirts, if you ask me. . . ."

Mrs. Armacost hurried in. "What's going on here?"

"Oh, nothing," Johnny said bitterly, opening the shirt to show his mother. "Dad and I will just go around looking like a couple of scarecrows, that's all. Look at this thing! I ask you. . . ."

Mrs. Armacost studied the shirt. "Mmm," she said noncommittally. Then, as they seemed to expect something

47

further, "After all, Anne has to learn, doesn't she? I should think you'd encourage her."

"I don't mind encouraging Anne. I can't think of anyone I'd rather encourage. But if you don't mind, I'd rather have you iron my shirts," Johnny announced definitely.

Mrs. Armacost and Anne looked at each other.

"Well," Anne said finally, "I'm glad you had a rest, Mom. Now I guess you can get the shirts and iron them all over again."

Johnny flushed. "Ah, I don't mean I won't wear what's done." He looked from one to the other. "I'm sorry, I suppose," he grumbled, and left the room.

Mrs. Armacost frowned. "Why do you and Johnny quarrel so much, Anne?"

"Quarrel? We don't quarrel. . . ." Anne considered a minute. "Don't worry about Johnny and me, Mom. We know what we're doing. You know," she went on contemplatively, "Johnny and I are good for each other. We're the only people in the family with tempers, so we blow up together and no one else gets hurt." She arranged silver on the table. "Fundamentally, I believe Johnny has a good deal of value, but he's in a difficult phase." Mrs. Armacost thought Johnny wasn't the only one, but held her peace. "I feel that at present," Anne was saying, "Johnny has barely enough intelligence to cope with the most rudimentary problems of life. But he'll improve," she concluded confidently.

Eight o'clock came.

Anne, in her new dotted swiss, navy blue, closely molded, with gently flaring skirt, her thick hair caught in a queue with a white ribbon, stood before her mirror. I look nice, she thought with simple directness.

"Mirror, mirror, on the wall," Theo said at the door. "You are," she added. "Fairest, that is."

"*Do* I look nice?" Anne asked.

"Very."

48

"Are you going out, Theo?"

"Uh huh."

"Anything special?"

"No. Just a date."

"Then could I wear your white coat?"

Theo nodded. "Is it Peter tonight?"

"Now let's see." Anne narrowed her eyes thoughtfully. "No, tonight it's Doug."

"How do you manage it, Anne? All these languishing males."

"I mystify them," Anne confided furtively. "To one, I am an odalisque. To another a lucent, wand-like maiden, and so forth," she nodded, pleased with the words, "according to their temperaments."

"Sounds like an excellent system. Do you ever get mixed up?"

"Never. I have notes and refer to them constantly."

Theo laughed. "Well, wear the coat, and have a good time."

"You too, and thanks."

But, after all, the coat made no difference.

Price's Beach wasn't, properly speaking, a beach at all. It was a large area of yearly transported sand dumped beside a lake. It had a wooden dance pavilion, a bubbly bright jukebox, a soft-drink stand. Mr. Price rented rowboats and canoes and patched-up tire tubes. During the day, young and very young and old flocked to the beach. But at night Price's Beach belonged to the high school and college crowd.

Day sank softly as Anne and Doug rode along in his old car. The sun, settling behind the evening plum-colored mountains, kindled a scarf of clouds that wound on the hilltops, crimson, violet, wisps of palest green. At the edge of town, the final slanting rays picked up bits of glass that clung here and there in the Wellman house, flashed briefly gold.

"I never pass that place anymore without thinking of you," Doug said, slowing as they passed the old wreck, now gently clothed in a garment of leaves. The stately ancient oak loomed in the lowering dark, and from its branches throaty songs of nesting birds gave it voice.

I never pass any place without thinking of you, Anne said silently. When she was with Doug, Anne still found she had little to say. Her being seemed so occupied with sensing, loving his nearness that words were too hard to capture. Through her mind images and wispy thoughts floated, disappeared. In books, she pondered, people seem to think such . . . consecutive thoughts. They start out with an idea and come up with a conclusion. I never do that. I don't believe I ever *start* to actually think anything through, much less do it. Just these reveries and day dreams coming in and out with no help from me at all . . .

Doug saving me from a burning building . . . or me saving him, that's really nicer. Or going up for a week-end at his college . . . a white dress, close and sparkly and cloud-like. Then the president of the senior class simply sweeping down upon me, with everyone watching . . . perhaps Dody Colman could be there with someone. Yes, she'd have to be there. And so this boy, with a name like Finlay Arden Todhunter, would absolutely brush away all competition and away we'd float, over the dance floor. Only really, all it would mean to me would be Doug seeing it. Proud at first, maybe. Then jealous, very very jealous. Only would he be? Anne sighed. Doug, so perfect . . . he'd never be jealous. He doesn't have to be. Certainly not over me. Because it's all very well for me to act gay and casual, but any fool could tell that I'm made of Doug, and without him I just am not.

She stared out the window at the fields waving slowly by, moonlight, like thin snow, on the wild hedges and trees.

Does he love me? He never says so. Does he? I think if Doug doesn't love me, I'll die. I wouldn't even have to commit suicide. I'd just melt, like that mermaid, just froth away to nothing. . . .

"What are you thinking about now, dreamy one?" Doug asked, putting his hand over hers.

Anne turned to him. "I was thinking . . . I was wondering, what do *you* think about? When you aren't actually thinking of anything special."

Doug lit a cigarette before he answered. "Well," he said, blowing a jet of smoke that spun out the window, "I guess I don't think about much. Football, maybe. Or work out a chemistry problem. Or think how proud Dad will be when I finally get that chemical engineering degree." He drove in silence for a while. Then, "I think a lot about you, Anne."

For this, for the strange elation that filled her breast and laved over her at his words, Anne forgave the hours of wondering and loneliness, when she didn't know where he was or whether he remembered her. Because Doug was so elusive, so apt to drift away . . . so uncatchable. But he wouldn't say this if he didn't mean it. Doug never did or said anything he didn't mean. Not to be polite, not to ease things, not for a passing idea, did he ever say anything he didn't mean. He wasn't rude. He just edged away. Even if he stayed right there with you, he took himself away so that there was no way to find him at all. She knew, too, that he seemed to do this when she herself was so trembling with love that it must show through, in spite of her caution. I must be slow, she thought. I must be very, very careful and slow. Nora Harrison got married when she was seventeen. The words flashed through her mind with no warning at all, and then, I want to marry you, Doug. . . . For a moment she thought she'd said it aloud, but Doug's calm profile remained fixed on the road.

"My sister, Theo," she said in a high voice, to drown out the still one before Doug should hear its faint call, "when I asked her that . . . you know, what you think when you aren't thinking . . . she said she thinks about poetry. Theo says she's never had an original thought in her life, that everything in her mind has already been said better by someone else. It isn't so, really. . . ." Her words slowed, the danger past for the moment. "Theo just says things like that."

"It's a good idea, that question," Doug mused. "Be fun to ask a lot of people. If they answered truthfully," he went on, "you'd probably have a pretty peculiar picture of your friends. But I suppose they wouldn't."

"Probably not," Anne laughed.

"What do you?" Doug asked suddenly.

"Think of?" Anne said, almost pleadingly. Please, what? What do I say? Oh, quickly, there must be something in the world to think of beside Doug. . . . No, there isn't. But something I could say? What? What? "Oh, all sorts of things," she fluttered. "I, ah, I think about books," she gasped.

"You have the readingest family," Doug said, shaking his head.

"Don't you like to read, Doug?"

"Sure I do."

"Are you reading anything now, this summer, I mean?"

"Uh huh. Organic Chemistry."

"Oh, Doug," Anne giggled, free again for a moment. She sank back into silence. I think a lot about you, Anne, she said to herself, turning the inflection, the deep ring of his voice, round in her mind. I think a lot about you.

A little past the Wellman place, the town road macadam yielded to hard packed dirt. Doug's car flipped confidently over ruts and rocks. Meadows, on either side, sloped away to blackness, dotted whitely with daisies. Buttercups and tiger lilies gave no sign. Peepers in the marshes chorused loudly, grew silent, welled up again. The air, fragrant here with country freshness, dusky and secret, swam in the open windows. Once, in the long pole of the headlights, a rabbit crouched, confused. Doug stopped, switched off the lights. When he put them on again, the rabbit was gone.

At Price's they found a crowd of people already dancing. Dody Colman, at a corner table, sat with Jack Raymond, Angela Byrd, and Peter Crosland. Dody waved vigorously, calling them over.

"Do you want to sit with them?" Doug asked.

"Do you?"

"Might as well, I suppose." He smiled toward the table. Anne summoned up a smile, beamed it in the same direction. I thought, she reminded herself unconvincingly, that I was supposed to enjoy Dody Colman and the way she throws herself at Doug. "Oh, of course," she said brittlely. "Much more fun with a crowd."

Then Doug made it all right again by saying, "Let's dance first." He held her off a moment, both hands on her shoulders, bending a prolonged gaze on her face. "Now what," he said, "did I ever do to deserve such a prize?"

"Just lucky, I guess," Anne replied, keeping it light. That was her part, wasn't it? To keep it gay and light as long as Doug did. It was really very easy . . . just answer the way you'd answer another boy. Just try not to show that the world had meaning only because Doug was in it. Very easy, if you guarded every answer, shuttered your eyes, and never let your thoughts show through.

"Come on," he said softly, pulling her close. "Let's dance."

Well, this was what the world meant, dancing close to Doug. Not speaking, skimming over the delicate surface of old, enduring, "Stardust." They danced, isolated, remote, spun round with a silk cocoon reeled from a garish box. Then the music stopped. Someone's store of nickels had gotten what it paid for, and the music stopped.

"Come along," Doug said. "Let's get a drink and sit down."

"Doug! Anne! What *fun!*" Dody cried as they approached. Doug pulled up a couple of chairs for them.

"Hi, Angie," he said. "Hiya Pete, Jack." He smiled at Dody. "How's blondie?"

"Oh, I'm fine, now," she said softly, so the others wouldn't hear. Anne did, and thought helplessly that Dody certainly had a positive approach, but what was there to do about it? I think I hate her, Anne thought with sudden fury. She makes me feel clumsy and flimsy and stupid. Perhaps it's because she's smaller than I am. Perhaps, perhaps . . .

"Oh, no," she said in answer to a query from Dody. "I *said* to Doug it would be more fun to sit with you people."

Brief respite.

"How're you, Anne?" Peter asked, delighted to see her and trying not to show it. Is that how I look, Anne wondered. Do I go on like a light when Doug comes near, so that everyone can see?

"You're going to college in the fall, aren't you, Anne?" Angela asked.

"Yes. Up near . . . upstate. Where are you going?"

"Out West. Dody's going to New York, to be a model."

"Really?" Anne glanced over. "You're going to New York alone?"

"Oh my dear, *no*. With a maiden aunt who has a simple dream of an apartment near Central Park. Actually, I can hardly *wait*, except for . . ." She broke off, glanced at Doug in dainty confusion. Jack Raymond looked annoyed, but resigned.

"But really," Dody pursued, "I think it's the perfect career for me. Oh," she clapped her red-tipped fingers to her mouth, "that sounds conceited, but I didn't mean it that way. . . ."

Well, *which* way, Anne wondered.

"You'll do, you'll do," Jack said, forgetting his irritation in the bright glance of Dody's eyes.

"Sure," Angela whispered to Anne, "she'll drive men mad with her moon-gold hair, she hopes."

"I like to be attractive to men, but I wouldn't want a lot of loonies following me around," Anne whispered back.

Angela giggled. Dody flicked a glance in their direction and smiled faintly, so that Anne flushed and Angela glared. But we're no match for her, Anne realized miserably, no match at all.

"How about a dance?" Peter asked Anne. "Okay, Angie?"

"Sure." The girl's strawberry lips curved pleasantly. Anne looked at her closely, saw that it was indeed perfectly all right. I'm getting so I suspect deathless passion everywhere, she thought, trailing Peter to the jukebox. Sometimes, just sometimes, I wish I were back there, free, the way Angela is. She looked over at Peter's date, happily chatting with Jack Raymond. Doug and Dody were laughing together, Doug with his head back, Dody with a hand on her throat, doubled up in delicate mirth. Anne looked away, before Dody should catch her gaze. Dody would like that, to see Anne's helpless eyes fixed on the two of them. I'm in a horrible, wretched, beastly, broken-down thralldom, Anne thought wildly. Then she made a sudden decision. I shall not, she thought, love him any more. I'll get over it, starting now.

She spun round to Peter, making his selection of records methodically, cautiously. "Put a quarter in, Peter," she teased. "I haven't danced with you in ages."

Peter responded with dazed delight, shoved in three more buttons at random, relinquished his quarter, and spun her out on the wooden floor before the music started. Oh, now this really isn't fair, she thought nervously, watching Peter's happy expression. I should have picked Jack Raymond, who doesn't much care whether I dance with him or not. Too late now. Peter glided, stamped, sashayed round. He danced beautifully, he beamed beautifully. Anne followed with expert indifference.

She saw Doug and Dody rise, melt together, pause a moment, swaying, then dip out among the dancers. Dody's pale hair swung in a molten coil. She tipped back now and then, her nose cozying up to Doug's chin. She chattered incessantly and Doug responded smilingly. Perhaps he likes to talk while he's dancing, Anne thought wretchedly, trying not to watch.

"Gee, this is great," Peter exulted. "I thought you . . ." He broke off, then continued, "Just great. You're looking marvelous Anne. I like your hair pulled back that way."

"That's nice, Peter. It's a new way."

"I thought so." They whirled apart, Peter's hand in hers. They wrapped together again. "You dance better all the time, Peter," Anne told him.

"I always dance better with you," Peter said without emphasis.

Anne didn't answer. I'm not being fair, she thought again. And oh, dear heaven, it's horrible to be jealous. I never was before. I never was in love before. She followed the smooth maze of Peter's steps.

Later, at the table, Jack Raymond said casually, "Hear they're going to tear down the old Wellman monstrosity this summer."

"That ark on Park?" Peter asked.

Doug looked up. "They are? Why?"

"Why not, if you ask me," Dody shrugged. "Ghastly old place."

"I think it's a marvelous old place," Doug said.

Dody blinked. "For heaven's sake, why?"

"Part of my past is in it," Doug answered, staring at the table. Anne's heart flipped over happily.

"If you mean you ran around scaring yourself to death in it, we all did. It's a part of my past I'd just as soon forget," Dody announced. "I mean, it's all very well to be sentimental about things, but you have to use your head."

If that's all *you* have to fall back on, Anne thought, I guess the rest of us needn't worry. Then she felt sort of sick. What am I turning into, she wondered. A snapping, suspicious, mean-minded creature. For a moment she hated Doug. Do you see what you've done to me, she accused him silently. Do you see?

She got up. "This place is an inferno," she announced at random, and started for the porch. Dody's voice drifted after her. "Is it hot? Funny, somehow I always feel cool." Jack Raymond replied admiringly, "You look it, too, like an ice-cream cone."

Anne went out on the porch.

The lake dappled silver and black under the moon. Near the small jetty a few canoes and rowboats swayed on the water, nudging, drifting apart. The hollow slap of waves under the jetty, a splash now and then as a frog leaped for some night insect . . .

Anne leaned her head against a pillar. Being pretty, and she knew she was pretty, was not enough. Not enough to be skillful in other relationships. Love removed weapons, left you disarmed, clumsy, at the humiliating mercy of the Dody Colmans. But how to go back to where she was before? How to get back her heart and her mind for herself? I'll stop. I'll stop loving him, she thought fiercely. Somehow, I'll make myself stop.

But she leaned against the pillar and wondered why he didn't come. Then, when she turned, walked into his arms. Oh, the wonderful, sudden, good-smelling closeness of him, the quiet, dear nearness of him. The churning ache subsided as she stood, very still, in his arms. In the dark mass of trees that ringed the lake, sudden fireflies winked fleetly gold. Anne sighed and lifted her head, because he had never kissed her, and now he would.

The next day rose in a bright vapor, but darkened as the hours passed. Doug didn't call that day, or the next. With uncomprehending pain, Anne watched the telephone, sitting on the hall table, ignoring her. Each time it rang, something hammered inside her, like a fist. At first she knew every ring would be his. Then four days had passed, and she hoped for nothing more from the telephone.

On Saturday afternoon she sat on the front porch glider, pushing back and forth to its unoiled, ungliding squeak, shelling peas into a pot. Johnny and Cooper Maloney in the street threw a ball back and forth. It slapped into their leather mitts with a sharp thud. A summer sound, Anne thought, like the piano a few houses down or the stirring leaves that Theo loves to hear. I used to love the summer sounds too. Now I don't love anything. I'd like to go away, like one of those sick animals, and lie in the dark.

She looked up at a footstep on the porch, and there he stood, watching her, hair bleached by the sun, T-shirt snowy against his brown arms and face. With no struggle at all, Anne yielded to happiness. Everything rocketed into brightness, and she went on shelling peas. They fell with a nice plop into the pan. Plop, plop, plop, they bounced into the pan.

"How are you, Anne?"

Her hands trembled a little. So did her smile. "I'm . . . fine, Doug. How have you been?"

"Not so fine."

He sat down on the glider, took up a handful of peas, shucked a few, tossed the pods into the pot. Anne said nothing. She picked out the pods, looking at him slantwise, as though he might disappear before a direct gaze.

t he was with her, beside her. . . . I love you, Doug, her heart cried. And if something warned her to be wise, to keep, if there was still time, some part of herself for herself, she didn't hear it.

"Anne, I've been experimenting."

"That must be interesting."

"No. It's not. I was experimenting to see how long I could stay away from you."

"Oh." They stared straight ahead. Then Anne said, "You did pretty well. Four days."

He shook his head. "I didn't last one day. The other three were punishment for not lasting longer."

"I couldn't have lasted through the punishment." She said it before she had any idea she had more than thought it. Her eyelids descended; she waited . . . because the words had come so naturally, so revealingly. Her eyes were still closed when he leaned over, so his breath surged softly against her ear.

"Anne, I love you," he said. . . .

Now, sitting under the apple tree, Anne dropped her head on her knees, rocking back and forth with pain. "Doug, Doug, don't do this again," she whispered. "Where are you? What are you *doing* to me?"

Her mother, at the kitchen window, looked down through the rows of sweet William and snapdragons, to where Anne, in pink shorts and white shirt, so young, so desperately faced her loss.

Mr. Armacost, coming in to abstract some part of the lunch for himself prematurely, forgot about food. "What is it?" he asked, moving over beside her in concern. His wife didn't answer. She nodded out the window, twisting a stemmed glass in her fingers. After a moment they turned away.

"There's nothing to do, you see. Nothing at all we can do." Mr. Armacost shook his head bleakly.

he
nge
plac-
that it
g in the
o wrecks,
be plunged
the floor.
, reaching for
all right, boys?"
re nods.
h his mouth full.
oor. "Pa!" she yelled.

shattered down the stairs

ant . . ." Mrs. Maloney in-
she could hear her husband's

ll he take us swimming," Cooper

know can you take them swimming."
boys. "Want me to pack you a lunch?
nterrupted herself as the upstairs voic

hey'll be ready to go in ten minutes
eavy, heels-first tread thudded over the k
the head of the stairs, setting up a ser

CHAPTER SIX

"CIGARETTE, JOHNNY?"

"Thanks, Cooper, don't mind if I do.

They lit crumpled cigarettes, caref
matches in their palms, drew bulging
blew long streamers into the air.

"You get any out of your nose ye
tapping his ashes vigorously.

"Not yet. You?"

"Nope."

They smoked in silent concen
en house in Cooper Maloney
jittered on the line. A droopy
fully, turning his head from s
something. This cock dutif
every morning and gave hi
ing. Then he remained hu
to know that one way o
Johnny watched him
dirt. A few yellow ch
but the rooster paid

"Sure wouldn't w
observed, examining

"Me either," Johnny agree
were different. If Mr. Maloney ca
Cooper'd catch it, fourteen years old or
was strong, too. Awash with muscles. But it
Johnny realized, caught me, the first thing I knew he
buying me a pack, inviting me to smoke with the family.
He pictured the scene shudderingly, the nonchalance, the
casual offer of a cigarette after dinner. Anne's remarks.

60

Mr. and Mrs. Maloney were big people. Mrs. Maloney
moved about the kitchen with aimless good intent, poking
at things, moving objects from one place to another and
back again, producing, in a placid way, miraculous cakes
and pies which Cooper handed out to his friends.
Johnny always felt uneasy here. Not with the Maloneys
—with their house. He was sure that the entire place
would someday topple and drop to the ground, that only
good luck had kept it standing this long. He eyed t
great seams in the wall, the door that had lost a hi
and never been repaired, the piece of cardboard re
ing one of the window panes. He was confident
had something to do with Mr. Maloney's bein
house-wrecking business. They're just used
Johnny told himself, waiting at any moment
to the basement through some eruption in
her cake tin as she did. "Devil's Food
Mrs. Maloney greeted them cheerfull
"Pop up yet?" Cooper inquired in
They nodded happily. "And milk?" M
Mrs. Maloney waddled to the
"Johnny and Cooper are here!"
"Whadda they want?" a voice
from a remote room.
"He says what do you w
terpreted, as though only
voice.
"Want to ask him w
supplied.
"Pa! They want to
She turned to
What, Pa?" she
sounded again
"I said, if
Maloney's h
en toward

tremors and reverberations in the walls that renewed all Johnny's fears. In a minute he came in, red-faced, over-alled, vastly good-tempered.

"Well, well, Johnny," he cannoned. "Howarya? How's the professor and your ma?"

"They're fine, thanks, Mr. Maloney."

"And the beautiful sisters?"

"Oh, you mean Anne and Theo?"

Mr. Maloney shook his head. Not in negation, in astonishment. "None other," he said. "How many others you got?"

"Oh, you know. . . ," Johnny said in confusion. "I mean, beautiful and all that. I don't think much about things like that."

Johnny looked at the floor, but Cooper rescued him. "How about swimming, Pop? You going out toward Price's?"

Mr. Maloney rubbed a finger under his nose. He stared at the ceiling, closed his eyes, opened them again, scratched his neck. He sat down heavily and pulled at his ear. Mrs. Maloney yawned widely.

"Well," Cooper's father said finally, "I suppose I could. I'm going out and look over the Wellman place. We're gonna start wrecking Monday. I told Mr. Gleebes over at Archetype that if we waited another year, the house'd fall down of itself. . . ."

Irresistibly, Johnny's eyes roved around the room in which they now stood. Then he watched Mrs. Maloney making roast beef sandwiches.

Gee, they're nice people, he thought. Then, struck with a sudden idea, he poked Cooper. "Hey, Mr. Maloney," he said, "you suppose Cooper and I could have some old wood from that place? I mean, just some pieces your boss wouldn't miss? They got some pretty good lumber in those old places, and if we got some maybe Cooper and I could start a carpentry shop. We could practice on it, and after

63

a while get to be cabinetmakers. Cooper," he went on excitedly, "that's some idea, don't you think? Really good. We could go into business later on, and . . ."

Mr. Maloney dropped to the table, leaned his head on his great muscular arms, and exploded into laughter. His shoulders heaved prodigiously, the strangled hoots muffled against the table top.

Johnny's jaw set.

"Now, Pa!" said Mrs. Maloney, slicing cake, wrapping it in oiled paper. "Stop it, Pa."

Mr. Maloney, still shaken with gusts of laughter, wiped his eyes with his sleeve, shook his head helplessly. "'Scuse me, Johnny," he choked. "Honest, Johnny, I wasn't really laughing at you. But you know, ever since you been five years old, you've been planning what you're going to be when you grow up. . . ."

"So?" said Johnny quietly.

With an effort Mr. Maloney grew serious. "So that's fine, boy. I really do think it's fine. It's only . . ." His mouth started to curve again, and he said hastily, "It's only that you change your mind so often, and the least little thing sends you off till in five minutes you got nothing to do but watch the gold pile up. . . ." He looked at the irritated Johnny with affection. "Remember when I got the chickens? You were going to . . ."

"All right, Pa," interjected Mrs. Maloney. "Johnny has ambition, and it's a good thing, too."

"Sure, sure it is," Mr. Maloney nodded emphatically. "I'm just saying . . ."

"Well, don't," advised his wife.

Mr. Maloney looked closely at Johnny. "Not mad, are you?" he inquired anxiously.

Johnny sighed. "Nope. I'm sort of use to it."

Cooper, peering into the lunch box, said, "*Could* we have some pieces of wood and stuff from the house, Pa?"

"Well now, I guess we could get some to you. And at

that, Johnny's idea is pretty good. Maybe you could make some things, lemonade stand or something. . . ."

But Johnny was not to be drawn. Cooper snorted at the lemonade stand. "That's kid stuff, Pa."

They stopped for Johnny's swimming trunks.

"See if Anne wants to go too, will you Johnny?" his mother asked. "She's in the garden."

Johnny scrutinized his mother. Then, "What makes you think Anne would want to go swimming with us? She never has before." Mrs. Armacost sighed and supposed he was right. Johnny lingered at the door, slapping the trunks against his leg. "It's tough," he said finally, and went out to the truck.

Mr. Maloney's machine battled its way along, a bit of the Maloney house come loose. Its fenders flared dashingly, one headlight drooped like a winking eye. From its interior unbecoming noises threatened sporadically. But somehow it managed to stay together, year after year. Cooper and his father had great confidence in it.

Past the Wellman house they lurched and sprang between dusty lanes of privet. The fields unrolled on either side, shimmering under waves of heat. Daisies, buttercups, clover drooped limp in the yellow grass. Beneath motionless trees cows stood or lay in apathy, their under jaws moving from side to side, their ropy tails ineffectually slapping at flies.

The cab of the truck sizzled. Johnny thought the odor of gasoline and hot leather would kill him, or the air sweeping through the windows, swollen and brassy. Perspiration trickled and poured from his forehead down. His arm stuck to the door, his legs to the seat, his thigh to Cooper. Drowsily he thought of Price's, of the clear green water sliding roundly over black stones in the rapids. The water going over stones looked motionless, like glass, until you put a finger in it. Then it surged up around the palm of your hand, broke in two smooth slabs that arched upward, joined, shot down in a little cataract, and bubbled away. He thought of the stepping stones that led to where the waters sloped, of his own body insinuating itself into the cool surge of the rapids, then sliding, serene and upright, bumping sedately on the slippery round stones, into the body of the lake itself.

Something stung him. He lifted a leaden hand to his neck. A fly. He picked it off, flung it through the window, blinking at the glare of the road and the air.

Then they were there, at Price's. Mr. Maloney braked without warning. Shuddering, his truck obeyed the order to halt. Johnny and Cooper peeled themselves off the seat, jumped to the ground.

"Thanks loads, Pop," Cooper said, reaching back in the cab for the lunch box. "Yeah, gee," Johnny echoed. Then, "You going to work today, Mr. Maloney?"

"Sure am. Why?"

"It's so hot," Johnny groaned. "How'll you stand it?"

"Ah, heat don't bother me none, Johnny." Or anything else, he might have added. The big man put his Juggernaut in gear. "Sure there're no hard feelings, son?"

"Oh, no," Johnny laughed. "It sure was nice of you to take us out here."

Mr. Maloney waved to the two boys, ground off in a fountain of dust. Cooper and Johnny ran for the boys' bathhouse, a rickety, gray wood structure, smelling of damp and moss. Laboriously carved initials, hearts, limp vulgarities wrinkled the warped walls. Johnny glanced at them briefly, wondering how so many idiots had found it worthwhile to linger in this stale cupboard long enough to produce such a fretwork. He went out to the now welcome embrace of hot sun and air.

Cooper sprinted over to the soft-drink stand, where Mr. Price leaned on a calloused elbow, perusing his beach.

"Keep this for me?" Cooper asked, anticipating the answer by thrusting the lunch box across the counter.

"Sure, Cooper. Wanna rent a tire tube?"

Cooper debated, clawing his head. "Hey, Johnny!" he yelled. "Got any money?"

Johnny sauntered over, tantalizing himself by remaining out of the water. There really weren't many people on the beach. A bunch of guys with some girls further up, a few mothers with babies. He thrust his chest out as he walked, then shrugged, letting it relax. Skinny, let it go at that. If that blasted course would only start coming, the whole thing could be fixed up by fall. Didn't the ad say you'd amaze your friends in a couple of weeks?

"A little," he replied to Cooper's question. "Hi, Mr. Price. Let's get a couple of tubes, Cooper."

"That's what I was deciding. Only I don't have any money."

Johnny produced a quarter from the pocket of his trunks, dropped it to the counter. "That's ten cents apiece, Mr. Price, for an hour. Two tubes, right? And a bottle of pop."

Mr. Price lifted the lid of an icebox, where colored bottles floated among water and great chunks of ice. "What kind, boys? Keep the tubes all morning. Ain't many people here."

"Cherry," Johnny decided for them. "Thanks a lot, Mr. Price."

"That's okay." He waved them to the water.

Johnny ran, a thin, brown streak, over the blistering sand. A few prancing steps in the water and he plunged like a freed arrow to the lake's heart, lashing and twining eel-like beneath the surface. He shot, showering droplets, into the air, arched and dove back, cutting into the water without a splash. Cooper, advancing somewhat ponderously over the lake's surface, watched admiringly. With a curvet, like a lean seahorse, Johnny disappeared before his eyes, emerged blinking and tossing his head at Cooper's side.

"Great, hah, Cooper?" he yelled exuberantly.

"Sure is."

Cooper clamped his fingers over his nose, sank beneath the surface. Johnny followed into the depths, where the water was yellow with reflected sunlight, and they moved through it, angled arms and legs waving in dream-like postures. They eyed each other solemnly, cropped heads with drifting mossy hair, slow-driving limbs, bubbles tipping at the nostrils, then spilling, shooting upward. Cooper sprang toward the air, Johnny bounded after. They splashed back in a thrashing tangle, then swam to shore for the tubes.

Johnny, drifting in his tube, legs and arms thrown over the slippery black rubber, revolved serenely, gazing about. He soaked and sponged up the sunlight that glittered in the wavelets like gold coins. The water closed coolly around his ankles and drooping wrists as he bobbed up and down. Willows on the bank looped their dreamy boughs to the lake's surface, where tiny bugs shot in triangular patterns. A kingfisher shot from the bank, sprayed the sun-spangled water in a shallow dive, rose and flapped away with a sequined fish.

Absorbed, peaceful, Johnny glanced obliquely upward. From this angle the sky seemed to tilt steeply, the birds to fly in shallow arcs against its blue curve.

"Douglasss!" a girl's voice shrieked in mock distress.

Johnny looked around quickly. On the beach Douglas Eamons and Dody Colman ran erratically through the sand, shouting and slipping. As Johnny turned, Doug scooped the girl up and dashed for the water, faltering when he saw Anne's brother. Johnny eyed them blankly, flipped his wrists to rotate away. He saw Doug ease Dody to her feet, walk off a bit, and fling himself down.

Johnny shrugged. "That pinhead," he muttered aloud.

"Which pinhead?" Cooper inquired, paddling along-side.

"Ah . . . that Eamons. Forget it."

"Doug Eamons? He's all right."

"*Sure* he is, the jerk. Acts like I put a pox on him. Let's go up to the rapids."

The sun didn't feel quite so radiant, and there was goose flesh all over his brown thinness. "I hate things that make me worry about things," he said obscurely. Cooper didn't answer. He had an idea what the trouble was, but no intention of discussing it. They went up to the rapids, and in a little while had forgotten everything but the transparent water streaking over the smooth round stones. They sat and bobbed calmly down the slippery waterway, back to the lake. Doug and Dody were gone by that time, but Johnny didn't look for them anyway.

CHAPTER SEVEN

TOWARD THREE o'clock the sun retreated behind a lifting mass of lavender cloud that swelled, billowed, darkened to purple, to black. Across the sky brilliant bursts of lightning flared and disappeared. The trees stooped trembling, turned up the silver under sides of their leaves, as the wind raced through them. Thunder cracked behind the hills, wavered, split the air, muttered away, charged back roaring like the ghost of a Celtic clan in combat. Then, maddened by delay, the gray rain cataracted down the hills, across the fields, surged through the town. In minutes, swirling tides careened in the gutters, gushed through rainspouts, rivered over the streets and gardens and driveways. Millions of jets sprayed up from the pavements and dashed off the rooftops.

Johnny, haring around from room to room, hurling down windows, shivered with pleasure. He liked the dark crackle of the air, the baying thunder, the sheeted water cascading down the panes, through which he could barely see struggling branches in the torrent.

July, stiff-legged, wary, stalked behind him, fur bristling, eyes dilated. Then with a sudden, satin, sideways leap, she decamped to the kitchen, where Mrs. Armacost was peeling fruits. Terrified of storms, Mrs. Armacost crouched into herself at every clap of thunder, started nervously at July's entrance, sprang to her feet with a stifled cry at the scream of the telephone. She heard Anne's quick footsteps.

"Don't answer that," Mrs. Armacost called desperately, without hope of sucess.

"Oh, Mother," Anne protested. She picked up the receiver, listened a moment. Then, with no betrayal of disappointment in her voice, "Oh, hello, Nora. When did you get back? How are you? Is the . . . ?"

Mrs. Armacost hesitated, turned back to the kitchen. She *knew* no one should answer a telephone during a thunderstorm, but how to make anyone else know it? "What do you think will happen?" they asked patiently. What Mrs. Armacost thought would happen was that they'd get electrocuted through their ears, but didn't feel quite comfortable about saying so. She contented herself with vague wavings of the hands and portentous nods. "Someday, during one of these storms," Theo observed darkly, "Mother is going to run screaming into the woods and no one will ever hear from her again." "Well," Mr. Armacost said, not agreeing with his wife, but defensive for her, "I've heard of odd cases where, hmm . . ." His illustration failed him. Mrs. Armacost realized that, like all atavistic fears, her abject dread of storms was a matter between her and nature . . . their battle. And a terribly one-sided affair.

She selected a peach with uncertain fingers, peeled it between sly glances at the window, as though to test from ambush the endurance of the enemy.

Then she laid down the knife and stared with unfocused eyes at the wall clock, the thought of her daughter surmounting the storm clouds. Anne has . . . courage, she was thinking. How very hard she tries to be natural. What a careful veil she spreads over her hurt. Perhaps if she were less courageous, she'd find the hurt easier to bear. This way, the way she is, all stiffened with pain inside and armor outside, she can't bend, like the reed in the adage, to let the storm pass over. She stands up to it, like the tree, to all the fury and buffetings. When it passes over, which it will, though there is no more use telling her so than there would be explaining to a baby that its stomach-ache will stop, Anne will be . . . scarred. Still standing, because she's a strong girl, but scarred. If something, someone, could teach her to bend . . .

"Learning to tell time, Mom?" Anne inquired, leaning against the door.

"Oh. Oh, my goodness. No, just thinking."

"About storms?"

"Yes, darling. I was thinking about storms."

Anne glanced at her mother curiously. "That was Nora Chapin."

"Oh, little Nora Harrison? Is she back in town?"

"For a while, except she's now little Nora Harrison Chapin."

Mrs. Armacost picked up the abandoned peach. "I know, dear, but it's so difficult to get used to her being married. A child-bride, really," she said distractedly, alert for some hideous display of power from the elements. The rain seemed to have diminished. But that, Mrs. Armacost knew, was just when the most violent thunderclaps would come. Lull you till you turned your thoughts away, and then knock you down with a cannon burst, that was the way.

"Oh, I don't know," Anne was saying. "She was seventeen when she got married. That's old enough to know what you want. Here, I'll help you with that. . . ."

Mrs. Armacost, now alert to closer dangers than the bolts of heaven, handed her daughter a bowl and a knife. "Peel some of these oranges, will you Anne?" she asked casually. "I'd planned a fruit salad, with no way, naturally, of guessing that a storm would simply roll up from nowhere, so we'll have to have it anyway."

"Oh, this'll be over in a while. Then it will be hot, and the sun will come out. . . ." Anne's voice trailed away and she smiled a little wistfully.

Mrs. Armacost realized, with a little thrill of wonder, that Anne must be thinking of herself . . . in a storm. Just the way I'm thinking of her, just the same way. As if . . . it were a heritage. My thoughts, her thoughts, mingling. She shook her head. It was a common analogy, and here indeed was the storm. But the sense of closeness warmed her.

"Why do you shake your head?" Anne asked.

"Oh?" A silence. Then, "Perhaps it isn't always a question of knowing what you want, Anne. About Nora, I mean. It's often a matter of having known enough to be actually making a choice, and that's difficult, at seventeen. As Nora was." Anne's eyes seemed to curve a bit at the repetition of Nora's name, but Mrs. Armacost continued. "When you are so young, you may be taking something that looks wonderful because you have no way of contrasting it. You may not be choosing at all." She paused, went on slowly, "And you may not know how much more you take, that you know nothing about, with this wonder. . ."

Anne nodded. "I see. I think you're probably right." But the reservation in her voice said as clearly as spoken words, you're right, for Nora, for everyone else in the world, but not for me. My wonder, my choice, was perfect. There is no contrast, because nothing is equal to him. The lost sadness stole into her eyes, but she blinked and nodded brightly.

Mrs. Armacost, wary of approaching directly, sighed back to the salad. "Melons," she stated, as though nothing else could possibly interest either of them. "I think I'll try to make those little melon balls."

The door of the small back porch opened, slammed shut. "Oh good grief," wailed Theo, invisible. A series of rustlings and stampings, and she appeared at the door, drenched.

"Darling!" cried Mrs. Armacost. "How ever in the world did you come home?"

"Rowed back in a bus."

"Couldn't you for once take a taxi?"

Theo shook her head vigorously. "It'll take more than a flood for me to spend money on a taxi. I'm all right. I'll run up and take a shower. Nobody struck by a bolt from Zeus?" she went on, studying her mother.

"No," said Anne. "But I narrowly escaped destruction by answering the phone at the height of the fury."

Mrs. Armacost nobly ignored them, contriving her salad. The furious rain had abated, but it dripped heavily from the eaves and the rush of water from the rainspout could be heard splashing.

"I'll go up and keep Theo company, Mom?" Anne inquired.

"Certainly, run along." Mrs. Armacost nearly asked that Theo defer her shower till the last signs of lightning were gone. But she didn't.

Up in their bedroom, Theo shed her dripping clothes, trotted off to the shower. The bottles and oils and sachets received no attention from her. Into the shower. At first she kept her head back, out of the spray, but then with a

73

shrug popped her red hair under the stream of water. Scrubbing vigorously with cake soap, she thought there was an advantage to having coarse curly hair. Anne recoiled in sincere horror from the sight of Theo rubbing her head with cake soap. "Don't you realize," she would cry, "that the hair consists of follicles? You'll drive all that soap right into them, and no amount of rinsing can get it out." Theo remained indifferent. "My hair," she would inform Anne, "is not made of follicles. It has threads, like a screw. Nothing can hurt it."

Returned to the room, she found Anne curled on her bed, reading.

Theo strolled over to the window. New sunlight sparkled wetly on dark, polished leaves. The smell of heliotrope waved in from beneath the sill. And, as she had hoped, a rainbow lifted in the distance—a soft-hued enamel bridge, spanning from hill to hill in the washed sky. "Look, Anne," she murmured, not taking her eyes from what was, like all the strange sky things, a miracle.

"Hmmm?" Anne murmured.

"Nothing." Theo turned back to the room. "What are you reading?"

Anne closed her book guiltily. "Oh . . . uh, *Wuthering Heights*," she said defensively.

"Oh, Anne, not *again?*"

"Well, so what? As I remember it, you read *Little Women* six or seven times."

"But that was different."

"How?"

Theo moved impatiently. "My dearest sister, if you can't tell the difference between *Little Women* and *Wuthering Heights*, you shouldn't be reading either one."

Anne stirred on the bed, glad that Theo hadn't seen the chapter she'd been reading . . . the scene in which Nelly Dean comes to Heathcliff, under the ash tree in the garden, the morning after Catherine's death. She'd read this

74

passage of violence, grief, and lost love so often it was almost unnecessary to glance at the words.

"Do you think, Theo . . . ?" Anne faltered, and stopped. Theo remained unnaturally still, so rarely did Anne speak in this voice. Supplicating, revealing. "Do you suppose," Anne continued in the same trance-like way, "that there ever were . . . people who loved that way, the way Heathcliff and Catherine did?" She was silent, waiting.

Theo felt uncertain, unsure of how to answer. To say yes, she thought, would increase Anne's unhappiness, with the figures of such star-crossed lovers to sanctify her grief. That Anne's suffering was real, Theo never doubted. But to aid it? She sighed.

"I think they were a pair of manic-depressives," Theo answered shortly.

Anne flung herself around on the bed. "You're a fool, Theo. You just don't understand." Her head burrowed into the pillow, escaping.

Theo sat on the bed, twined one of the long brown curls in her fingers. "I'm not a fool, darling," she said softly. "I may never have known love, but I know . . . of it."

Anne turned back, suddenly contrite. "Theo, I'm sorry. And I'm a pig. Making everyone suffer with me. Poor mother," she added ruefully.

"Anne," said her sister, searching for words, "Anne, you aren't a pig, as you say. And if we wouldn't help you in any way we could when you're . . . sad, then we're a pretty pathetic family, wouldn't you say?"

Anne smiled a little. "You do. Even poor Johnny, who thinks I've gone mad."

Theo stared abstractedly through the window at the dripping branches of the elms across the street. "I think," she said at length, "that Heathcliff and Catherine were symbols. Sick, savage symbols. Not people who could ever have lived. . . ." She picked up the book, leafing

75

through idly, noting without comment the page at which it opened naturally. She read the last page, the last paragraph. She read aloud, softly: "I lingered round them, under that benign sky; watched the moths fluttering among the heath and harebells, listened to the soft wind breathing through the grass, and wondered how anyone could ever imagine unquiet slumbers for the sleepers in that quiet earth."

Anne was silent.

"It was kind of her," Theo mused, "to end it that way. After lacerating your nerves so long, to gently close the book with her moths and harebells."

Anne seemed to be asleep. Theo dressed quietly and went downstairs.

Mrs. Armacost surveyed her salad dolefully. The bananas, in spite of lemon juice, were beginning to brown. The melon balls were only round on top. "I'm ashamed to have the *Ladies' Home Journal* in the house," she observed as Theo entered.

"Why?"

"Look at that thing. Probably their garbage pail is better arranged."

"Well, they have fancier garbage than we do."

"*Theo*, don't talk that way! This isn't garbage, it's dinner. And your poor father . . ."

"Just pour a little salad oil on the sports page, and Dad'll eat it with relish."

Mrs. Armacost's brow furrowed. "Your father is an intellectual. He needs relaxation."

"Don't call him that. He wouldn't like it."

"What *is* an intellectual?" Mr. Armacost inquired, coming in with the sports page.

"An intellectual," Theo replied, "is someone who has to sit on the floor to read poetry."

Mr. Armacost selected a flat melon ball, popped it into

his mouth. "Epigrams?" he inquired. "Or is this the voice of the redoubtable Mr. Coombes?"

"Not his voice, but no doubt his influence."

"And how is the old sesquipedalian?"

"I took another letter for him this morning. But then the nephew came after all."

"About time," said Mrs. Armacost.

"Oh, no," Theo said hastily. "He's been away on vacation and his mother never told him about it."

"Hmm," said Mr. Armacost. "Well, it's probably unnerving to have an uncle who thinks he's Dr. Johnson."

"Or Lionel Barrymore," his wife commented suddenly.

Theo glanced similingly at her mother. "He said to me today . . . let's see, what was it in reference to? Oh, yes, about some rule or other in the hospital that he didn't like and had to obey, he said, 'Do you feel, young lady, that a course of action must be correct in order to secure the approbation of the righteous? On the contrary, as witness the dismal condition of our political structure, to which we cling the more firmly as it sinks beneath us. Disastrous . . .'"

"What are you talking about?" Johnny demanded, squashing across the floor in wet sneakers.

"John Armacost!" his mother shrieked. "What have you been doing?"

Johnny glanced down at his sneakers. "Well . . ."

"You don't have to look at your feet. You're soaking wet all over. Did you go out in the rain?"

"Well . . ."

"You could be struck by lightning! A tree could fall on you! What ever in the world possessed you?"

"Well . . ."

"Go up this minute, this *minute*, and get into dry clothes." Mrs. Armacost glared about, including Theo and her husband in her displeasure.

"Don't look at me . . ." they said together.

Johnny disappeared.

"It's a very funny thing," Mrs. Armacost declared in the silence after dinner, as they sat in the living room, "that no one woman can be all things."

"Cleopatra was," Anne remarked.

"Darling, I'm talking about normal women. Cleopatra was *not* a normal woman. Anyway, what I had in mind was housework."

"Oh well, I imagine she didn't know much about that."

"What I meant," her mother continued firmly, "was that some women are good cleaners and some are good cooks, but none of them seem to do both well. Why is that?"

"You do," Johnny said, honestly surprised.

His mother smiled at him. "You say that because of the muffins." Then she sighed. "No, it's really quite a problem."

Her husband and children seemed to have no thoughts on the subject, so she abandoned it. Nevertheless, she said to herself, that salad was terrible. Tasted all right, I suppose, but good heavens, what a mess. I wonder, she mused, what they make melon balls with in restaurants.

"What do they make melon balls out of?" she asked the silence.

"Melons," Johnny answered.

"Excellent example of what is considered rollicking humor, circa fourteen years," Anne observed moodily.

Johnny glanced up with interest, thinking to find Anne in her old manner, but she had already lapsed into reverie. Shaking his head, he went back to *The Cruise of the Cachalot*.

Mr. Armacost sat at his desk near the window, writing checks. From time to time he groaned. Now and then his eyes widened as he pulled some bill from its envelope. The scratch of his pen, the turning of pages as Johnny pursued the sperm whale, Anne's occasional not quite suppressed sigh, the pendulum beat of the clock . . . Mrs. Armacost listened, thinking how muted the evening sounds are. She tipped her head slightly harkening to the outside rumors . . . *a cappella* of nesting birds, dark grass chorus of crickets, swirl of tires over still wet pavements. Twilight nudged up to the windows, deepening.

"Dad?" Johnny questioned suddenly. Mr. Armacost, lost in papers, did not reply.

"Dad, what's a whelk?"

"Hmm?" his father murmured. "Oh, just a second, Johnny, I have a form to fill out."

"So has Johnny," Anne said, and instantly regretted the words. She looked up cautiously, encountering her father's grave eyes, her mother's shocked ones. Johnny seemed not to have heard, but his face reddened, his concentration on the book became intense.

After a long moment of nervous silence, Johnny got to his feet, slapped his thigh once or twice, then strode from the room.

Anne, swallowing jerkily, made a motion to follow, huddled back against her chair. "What a hateful thing to say," she implored, staring at the rug, where July curled in a loop of gray and silver fur.

"Anne," Mr. Armacost said thoughtfully, "Anne, there are people who will sacrifice any loyalty for a well turned phrase, and in most cases the value of these so-called witticisms is dubious. I wouldn't want you to be like that. I don't think you are, really." He turned over a few papers before continuing. "You don't seem to be very happy yourself right now. . . . I know you don't want to talk about it. But, Anne, don't take it out on your brother." He paused, pondered, smiled at her softly, then got up and fiddled with the T.V. Mrs. Armacost watched her daughter carefully, hoping to give some support if their eyes should meet, because surely this was very hard for Anne. But the girl sat like a statue of stone.

Horrible, horrible, horrible, Anne was saying to herself, an incantation to ward off further thought. The thoughts tumbled on her anyway, crying "mean, unloyal, hateful, I hate them. . ." in an undirected jumble. Hot-cheeked, unable to move, she sat impaled by her words, "So has Johnny." Three words . . . said. And now I'll have to apologize, she thought. Only I hate to. I won't. I must. Poor skinny little Johnny. How could I ever . . . ? Poor thin Johnny. Over and over. Why does he care so much? He's so graceful . . . only he doesn't care about that. He wants muscles. . . . And I, said her mind, turning as minds do, back to its own concern, I want Doug. Only Johnny doesn't lash at other people. I do. . . . Oh, horrible, horrible . . .

Just to get out of the room, Johnny turned in the first direction that occurred to him. So now he sat on his bed, thinking that after all he'd go over to Cooper's. He didn't move. July pushed in through the open crack of the door, eyed him with imperious affection, vaulted to his lap.

"You're a silly cat," Johnny said softly, aloud. "You think you're a dog, following me around this way?" His brown fingers flickered at her ears and she arched against them, slit-eyed, purring, like an Egyptian cat in the brown clasp of Pharaoh. Then, bored by fondling, as if Pharaoh's cat should suddenly remember yellow lions lapping at the Nile and weary of the docile role, she evaded him and leaped lightly to the floor. Johnny watched her idly. Then he lay back, hands clasped beneath his head. "What a dopey thing!" he muttered. July pricked up her ears, returned to him, settling on his chest. I'd have sworn, Johnny thought, that nobody knew. Wonder if she's been reading my Journal. But he knew she hadn't. Families, he decided dully, just have a way of ferreting things out. He considered the Course rather halfheartedly. It didn't seem too promising right now, but there was no telling what it would do for him. . . .

"Hop off, July," he ordered, sitting up so that she fell off and lay staring at him with astonishment. He laughed suddenly. "How important you are to you, July," he told her. "And me to me. And Anne to Anne." He pondered this a little. "Theo?" Well, he decided, it must be because Theo's older, like Mom and Dad. They can find something important besides themselves.

He closed the door, took the Journal down from its cache, opened it to a back section, entitled, "What People Would Be if They Weren't Already What They Are." He had a page for each person in his family. There were several entries, on different dates, for each, the greatest number for Anne.

Nibbling on a pencil, he read here and there, turning the pages.

Mother: A flower. A crocus, I think.

A tennis ball, very new, very white, lying on a patch of very bright, green grass with the sun shining on it.

Dad: One of those books people take with them to desert islands.

Theo: I think and think, but I cannot think that Theo would ever be anything but Theo. I am not sure whether this is good or bad, for her that is. It's fine for other people.

When he came to the page labeled Anne, Johnny held his pencil poised as he glanced at the recent entries. He shook his head over one dated April sixteenth. "A butterfly, only a talking one. Fanning around from place to place, colored blue and green, talking away in a sort of fluty voice."

The last remark he'd written a few days earlier, "A goldfish. About to be eaten by a cat."

Now he sucked his pencil, made one more entry for Anne. "A boomerang," he wrote.

Then, turning back to the Journal proper, he wrote

hastily. "I did go swimming today. I'm going to swim every day I can and not bother about the other business any more. What the he . . . ck. Anyway, I'm sure to get the first two lessons of the Course pretty soon, including the over-all explanatory booklet, so I can get started and won't have to worry about it any more. I wish Anne was back the way she used to be. She's sad and she's getting mean. If that Course ever does get here I'll work at it fast and then I'll go out and knock Doug Eamon's block off."

He sighed, closed the ledger, tilted back in his chair, then dropped back to the floor, stored the Journal away, ran downstairs.

His mother and father were looking at T.V. in the living room. At any rate, Johnny smiled to himself, Dad's watching, and Mom's pretending she's one of those women who really loves baseball but doesn't like to show it. Theo had gone out with Dr. Dolan after dinner. He was relieved to see no sign of Anne.

"I'm going over to Cooper's, okay, Mom?" he asked from the hall.

"Mmm," she replied absently, bending her head toward the T.V. as though fearful of missing a play. "Be back soon, Johnny. . . ."

As he stepped on the porch, the street lights lit up, flinging sudden shadows on the sidewalks and lawns. The glider squeaked.

"Johnny?" Anne called.

"Oh . . . yeah, Anne?" He half turned toward her. In the darkness she seemed almost to glow . . . white dress, white skin that never tanned . . . something misty, milky, in the shadows.

"Johnny . . . ," she repeated on an outgoing breath, so that it sounded almost like a gasp, "I'm . . ."

"Oh, let it go, Anne," he interrupted uncomfortably. He perched on the railing and tried to think of something else to say.

Anne went on, "I don't guess I want to let it go, so . . . I'm sorry, Johnny. Really very sorry."

"It's all right."

They sat still, feeling that, so far as they could, they'd dealt adequately with the situation. Nothing more to say, nothing that could be unsaid. One more line added to the network of small hurts. One more hopeful attempt at erasure.

"Well," Johnny got up, "I'm going over to Cooper's for a while." He hesitated, descended the steps. "So long, Anne."

"Night, Johnny."

She watched him walk down the wide street arched over by the branches of the great trees. When he passed under a street lamp, the leaf shadows dappled him, the way they dappled the sidewalk. Leggy and springy he was, moving down the street, into the shadows, under the lights, out of sight.

Theo got home about midnight. By then, everyone else was in bed. She turned off the hall light, edged up the stairs, at the side where the squeaks were not.

Her bed was turned down, white pillows fluffed. The spriggy flowery wallpaper, dark on the dormer slopes, glowed in a roundness on the wall behind the bed lamp. Anne, in bed, was filing her nails.

"Have a nice time?" she asked, turning her hands before her, as though wondering whether or not to take them.

"Oh, yes." Theo grinned. "But I believe Dr. Dolan and I will be seeing less of each other from now on."

"Why?" Anne asked, and added, "You don't care, do you?"

"Not very much. I like him, and I hate to see him floundering in a trap, but there's nothing to do about it."

"Nothing," Anne said wisely, "if you can't think of anything. Whose trap?"

"Oh, a siren in the hospital. Lydia Colman. Did I ever mention her to you?"

"You don't have to," Anne said wearily. "I know her only too well, and her sister Dody." She stared at the nail file a minute, and then said tightly, "Blood may be thicker than water, but those two are thicker than either one."

Theo wasn't really interested. She was wondering again what had become of Anne. I miss her, Theo thought, that Anne with her stagy ways. Not quite real, but very pretty make-believe. This girl we've had since, well, ever since she met Douglas Eamons, who's hurt sometimes, exalted sometimes, but different always from what she was . . . this girl is real enough. But not Anne, I think she isn't Anne. Or is this Anne, becoming a woman, and the girl gone?

". . . waiting for, Theo?"

"What's that, Anne? I wasn't listening."

"I just asked what you're waiting for."

"Waiting for?"

"You know what I mean, Theo. Men. All women want a man, don't they? Oh, well," she added at Theo's expression, "most of them. Don't you at all?"

"Of course I do. I'm not sure that all women do. I do. But, as you say, I'm waiting."

"And if no one with the proper specifications comes?"

"Oh, Anne," Theo protested, "I don't have specifications. At least, no form for someone to fill out. . . ." Anne winced at the phrase. "Perhaps I have them, but it's not at all clear to me what they'd be." She thought of Mr. Coombes' nephew. It wasn't the first time today she'd thought of him. But how very peculiar. She frowned. A man I've spoken to once. She said nothing to Anne. What a reserved family we are, she realized. Talk all the time, but with so many reservations.

"If no one comes," she said at last, "then no man." She stretched her arms high in the air, yawning till the only sound she heard was the roaring in her ears. "I don't have to get up till any time tomorrow," she murmuring, sinking back on the pillow. "On at three."

"That's nice." Anne put the file away. "Want the light out?"

"All right. Did you do anything tonight, Anne?" she asked in the dark.

"Stayed home."

They heard their mother turn over in bed. She always does that, Anne thought. Not that she lies awake, listening and waiting. But when everyone's in, she turns over in bed, as though something whispered to her, "There, all of them safe. Sleep sounder."

"Night, Theo."

"Night, little one. Sleep well."

"You too."

Theo, drifting, nestling in the cool sheets, sniffing dreamily the moving dark night, thought again of Robert Frost's poem. To go up that way, she thought, if you do your own climbing, is good, going and coming back. But what of poor Anne who seems to be carried into the air by no act of her own at all? And certainly her tree doesn't dip its top and set her down again. She gets thrown out, over and over again. That's no way to be a swinger of birches. Or Johnny? Theo smiled in the dark. Yes, Johnny, I think, is like the boy in the poem. He'll climb of his own accord, and come down gently to earth again. Me? Well, if earth's the right place for love, here I am, on it. I've never climbed a birch tree.

She wondered how one writes letters to poets. People do, she thought, lots of people write letters to poets. "Dear Mr. Frost," she composed drowsily, "thank you for your poems. I love them. Especially the ones about trees. I should like to grow into a tree one day myself, like

Thisbe, who did not love a wall." Theo turned that happy phrase over a few times. "Only I can't find a Pyramus. I cannot find . . ." She dreamed away.

CHAPTER EIGHT

WAKING UP was the hardest part. Before, it had been the nicest part. For days, for several weeks after Doug had sat beside her on the glider and said he loved her, Anne had opened her eyes each morning to an almost unbearable happiness. In a sense she could never quite believe it. How could she, out of all the girls there were, how *could* she have had the incredible good fortune that was Doug's love? Her last thought at night, her first thought in the morning, and usually her bright vapory dreams . . . all Doug. Once she dreamed he changed his mind, that when she approached, he turned away . . . the dream was terrible. The waking was a wave of delight. He loved her. Because he said so. He said, "Anne, I love you." And when he said it, his eyes said it too, and the fingers that pushed the curls back from her forehead. When they danced, when they swam, when they sat with two other people, ten other people, Anne heard his voice now bantering nothings with other voices, whisper in her mind, "I love you," and the joy of it bubbled in her till she laughed and people looked at her smilingly, for no reason but that such laughter reels out to enfold everyone near. She had liked them to be with other people sometimes . . . so she could watch him, hear him saying the easy exchanging words, being the handsome, well liked Doug Eamons she'd watched in high school when he'd never looked her way. But with the one wonderful difference—he loved her. And when his eyes rested on her, in the midst of all the others, she could hear him say it.

He hadn't said it often . . . altogether, three times . . . and Anne, helplessly humble where Doug was concerned, began to wonder and to ache. Because love must be told.

He had said it the afternoon on the porch, and once when they'd come home, about midnight, and his dilapidated car had crackled to a stop before her house. He'd turned the ignition key, but the motor sputtered and muttered before it agreed to rest. "Marvelous old car," Doug had approved, listening to the engine's protest. "Eisenglass and the American Can Company," Anne said. Then he quite surprised her with his sudden laugh. His arm went around her shoulder, and he pulled her close. "Oh, Anne, I love you," he said.

The third time she'd asked him to tell her. That was a week ago. And every morning for a week now she'd awakened to misery . . . pinching, gray, bewildered. What have I done, she cried, what did I do? Doug, Doug, *what* did I do? Sometimes it seemed she couldn't stand it at all. I'd like to die, she thought, opening her heavy eyes to the day. Or faint, for a long time, and then when I woke up it would all be over. I'd have forgotten. Forgotten, or, though she tried frantically to keep the thought away, perhaps he'd come back. But that was really harder to bear, the small persistent hope that crowded back. "What of the things he said? How could he forget?" hope asked, returning against her will. Dully she realized he *could* forget. And the things he said? Well, things get said and said . . . nothing is easier to say than a thing. I can say a thing myself. I can say, "I hate you, you're a liar, I hate you. . . ."

A week ago this morning Anne had risen to the radiance of a whole day to be spent with Doug. With Doug and three other couples, including Dody Colman. They were going huckleberrying on Hungry Hill.

When Theo awoke, she found Anne already dressing.

"What in the world? What time is it?" Theo shrieked, bounding out of bed.

"Relax. It isn't even six ye—"

"Then what are you doing, sleepwalking?"

Anne, dressed in blue jeans rolled halfway up her calves, white shirt flopping out, white ribbon holding back her hair, laughed. "Is this accepted raiment for a sleepwalker?"

Theo rubbed her eyes sleepily, going to the closet for a uniform. "Not quite," she conceded, poking about. "Darn it, no fresh ones. What *are* you doing?"

"Doug and I, and some other people, are going over to Hungry Hill and pick huckleberries," Anne announced.

"That should be nice," her sister remarked without enthusiasm. Anne laughed again.

"I can't understand why you hate to get up in the morning. Such a beautiful time, Theo, with the risen sun blazing on the dew-drenched grass, the birds in joyful chorus, the . . ."

Theo cut her off with a skeptical stare. "Try," Theo offered dryly, "try, for say three mornings, rising to the blazing dew and going to work. Then come back and tell me how you like it."

"Well, put that way . . ."

"That's the way it's put to me every morning." Theo yawned again, departed for the bathroom.

Anne painted on a careful scarlet mouth, considered powder, and decided against it. Her skin had a mat quality, a lovely freshness that never got shiny. Powder was a fillip, hardly necessary for huckleberries. "Don't you think huckleberry is a lovely word?" she asked Theo as they met in the hall.

Theo said huckleberry was a beautiful word, Anne a beautiful girl, the morning was beautiful. "Oh, and one more beautiful," she added. "A beautiful berry pie tonight, I hope." She went into the bedroom, stuck her head out

88

the door, and called after Anne, "Made by Mother, not you, beautiful."

Anne lilted downstairs to the kitchen, where Mrs. Armacost was packing sandwiches for her in Johnny's lunch box.

"Morning, Mom," Anne said, kissing her mother's cheek. "Would you put iced tea in the thermos, not milk? Is there any?"

"There's some left over from last night, if that will do."

"Just fine. Do you get up early or stay up all night?"

Mrs. Armacost, gazing abstractedly into the refrigerator, said, "I suppose so." She frowned. "Anne, did you eat that chicken that was in here?"

"No. As a matter of fact, I was hoping to eat it today."

Mrs. Armacost shook her head. "Well, you can't. It's gone. I suppose Johnny . . ."

"I suppose Johnny is right. Is there anything else, or just sandwiches?" Anne joined her mother and together they peered into the refrigerator. Anne found a couple of plums and a tomato, which went into the lunch pail. She poked about the kitchen till she located some cookies. "By the way, Theo is hoping you'll bake a beautiful pie when I bring home the berries."

"Is she?" wailed Mrs. Armacost. "Why do people think I can do things like that?"

"I think your pies are very good, except for the crusts, and we don't have to eat those."

Mrs. Armacost thought this rather scanty reassurance. "I'll try," she sighed, thinking of pie-crust mix. Now she'd have to make one of those secret trips to the A.&P. Unless Mrs. O'Brien next door . . .

Anne put cream on Grape-Nuts, poured a glass of milk, a glass of orange juice, and sat down. "Have some coffee with me, Mom," she invited. Then, "Where's Dad?"

"Out among the birds and bees."

"Is Johnny up too?"

"Heavens, no." Mrs. Armacost poured two cups of coffee, sat down opposite Anne.

"He's the only normal member of the family. All this getting up at dawn just isn't natural. Unless for something special, like huckleberries."

"How are you going?"

"Four of us in Doug's car and four in Jack Raymond's."

Mrs. Armacost shook her head. "I hope those old things are safe, Anne. They look extremely doubtful to me, to say nothing of how they sound."

"Oh, the boys are good drivers. Doug is especially," she said, sure that the pride she felt was not echoed in her voice, quite sure she didn't actually linger over his name when she said it.

Mrs. Armacost glanced out to the garden, where her husband, on his knees, was keeping his bird vigil, flower in hand. His broad determined shoulders gave her support, even at this distance. Glancing back at Anne, she smiled. "I'm sure he is . . . they are."

A crunch of tires on gravel, slam of a tinny door, and there was Doug at the back porch. He wore jeans with his inevitable white T-shirt. Looking at him, Mrs. Armacost could understand how Anne could be so lost in love. Looking at him, she repeated to herself. But what sort of boy he was, she couldn't tell. Polite enough, pleasantly at home when he visited them. This, of course, meant nothing. Anne's first love, the one that never leaves. Whatever comes after, this first love is always there. The measuring rod, the lost beauty, the one for whom her husband suffers all his life. Even, she thought, if he happens to be the same person. Because what we love the first time is a feeling and an age. It remains inviolate, unchanged. The person cannot. The man of thirty who comes home to shrieks of, "Daddy, Daddy!" cannot be the boy of nineteen who took you dancing by a lake. And if he looks the same,

90

only older, and talks the same, only less, he is still forever losing a most unequal battle with himself.

"Morning, Mrs. Armacost," Doug greeted her in his deep-toned voice. "Hi, Anne. All set?"

"Right with you," Anne answered, rationing the length of time she looked at him.

"Good morning, Doug," her mother said. What sort of boy? Polite, handsome, clever at his schoolwork. Very mercurial. A boy who slipped away and reappeared. His mother dead, his father a fireman, who only cared for his son, who had, apparently, sacrificed much so that Doug could go to college. Still, Doug worked hard. He'd worked after school since he'd been thirteen, a tow-headed boy delivering groceries. (She grinned a little, remembering a recent comment of John's. "Tow-headed?" Johnny had said. "Two-headed is more like it." Johnny, militantly defensive for Anne, with whom he fought constantly.) Doug worked in college too, waiting on tables, tutoring. Mrs. Armacost ran her finger round the tip of her coffee cup, thinking about him. She sighed, realizing that, consciously or unconsciously, Doug gave nothing away to show what sort of boy he was at all. After they'd gone, she went out in the garden, to be with her husband whom she'd come to understand.

Doug pushed through a gap in a hedge, holding it back for Anne. On the other side, the slope of the hill ran gently away and up. Daisies and clover, melting buttercups, spangled the meadow grass. The tangled, many-branched berry bushes, rich with their deep blue fruit, sprang lavishly, everywhere. Broad swath of the sunlight, darkened with pools of shadow where rock or hummock rose, fell over the hills and fields. Far off, below them, they could see their two cars parked side by side, at the edge of a dusty road. Nearby, but out of sight, were the other berry pickers, their voices clear in the still air. It was nearly noon.

Doug looked at their two full baskets. He studied the new field, apparently untouched. He sighed. "There's a heck of a lot of berries around," he remarked with resignation.

"Mmm. But we haven't any more room in the baskets," Anne offered hopefully.

Doug glanced down at her. "Shouldn't we offer to help the others?" he asked dubiously.

"Why?"

He didn't answer right away. Then he said, "Why, indeed? I guess I'll have a smoke." He pulled a pipe from his pocket, produced a tobacco pouch, dropped to the grass. "Come on, Anne," he said, patting the ground beside him.

Anne sank down slowly, eying the pipe. "I didn't know you smoked a . . . pipe, Doug."

"Oh, sure, have my pipeful once a week."

With anyone else, Anne thought, I'd be laughing by now. But since it's Doug, I take it seriously. He looks wonderful smoking a pipe, because he's Doug. If this were Peter, I'd roar. It isn't, she went on dreamily, fingers clasped on her knees, so much that I love him for the things he does. I love anything that gets done by him. Just because Doug does something, it's wonderful to me. Doug. Douglas Eamons. The sound of his name, the look of it written down . . . different from any other sound or writing in the world. I'd rather hear or see his name, she realized with a sense of discovery, than my own. That man who lectured on psychology last year said each person's name is the most important combination of syllables there is, to himself. But Doug's is more important to me. I guess it's rather like Theo feels about the word "poet." She says it's a word separate from the rest of language, its form and its sound above all others. What did she say?

"A complete language of one word . . . poet." Or, for me, "Douglas."

Bees boomed past on their airy paths, trips from clover to clover. High, high in powder-blue space a buzzard wheeled on ragged wings. Round Anne and Doug a heavy redolence rose, sweet smoke from his pipeful of the week. It's certainly, Anne decided, a . . . substantial tobacco. She didn't say anything.

Dody and Jack Raymond burst through the hedge, laughing and spilling berries. "Hey, stop it!" Dody shrieked, trying to right her basket as Jack laughed at her. They collapsed giggling on the grass.

"For the luva Mike!" Jack exploded, directing a stern glare at Doug. "That's *you*! We thought a bunch of honey-combs had caught fire."

Dody looked at Doug, then at Anne, then cascaded into renewed laughter. "Oh my goodness," she sputtered, covering her face with her hands, shaking her thick pale hair from side to side. "You look so terribly funny, you do."

Anne felt herself stiffen with indignation. How dared they, how did they *dare* to laugh at Doug? "I think it's nice," she said with a faint tremor.

"Do you *really*?" Dody choked. "Ah, well, a comfortable briar . . ."

Anne glanced nervously at Doug. He was grinning broadly, knocking the tobacco out on a little rock. "Preparation for the sophomore circle," he nodded calmly. "All the blades smoke these things, and I don't intend to be a wallflower." He was laughing at himself and, in a way, at Anne, for being so serious about it.

"What I want to know," Jack persisted, "is *what* do you smoke in it?"

"Hershey bars," Doug said grandly, and the three of them roared. Anne, in wretched amusement, contributed a dismal cackle. Her face and neck were moist with embarrassment. I hate her, she cried inwardly, not looking at Dody. She makes a fool of me without even trying. Or perhaps, she went on, forgetting to laugh, she is trying. I shouldn't have thought she'd be so clever. Or myself so utterly clumsy. Oh, horrible, horrible . . .

Angie, Peter, Susie Holmes, and Buster Hopkins trailed through the now permanently parted gap in the hedge. Buster and Peter were lugging a small icebox, which they set on the ground with a sigh of relief. Angie and Susie had some lunch pails. They were all grimy with perspiration and dust.

"Somebody else can get the rest of the lunches," Angie announced firmly. "I refuse to carry anything or move me for quite a while."

The four boys exchanged glances, without speaking.

"Oh well," Doug got to his feet. "Come on, Anne. But I warn you," he said to the recumbents, "on the way back to the cars, I won't carry more than two people on my shoulders. Two girls," he added.

"I get firsties," Dody called.

"Come off it," Jack told her. "Anybody carries you, it's going to be me."

"Darling!" Dody squealed. "Just like a knight dashing up to me!"

"Kinda late night, if you ask me," Peter observed.

Their voices grew fainter as Anne and Doug went toward the tree where the rest of the lunches lay. The smell of the grass rose fragrantly, grasshoppers scattered in shooting sprays before their feet, little earth voices stilled as they approached, rose again behind them.

Anne stumbled along mutely, nibbling nervously at the inside of her cheek. Doug ambled, jumping into the air now and then. Once he let out a high yodel, which was instantly answered by an invisible chorus from behind the far-off hedge.

They reached the tree. Anne stooped for a basket,

94

straightening as Doug said, "Wait a minute, Anne." She waited, quite still. But her heart slammed around till it echoed in her ears.

Doug looked at her for a long minute. Then, "Let's sit down a second," he asked quietly.

Anne, who thought she was going to fall down anyway, crumpled beside the lunches. Doug lowered himself beside her, stared across the fields, carefully pulled a blade of grass from its green sheath and bit off the tender white tip. "All right," he said at last. "What's the matter?"

Anne, feeling miserably close to tears, shook her head, not answering.

"Something is," he said.

Anne took a deep breath, opened her mouth, closed it again, and smiled weakly.

"Anne, you can't let those people see you this way," the boy pleaded.

"What way?" she asked, and then coughed because something seemed to be stuck in her throat.

"You know what way," he said in a louder voice. "All stony and closed up. And . . . unhappy," he added. They sat in silence. Then Doug blew out a long breath. "Look," he tried again. "How do you think I feel when I see that almost everything I do either hurts you or embarrasses you?"

"Nothing embarrasses me that you do. . . ."

"Well, indirectly. That pipe, for instance. Everyone else thought it was a joke. Why couldn't you?"

"I . . . thought you were hurt," she whispered.

"But that's just what I mean. *You* get hurt, and it's always because of me, and I have no way of telling when it's going to happen." Doug shook his head, became silent. He stared thoughtfully into space, and Anne stared at him. "I don't think I'm good for you at all," the boy said very sadly.

Doug had two lines running from his nostrils to his

mouth. Sometimes Anne traced these lines, which she loved, with her finger. She didn't dare to now, though she ached from the wish. His mouth looked very wistful and very dear. She would have liked to kiss it, but couldn't. She was, actually, a little afraid of him—or of what he'd do. Afraid that he'd drift away again, and maybe this time for good. She sat, not daring to speak or move, for fear of saying or doing the wrong thing. It was clear enough what he wanted—for her to be gay, sure of herself, the way she used to be. She didn't blame him at all. It must be, she thought, boring for him to be around me when I get this way . . . tongue-tied. And jealous of . . . I suppose really of everyone who turns his thoughts from me, even for a minute. That's why, she thought suddenly, he laughed that night in the car and said he loved me. Because for a change I had something light to say. Oh dear heaven, she prayed silently, why is it that I can know how I should be, only I can't make myself be that way?

Then, to her horror, she heard herself saying, "Doug, *do* you love me?"

He turned around to face her, and for a long time they gazed in each other's eyes. "Of course I do," he answered at last.

"Well then, say it," she almost sobbed.

"I love you," he said.

Anne, sifting her victorious ashes, closed her eyes and hoped she wouldn't cry.

Waking up was the hardest part. Once she'd shouldered up through the clouds of sleep, where sometimes Doug was still hers, once she'd shaken off the deceptive peace and promise of dreams, she found a little courage to face the day.

It was, simply, a matter of moving from nothing to nothing, till the day was over.

She had a shaky remedy with which she tried to help

herself. If, she said, I were going to see Doug in the next hour, I could stand the hour till he came. So if I just take one hour after another hour, not looking further, I can get through any day. And sometime, maybe, it'll be a day, and then a week . . . but no, no. Not a day, not a week . . . not even an hour. Well, a minute then. . . . Try it with a minute.

What have I done, she cried. But she knew. She'd made a simple error. She'd loved him too much, and told him so, if not in words, in every other way. What was that poem Theo read to her once? "Never seek to tell your love, love that never told can be . . ." Something like that.

Anne got up to face her nothing.

CHAPTER NINE

Theo, walking for the bus at two-thirty in the afternoon, became aware of a car edging slowly along beside her. She lifted her head, stared with purpose at the bus stop, walked faster.

"Hello," said the occupant of the snailing car.

Theo frowned. What in the world, she thought, does this character think he's doing? I am certainly not the type who gets into strange automobiles to go buy a bag of candy. Especially not in a uniform, she added, a little uncertain of what the type actually is.

"Look, I'm going down to the hospital too," the voice went on.

Theo turned. The nephew looked marvelously cool in a cord suit, panama hat over his black hair. He lounged in a blue convertible that seemed to drive itself. From beneath his wild brows the green eyes smiled up at her, aware of what she'd been thinking.

Theo began to frown again, then smiled. "Is this an invitation?"

"It is." The car stopped, he leaned over and opened the door for her. "You are Miss Armacost," he said when she was settled and they'd started along, at a barely faster pace.

Theo smiled again. Isn't this fun, she thought. Then, I wish I were better at flirting. If I were Anne, I'd ask him, "How do you know?" with demure surprise. But since I'm not . . . "You asked your uncle?" she said.

"I said, 'Who's the red-haired nurse who knows you like Boswell?' and he said, 'Ah, you have reference to Miss Armacost. A delightful young woman who has been kind enough to take a letter for me to . . . ah, she has most kindly attended to a vital piece of correspondence in the absence of anyone else who would. . . .' So then I said, 'Very nice of her, and what were you writing to me?' Shall I go on with this?" he asked, sliding competently between a truck and another truck, which loomed hugely as they passed.

"Oh, yes," Theo answered. "I want to hear what he said to you after that. Although I have an idea . . ."

"Yes. Well, he said, 'Paul, I am in imminent danger of losing my patience with you. You have the most unwarranted cheek it has been my misfortune to encounter in a member of my family, which insolence I cannot but feel hearkens back to a misalliance, conceived, if memory serves, about the . . .' Do you wish to hear any more?"

"No, I can fill in the rest for myself." Theo laughed, picturing the big old man firing broadsides from his bed. Her face softened.

"You like him, don't you?" the nephew said.

"Oh, I do. He's an extraordinary man. I like him very much."

"I'm Paul Favor, or did you know?"

"Yes. How do you do, Mr. Favor?"

"Very well, and you are Miss What Armacost?"

"Theo."

"What a nice name. You're my first Theo. May I call you Theo?"

She turned, a little suspiciously. All very well to be dashing. But rather unbecoming to be so . . . confident of it.

He halted for a red light. "Oh, don't," he said smiling, then serious. "Don't look at me that way. I really mean it, about calling you Theo. It's a nice name so why waste it?" He sounded, oddly, a little shy now.

"It's not wasted," Theo assured him slowly.

He shifted, drove on. They approached the hospital. Theo felt a little desperate. A prig, that's what I am, a prig, she told herself angrily. He was friendly, that's all, and I behave like a vaporing nineteenth-century maiden. She cast about for some way to retrieve her position, but her mind continued to revolve about her own folly and her tongue lay unmoving. They drew up before the hospital.

"Well," Theo said dismally, "thanks a lot for the ride." She reached for the door handle, but he sprang out, ran around, and opened it for her.

"Look," Paul said as she got out, "I didn't mean to be rude."

"You weren't rude," Theo told him. "I was. Thanks again." She started for the side door.

"May I go in this way too?" he asked, pacing up beside her.

"What? Oh, of course. It's easier than the lobby for me. Just keep on till you reach the center hall." What a lot of nonsense we speak, she was thinking. Words, words.

"When is your day off?" Paul asked, as she paused at the Nurses' Room.

Theo felt a bit weak with relief. "Friday," she said expectantly.

"Well, Miss Armacost, may I take you to dinner on Friday?"

Theo nodded. "I'd like that."

Still he lingered. "Is your father Alec Armacost, the teacher?"

"Yes, he is."

"I had him in high school, quite a while ago that was. I'll be glad to see him again. He's a fine teacher."

"Yes, he is," Theo repeated. "I think he'll be glad to see you."

"If he remembers me."

"Oh, he'd remember you," Theo said, and then thought, that's the sort of thing you say to flirt, only I'm not flirting.

"I'll call you tomorrow, Miss Armacost?"

"All right," she said happily, then added, "You don't have to overdo the Miss Armacost part." She went into the Nurses' Room, got her cap out, clamped it on her head, glancing idly in the mirror, as usual, to see that the cap was on right. Today she leaned forward, studying her face critically. Well, it was a face, but after you'd said that, there wasn't much more to remark. Why does he want to take me to dinner? I haven't had time to grow on him at all. And I, of course, am the type that must grow on people. My values emerge with continued contact, everybody says so. How nice of him to ask me to dinner before my values had a chance to emerge.

"Good afternoon, Judy," she greeted the entering supervisor cheerfully.

Miss Tracy looked at her askance. "What's perked you up? Don't tell me a morning's sleep can put that sparkle in an eye," Judy inquired, plopping her own cap on without looking in the mirror at all.

"Oh that. And other things," Theo said evasively.

They went up to the third floor, received the report of the limply departing morning nurses. "Mr. Coombes," one of them observed as she got up to leave, "is in a

100

strangely pleasant mood. No trouble at all." Theo smiled. He does seem to have a good effect on people, she was thinking, her mind on Paul Favor.

Dr. Dolan and Mrs. Bacon, in her walker, were emerging from the ward, chatting happily. The doctor patted one plump old hand, smiled softly, and started down the hall, his white starched back to Theo and Judy. He neared room 320, the door opened, and Lydia Colman, swathed in pink chiffon stepped dreamily into the hall, blinked in astonishment. "Why, Dr. Dolan," she murmured in a low tone, like honey dripping from a warm jar. The doctor jammed still in his tracks at the sound of her.

"Well . . . well, hello," he floundered.

"I was just going down to the solarium. Perhaps . . . would you have a few minutes, to beguile the tedium for me?"

"I can't now," he said in a distressed way. "If you'll, that is, after my rounds . . ."

Lydia understood. Her violet eyes told him how deeply she respected his firm male devotion to duty. "Of course," she told him, gently releasing. "I'll just go back in my room here and perhaps, in a little while . . ."

"Oh, yes, yes," Dr. Dolan assured her intensely. He sagged off to continue his rounds. Lydia swept the hall with a wide glance that slanted obliquely off the two nurses and Mrs. Bacon, and retired.

"I feel like a piece of ectoplasm," Judy complained.

"Poor man . . . he's gone, finished," Theo mourned, adding curiously, "You'd think he could put up a *little* more fight. She's so really corny."

"He was all ripe and ready to fall when she came along," Judy analyzed. "All she had to do was stretch out her hand and down he plopped."

Theo nodded. "I wonder what sort of problem she handed him?"

"Problem?"

101

"Oh, you remember. Yesterday, all that maidenly confusion and dependence . . . plus the problem that only a Dolan could comprehend."

"She'd have thought one out. As a matter of fact, I imagine her life would be one problem after another."

"Not the kind she could tell Dr. Dolan. This one would have to be special. . . . Let's see. How about, 'Oh, Dr. Dolan, my convalescence . . . what shall I do? I don't mean to complain, I know there are others worse, oh, so much worse off than I am. But what shall I do with my life? No more riding, sailing, tennis . . . just to sit, to sit helplessly by . . . oh, doctor, how can I bear it?' Will that do?" Theo inquired.

"Except it sounds as if she'd lost both legs. After all, she only had an appendectomy."

"A girl like Lydia can do a lot of swooning and lying about on couches like E. B. Browning on less than an appendectomy."

Judy agreed. "I never saw such a woman for appearing at the opportune moment. You know, I really think she skulks at the door, waiting for him. Every time he gets on the floor she shoots out of her room like a torpedo, and then couldn't be more surprised to find *Dr. Dolan*, of all people. All duked up and trailing perfume like a broken bottle . . ."

"I hear it runs in her family," Theo said restlessly.

"What does?"

"This lining them up and shooting them down." She yawned. "I have that infusion to do. See you later."

Theo set up the infusion for Mr. Warren, who lay curtained in a cubicle in the men's ward, so still that the air seemed hung in a motionless suspension, so thin that the white bedcovers were almost flat. Theo called him gently, "Mr. Warren?" She waited. In a few seconds the bony head turned toward her. "Another infusion, Mr. Warren," she told him. The gaunt head, yellow-skinned, nodded

102

slightly. When he blinked, the lids closed over his pale blue eyes slowly, as though each time were the last. He said nothing, though he watched her preparations vaguely. She strapped the ropy arm to a board, rubbed with an alcohol swab, inserted the large needle, adjusted the bottle, then looked down at him. He returned her glance with no expression at all. Eyes like flat glass, mouth drooping but immobile. The saline solution dripped from the bottle through the tube. Each drop hung shuddering a moment, then fell as another welled behind it.

"How are you, Mr. Warren?" a resonant voice inquired. Theo turned to Dr. Jordan. "Good afternoon, Miss Armacost," the doctor murmured, his eyes on the still figure lying before them. The wan face deepened with expression as Mr. Warren gazed at the big, iron-haired figure beside the bed. Theo had seen this happen many times with doctors like Jordan, Patients who lay accepting alike pain and treatment with small response would lift their heads a little, find somewhere the strength to smile briefly. The doctors' visits were short, noncommittal. But their pauses at the bedside seemed sometimes, and not rarely, to do more than all the nursing care or medicine could. Theo thought perhaps the calm assurance of Dr. Jordan, his dignity and impersonal kindness were medicine too. She considered Dr. Dolan. The comparison was not good. For all Mrs. Bacon's slavish devotion, Theo knew that poor Dolan would never, at any age, reach the stature of this one. She tried to think of Dr. Jordan touched, even remotely, at any time, by the devices of Lydia Colman. It was quite impossible. And that, she was thinking, must come, in part anyway, from Dr. Jordan's utter self-respect. He doesn't need any Lydias to cling and claim and glorify. Whereas poor Dolan can never be praised enough or reassured enough . . .

Later, as Theo went toward the diet kitchen, she saw Mrs. Bacon proceeding mountainously down the corridor.

"Dinner in a little while," Theo reminded her. "Don't stray off the reserves."

"Not at all," Mrs. Bacon said reassuringly. "I have a little route all planned."

Theo looked at the placid round face with surprise. She smiled. "That's nice, Mrs. B. Have a good route."

"I will," Mrs. Bacon said with conviction. Once again Theo darted a speculative glance at the serene countenance. But she was too busy to inquire further. "'By," she said to the slowly moving back.

About the time that Dr. Dolan should finish his rounds, Lydia Colman opened her door. And at that moment Mrs. Bacon, in a final determined spurt, arrived before it in her walker. With a long sigh Mrs. Bacon relaxed her hold on the sides, sank laboriously to the bench. Then she smiled brightly at Lydia, completely blocked inside.

Lydia's mouth dropped open. She shut it quickly, glared at the great lounging figure. "Please, get out of the way," she said irritably, gazing anxiously about the hall. Dr. Dolan came out of the solarium, started for the stairs, apparently forgetting his appointment. Lydia eyed him with frustration. "Will you *move?*" she demanded.

"In a moment, dearie," wheezed Mrs. Bacon. "Tiring, this is. I shouldn't really have come for a walk this afternoon at all. But I said to myself, 'Lucy Bacon,' I said, 'you're getting lazy. A good brisk walk will . . .'"

"For heaven's sake, get out of the way!" flared the furious Lydia in a harsh and carrying voice. But Dr. Dolan had disappeared through the stairway door. Lydia gave a final withering eye to Mrs. Bacon, who stared back in innocent offense, and shut her own door, attempting, without success, to slam it.

Judy and Theo, at the nurses' station, watched speechlessly as Mrs. Bacon hoisted herself to unsteady feet and moved toward them. Together they advanced upon her.

"Now what, will you tell us, was the meaning of that?" Judy inquired.

"Of what?" Mrs. Bacon asked blandly.

"You know of what." The two nurses eyed the patient expectantly. She, however, continued her slow path to the ward, so they paced beside her.

"Mrs. Bacon," Theo started, "you can't do things like this, it isn't good for you. . . ."

"Dr. Dolan said I was to walk."

"I'm not talking about walking and you know it."

"I don't know what either one of you is talking about."

"You did that deliberately, to keep Dr. Dolan away from her," Judy said assertively.

"Oh, you're talking about that . . . me getting stuck in front of her door. Wasn't that a sketch?" Mrs. Bacon cackled.

"Sketch my eye. It was a plot."

Mrs. Bacon shook her head. "Not at all," she said calmly. "Funny how it worked out, though. Well," she sighed, "Dr. Dolan will be on his rounds downstairs by now. I'll be getting ready for dinner."

"But you can't hope to do this all the time," Theo implored.

"I shouldn't think so," was Mrs. Bacon's final word, "but then, I can be an awful nuisance."

Theo and Judy stared at each other.

"Well," Judy commented as they went back to the desk. "I can see she's going to do her best to break up that combination. And, furthermore, it wouldn't surprise me if she pulled it off."

"Mmm," Theo agreed absently, losing interest. "I think the trays are coming up."

She took Mr. Coombes' tray and went to his room, feeling her arms grow watery. Nearly two hours. He'd probably be gone. But Paul Favor was still there. He got up from an armchair, took the tray from her. "I was just talking to Uncle about you, Miss Armacost," he said, settling comfortably beside the bed to feed his uncle.

How easily he does that, Theo thought. As if feeding an uncle were just one of those pleasant things that turn up. She was reminded of the many relatives who shuddered away from the trays, licking their lips nervously at the task of spooning food for an adult.

She looked from uncle to nephew, smiling, not speaking. It's like taking nembutal, she decided, this drifty, dreamy feeling. She didn't ask what he'd been saying, and made no move to leave. How silly I must look, she thought, not in the least perturbed.

Mr. Coombes prepared for speech. "My nephew has fully explained his dereliction, Miss Armacost, and I am satisfied to say that no blame can be attached to him." He spoke as though some explanation were due Theo. So he's probably, she realized, told him about the letters.

"My uncle, Miss Armacost," Paul said, answering her thought, "is in the habit of sending me the most sinister communications on the flimsiest pretexts. You must not attend to any of his slanders."

"Good heavens, is it catching?" Theo inquired.

Mr. Coombes looked blank, but Paul laughed. "Everyone in the family talks like that around Uncle. We're the haunters of a ruined century."

"Well, you picked a good gone one," Theo remarked. "I'll have to go now. Someone will be in for the tray in a while."

"Don't you want to hear what I was saying about you?"

"Well . . . yes, as a matter of fact."

Now Paul seemed at a loss. Probably, Theo said to herself, he expected more tact. Oh dear, *how* do people do this sort of thing? Annie just naturally says all the right things. . . . An instinct, is it?

"I was asking him where to take you for dinner. Uncle is a great diner-out, you know."

"Are you, Mr. Coombes?" Theo said, wondering how long they'd continue to hide behind Uncle.

"Paul was telling me, rather fancifully, how deeply he admires your . . . ah, father." Mr. Coombes seemed to be as deeply in the maze as either of them. How in the world did we get started on this, Theo thought confusedly. And why? If he has to consult his uncle before taking a girl out, perhaps we should wait till all three of us could go together. "I really must go," she said crisply, and left before they could tangle her in any more words.

Half an hour later she asked one of the aides to pick up Mr. Coombes' tray. "Oh, wait a second," she added quickly, "I'll do it myself." She strode down the hall, narrow-eyed with irritation at herself. Most ridiculous thing I ever heard of, she rasped inwardly, simply ridiculous. As she lifted her hand to knock, the door opened, and Paul Favor, holding the tray, was confronted by her upraised fist.

"Don't blame you in the least," he said, then called over his shoulder, "See you tomorrow, Uncle." Balancing the tray on one arm, he shut the door firmly behind him.

"My uncle, to speak once again of a very strong character, is so used to being part of everything that he can't bear to be left out even when he's flat on his back," he explained, walking beside her.

Theo glanced up at him mildly. "You needn't make any apologies to me," she said, thinking how very black his hair was. Not a trace of brown or red.

"But I do need to. You're thinking I had to get his permission to take you out. . . ."

"Not at all," Theo replied untruthfully.

Paul put the tray on a stretcher. "See here, are we going to quarrel all the time?"

"All what time?"

"ere, you see what I mean? Like that. Is that the swer I can expect from you?"

107

My, thought Theo, you *are* used to having your own way. "Nobody can expect anything and I'm tired of people expecting something."

"Who expects what? Are there a whole lot of men I'll have to dispose of?"

Theo almost laughed, but she felt a little confused. "I don't know what you're talking about. I don't know any men at all. Or at least, I thought I did, but now I see I don't."

Paul looked at her for a long moment. Then he smiled. "Fine," he said. "You can forget about the others, since you admit yourself you don't know anything about them. As for Uncle, he just likes to be in on things. You won't mind that."

"No, I suppose I won't," Theo agreed meekly.

"He likes you," Paul said. He thought a minute, and added, "too."

This is what they mean, Theo thought happily. Just this. Whoever loved that loved not at first sight? This is what they talk about. I feel like one of those heroines who waited for Mr. Right. I waited till I was twenty-three and then took two days and half an hour's conversation to fall in love.

She smiled serenely up at him. "Where," she asked, "did Mr. Coombes decide we should go?"

CHAPTER TEN

DURING DINNER Mrs. Armacost suddenly reme___
something. "Dear?" she addressed her husband, ___
thinking about hummingbirds. Her eye slid ___
Johnny, in the act of smuggling meat to July. "D___
that," she said sharply.

But he was with her, beside her. . . . I love you, Doug, her heart cried. And if something warned her to be wise, to keep, if there was still time, some part of herself for herself, she didn't hear it.

"Anne, I've been experimenting."

"That must be interesting."

"No. It's not. I was experimenting to see how long I could stay away from you."

"Oh." They stared straight ahead. Then Anne said, "You did pretty well. Four days."

He shook his head. "I didn't last one day. The other three were punishment for not lasting longer."

"I couldn't have lasted through the punishment." She said it before she had any idea she had more than thought it. Her eyelids descended; she waited . . . because the words had come so naturally, so revealingly. Her eyes were still closed when he leaned over, so his breath surged softly against her ear.

"Anne, I love you," he said. . . .

Now, sitting under the apple tree, Anne dropped her head on her knees, rocking back and forth with pain. "Doug, Doug, don't do this again," she whispered. "Where are you? What are you *doing* to me?"

Her mother, at the kitchen window, looked down through the rows of sweet William and snapdragons, to where Anne, in pink shorts and white shirt, so young, so desperately faced her loss.

Mr. Armacost, coming in to abstract some part of the lunch for himself prematurely, forgot about food. "What is it?" he asked, moving over beside her in concern. His wife didn't answer. She nodded out the window, twisting a stemmed glass in her fingers. After a moment they turned away.

"There's nothing to do, you see. Nothing at all we can do." Mr. Armacost shook his head bleakly.

CHAPTER SIX

"CIGARETTE, JOHNNY?"

"Thanks, Cooper, don't mind if I do."

They lit crumpled cigarettes, carefully cupping the matches in their palms, drew bulging mouthfuls of smoke, blew long streamers into the air.

"You get any out of your nose yet?" Cooper inquired, tapping his ashes vigorously.

"Not yet. You?"

"Nope."

They smoked in silent concentration, behind the chicken house in Cooper Maloney's yard. A huge washing jittered on the line. A droopy rooster strutted about fretfully, turning his head from side to side, as though seeking something. This cock dutifully flapped to the fence post every morning and gave his lonely call. Unless it was raining. Then he remained huddled in the henhouse, seeming to know that one way or the other it didn't matter much. Johnny watched him scraping his orange claws in the dirt. A few yellow chicks ran past on their spidery feet, but the rooster paid them no heed.

"Sure wouldn't want Pop to catch me at this," Cooper observed, examining his cigarette closely.

"Me either," Johnny agreed. But his reasons, he knew, were different. If Mr. Maloney caught his son smoking, Cooper'd catch it, fourteen years old or not. And Cooper was strong, too. Awash with muscles. But if my father, Johnny realized, caught me, the first thing I knew he'd be buying me a pack, inviting me to smoke with the family. He pictured the scene shudderingly, the nonchalance, the casual offer of a cigarette after dinner. Anne's remarks.

Mr. and Mrs. Maloney were big people. Mrs. Maloney moved about the kitchen with aimless good intent, poking at things, moving objects from one place to another and back again, producing, in a placid way, miraculous cakes and pies which Cooper handed out to his friends.

Johnny always felt uneasy here. Not with the Maloneys —with their house. He was sure that the entire place would someday topple and drop to the ground, that only good luck had kept it standing this long. He eyed the great seams in the wall, the door that had lost a hinge and never been repaired, the piece of cardboard replacing one of the window panes. He was confident that it had something to do with Mr. Maloney's being in the house-wrecking business. They're just used to wrecks, Johnny told himself, waiting at any moment to be plunged to the basement through some eruption in the floor.

Mrs. Maloney greeted them cheerfully, reaching for her cake tin as she did. "Devil's Food all right, boys?" They nodded happily. "And milk?" More nods.

"Pop up yet?" Cooper inquired with his mouth full.

Mrs. Maloney waddled to the door. "Pa!" she yelled. "Johnny and Cooper are here!"

"Whadda they want?" a voice shattered down the stairs from a remote room.

"He says what do you want . . ." Mrs. Maloney interpreted, as though only she could hear her husband's voice.

"Want to ask him will he take us swimming," Cooper supplied.

"Pa! They want to know can you take them swimming." She turned to the boys. "Want me to pack you a lunch? What, Pa?" she interrupted herself as the upstairs voice sounded again.

"I said, if they'll be ready to go in ten minutes!" Mr. Maloney's heavy, heels-first tread thudded over the kitchen toward the head of the stairs, setting up a series of

He shook his head at that. Then, puzzled, he thought that perhaps Anne wouldn't say anything after all. She's changed, he realized, not liking it. Not like she was at the beginning of the summer, either, all sweetness and sop. She's not happy, Johnny defined for himself suddenly. He didn't want to think about it.

"How many of these things have we got left?" he asked Cooper.

"Well, there's twenty in a pack, and we bought it a week ago. So that's one a day for each of us, except Sunday. Twelve. We've got eight, I guess. Four days to go."

"Whew." Johnny pushed the cigarette into the ground. "Do you like them?"

"Not much. We'll be through pretty soon." Cooper disposed of his and they got up. "Want to throw a ball around?"

Johnny made a quick decision. "Let's see if your dad'll take us out to Price's." It was early in the day. There wouldn't be too many people at the beach yet, and anyway, you have to swim. Skinny or not skinny, you have to swim.

"Okay," Cooper agreed. "Let's go see if he's stirring yet."

Cooper's father was associated with the Archetype Wrecking Company. He also drove a truck with which he did odd jobs on his own. Once he had taken Cooper and Johnny along to New York City. They'd bumped around the Bronx on a sweltering afternoon, delivered some furniture, Cooper and Johnny carrying chairs, Mr. Maloney singlehanded dealing with the rest. They'd had dinner in a diner and gotten home after midnight. Swell, Johnny remembered, that was swell.

"I don't know whether he'll be awake," Cooper repeated as they walked to the back door. Mr. Maloney had been out late the night before hauling a load of bricks upstate.

to the hall. In a moment he was back. "Guy on the phone for you, Anne." Seeing the color actually drain from her cheeks, he added hastily, "Pete Crosland, I think."

Anne shuddered a little. She went to the phone, picked it up in still soapy fingers. It slid a bit, so that she had to steady it with the other hand. "Hello?" she said.

"Hi, Anne," Peter replied. There was silence, so he went on, "I just saw . . . I mean, are you busy tonight?"

He just saw Doug—with somebody else. So he knows I'm not busy. The little sentences chopped in her mind. She took a deep breath and literally lifted her chin in the air. It seemed to help. "Why, no, Peter. I'm not busy," she said, and her own voice fascinated her, sounding so clear and untroubled.

"I thought we might think of something to do. How about Price's?"

"No!" Anne swallowed, went on more composedly. "Not Price's. What else you got?" she asked in an attempt at lightness.

Pete considered. "Just as well, anyway," he said. "I don't think Dad wants me to take the car tonight. Would you mind taking a bus? We could go to the movies."

"That would be nice, Peter."

"Okay. I'll be right over. We can make the whole last show if we hurry." He started to hang up, then yelled," "Anne?"

"Yes?"

"It'll be good to see you. 'By." He was gone.

"You going out?" asked Johnny, lounging in the doorway.

"To the movies. I'll finish up and get dressed."

"The dishes? I'll do them. Run along."

Anne studied the bony young face. "What a nice person you are," she said suddenly, and ran up the stairs.

She was still upstairs when Peter Crosland arrived.

"Hullo, Pete," Johnny greeted. "Anne isn't dressed yet.

111

Come on in and watch the game." They went into the living room. Pete immediately gave himself to Red Barber. Johnny scrutinized him for a while. Sure is hard to tell, he thought, what makes one of them different from the other. Peter wasn't too tall, but he was broad and muscular. He'd been a two-letter man in high school. Of course, Johnny remembered, that Eamons is no slouch for biceps himself. But this guy's better looking, and what's more, he seems to know what he's doing. Eamons is off in a trance half the time. He'd have to be in a trance, Johnny thought with fierce loyalty, to like that bleached stick Colman better than Anne. He looked again at Pete's huge shoulders. Power-packed, Johnny sighed, he sure is power-packed.

Pete and Anne cut through several backyards to arrive at the corner where the bus stopped. There was no sign of it yet, so they leaned against a street lamp, waiting. About the luminous globe blundered soft-winged moths. Branches lifted, soughed, sighed in the high darkness. The headlight beams of the bus streaked round a curve, angled, straightened as the bus itself appeared. It drew up beside them with a squeal, pulled away as soon as they boarded.

There were few passengers. Pete and Anne sat together toward the back. Peter nudged his shoulder into hers, looking up at the ceiling and whistling softly through his teeth. Anne jerked nervously, leaned over to scratch her ankle, edging away when she sat back.

Peter glanced at her sidelong. "Why're you so jumpy?"

"Jumpy? I'm not jumpy."

"You certainly are. Hopping around like one of those beans."

"What beans?"

"You know, those little brown beans. Mexican jumping beans."

"I never heard of such a thing."

112

"You didn't?" Pete was uninterested.

"What do they do?"

"The beans? They jump. I had lots of them when I was a kid. Used to keep them in a bowl and look at them."

"Were they pets?"

"Pets? He looked pained. "How could you have a bean for a pet?"

"How could you keep beans in a bowl and look at them?"

Peter's jaw set. "I kept them there because they jumped."

"How long would you look at them, at one time, I mean?"

Peter stirred angrily. "What's the matter with you?" he demanded.

"Nothing. You said yourself you looked at them in a bowl."

"For the luva Mike, just because you say something doesn't mean you do it all the time!"

"No," she repeated slowly. "Just because you say a thing doesn't mean you do it all the time. . . ." Everything, she thought, seems to be an allegory to me. She felt ashamed of talking to Peter this way. "I'm sorry, Pete," she said to him softly. "I didn't mean to . . ."

"That's all right, Anne," he said quickly. His voice had an eager forgiveness that maddened her.

Downtown they walked slowly, since there was still time, looking in the shop windows, at dresses and argyle socks and tastily stacked boxes of candy. When they got to Dublin's Drugstore, Peter dashed in to buy the huge box of popcorn without which he couldn't go to any movie, then across the street to the luridly lit Paramount Theater.

Anne disliked the first moment in a movie—the stumbling through the murk, the heated whispered controversy in the aisle as heads craned and obscure mutters reached

113

out of the dark, the eventual clumsy achievement of anonymity. She sank down gratefully. Peter immediately seized her hand and held it.

The newsreel ended in a brassy blare, the Western galloped on. Gazing indifferently at the inevitable stagecoach, Anne became aware that Peter was having difficulties. He wanted to start eating his popcorn, but his right hand was clutching Anne's left, he didn't know how to manage, not wanting to appear ungallant or desert the pleasure of contact with her for food.

Feeling they'd never get to either the popcorn or the picture unless she did something, Anne gently disengaged her hand, patting his as she did so, to make her withdrawal seem reluctant. Peter gave a grateful sigh, offered her the box, settled back comfortably munching. When the popcorn was gone, he repossessed her hand, held it through the rest of the Western, the Coming Attractions, and the Feature. By the time the heroine had explained it all away and wed the hero, Anne had no feeling left in her fingers at all.

When they emerged, the heat of the night swarmed all over them, breathtaking after the chilly air-conditioned theater. They walked toward Dublin's.

"I don't think I like Tyrone Power much," Peter said, taking her arm as they crossed the street.

"No?"

"Nope. Too sort of fluffy."

"I don't know. He's all right."

"Think I'll have a frosted. I'm hungry."

"I don't see why, after all that popcorn."

"I'm always hungry," Peter replied good-naturedly.

The drugstore was full. All the tables were already taken. They had to wait for two people to finish at the counter before they could sit down.

Anne glanced at herself in the big mirror behind the soda fountain, thinking that Doug had never seen her in

114

this blue piqué dress. She shifted her eyes to Peter and found him already looking at her. Staring into each other's mirrored eyes made them uncomfortable and they were glad when the drinks came, looking down at the glasses quickly, as though they'd been spying.

Anne swirled coke with a straw, thinking how long the night seemed. I'd better not go out with him any more, she decided. It isn't fair, and I can't stand it. She glanced slyly at him again. He was leaning over, his lips thrust out, spooning ice cream into his mouth. A shudder of revulsion flashed through her at the sight. But why? He's just having a frosted. I don't like to be out with him alone, she answered her question. He's all right with a lot of other people, but I don't like him alone. Loudly his straw gurgled in the pit of the glass.

Anne jumped. "Peter, let's go. I'm terribly tired."

When they had gotten off the bus and were walking toward the house, they still hadn't spoken another word. In silence they recrossed the yards to her house.

"Peter?" she said suddenly.

"What is it, Anne?" His voice was dull.

"Where do you get those beans?"

Peter stopped walking. "What beans?" he shouted.

"Peter, don't yell so, you'll wake people up. Those Mexican beans."

"I don't know where you get them," he snapped. "I haven't seen any for years."

"Why do they jump?"

"Worms."

"*What* did you say?"

"I said, 'Worms,'" Peter repeated slowly. "They have worms in them, and that makes them jump."

"Why, I wonder?"

"Anne," said Peter between his teeth. "I don't want to talk about it. Here we are practically home and the only thing we've talked about all night is beans."

"I'm sorry, Peter. I just thought I'd like to get some for Johnny. After all, if you liked to look at . . ."

"Will you keep still!" Peter rasped. Then suddenly he grabbed her shoulders and with his eyes forced her into silence. They stood there, close to the back porch, staring at each other. Peter's grip softened. Quite tenderly, he tried to draw her to him. Anne turned her face away, and again, for a long moment, they stood unspeaking.

Finally Peter stepped back. "Hopeless, isn't it?" he asked flatly.

Anne didn't answer, so he turned away.

"Peter?" she whispered unhappily.

He kept walking. "It's all right. See you around, Anne," he called over his shoulder. His footsteps on the gravel crunched, then died away.

Johnny was in the living room when she went in. He looked up, as if to speak, but after all, only closed his mouth more firmly. Anne went upstairs. Johnny thought he'd wait till the folks got in. Maybe over at the Robinsons they wouldn't get the results of the game.

CHAPTER ELEVEN

MR. ARMACOST took the morning mail, shuffled through it quickly, stopped midway between a frown and smile at a thick battered piece of mail addressed to his son. The envelope bore in its upper left-hand corner the legend, "Thor Savage." Beneath this impressive name was a line of script, "Muscles for the Mighty." In the lower left-hand corner was a sketch delineating a great fist in the act of pulverizing what was apparently the Rock of Gibraltar.

He walked slowly into the kitchen, presented it to his wife without comment.

"Oh my," she said. "My goodness. This must be what he's been lurking about at mail time for. . . ."

Mr. Armacost slumped into a chair, smiling undecidedly. He swept a hand roughly over his head.

"Well, yes," Mrs. Armacost agreed. "It's sort of funny. But did you think it meant this much to him?"

"Did I? I don't know. It can't hurt him, I guess."

"Are you sure? Some of those things they pick up are pretty heavy. And anyway," she added firmly, "I do not want Johnny to burgeon suddenly with those repulsive muscles. I've seen pictures of weight lifters. Definitely, no. I don't mind if he's strong, but not in bumps."

"Oh well, I wouldn't worry. He'll never stick it out. . . ."

They looked at the envelope, at each other. "I think," said Mr. Armacost, "I'll take it up to him. I shouldn't think he'd want the girls to know about it. Rather take them by surprise, eh?"

"Goodness. You don't think . . . he wouldn't be planning to run for Mr. America, do you suppose?"

"I think he has more immediate plans. You wouldn't know because you're a woman." He got up, taking the envelope. "It can mean a great deal," he reflected, heading for the stairs.

Johnny was still asleep. Mr. Armacost thought he could still see the faintest trace of the little boy he used to wake, who now, of course, was gone. Where do little boys go to?

July slept at the foot of the bed. She opened her amber eyes when Johnny's father entered, studied him a moment, turned away aloofly. Johnny stirred as Mr. Armacost leaned over, shaking him gently by one bony brown shoulder, smiling slightly at the fate in store for the slender body . . . muscles by mail.

"Johnny? Wake up, boy."

"Huh? Whatcha want?"

"Some mail for you, John."

The boy sat up abruptly, shaking away sleep. July

reared like an antelope, ears leaning forward. Johnny took the envelope, regarded it with frank rapture. Then he frowned. "Who's downstairs?" he asked his father suspiciously.

"Your mother and I."

"Hum." Johnny nodded. "Girls asleep, I suppose."

"Sound asleep."

Turning the long-awaited matter in his hands, Johnny studied what to say next. "Well, what do you think of it?" he inquired at length.

"Seems like a good idea," Mr. Armacost replied mildly.

"Mom?"

"Your mother hopes you won't run for Mr. America."

Johnny grinned. "Fat chance." He got out of bed. "What it is, you see, Dad, is just an idea I had. . . ."

His father nodded. There again came that flash of the lost small boy, asking, "Is it all right, Dad?" in an anxious voice.

"Sure it is, John. I knew a fellow once," he went on reflectively, "who took one of these courses."

"Yes? Did it work?"

"It worked. He finally had to keep sitting up to keep from strangling himself with his own muscles."

"No kidding!" Johnny breathed reverently.

"That's right. And I remember when he ordered some bar bells." Mr. Armacost began to laugh. Johnny, half grinning, waited expectantly. "He ordered them," his father chuckled, "and then they called from the post office telling him to come down and get his own packages. Nobody in the place could lift them." He wiped a hand over his face, delighted with the sudden recollection. "You go ahead and work at it."

"Okay, Dad." Johnny started for the door. "Gee, I almost forgot . . . Cooper and I are attending a pet show in Easy Register's barn today." He looked around for July. "Where'd that cat go?"

"In *whose* barn?"

"Easy's. Oh, I see. Well, you see, his name is Edwin Cahill Register. E.C. Get it? So they call him Easy. Oughta call him Greasy." He shrugged. "July go downstairs?"

Mr. Armacost glanced around. "Guess so."

Johnny bounded into the hall. "Mom! Hey, Mom!" he shouted down the stairs.

"Johnny, you'll wake the girls . . . ," his mother's voice called.

"Oh. Sorry. Look, keep the cat in, will you? I need her."

"For what? Oh, all right, I'll keep her here."

Johnny turned back to his father. "Gotta brush her up, you know."

"Are you doing this with July's consent?"

"How's that?"

"Do you think July will submit gracefully to being an exhibit at a pet show?"

"Oh, sure," Johnny said confidently. "She'll do anything I tell her to."

Mr. Armacost was doubtful. Not, he thought, that I need worry about possible dogs. That cat is built on lines that would give pause to a Great Dane. But he couldn't fancy July's regal figure at a pet show.

The girls' door opened, and Theo made a sleepy entrance into the hall. "Johnny," she said huskily, "could you put a muffler on that voice of yours?" Without waiting for an answer, she went into the bathroom and closed the door.

"Well, I'll be darned," Johnny exploded.

"You shouldn't," his father advised, going down the stairs, "make so much noise. Just be glad it wasn't Anne," he added.

Johnny scratched his head, lifted his shoulders, then

shot back into his room, closing the door carefully. The brown envelope lay on the dresser. For a minute he just looked at it, then gingerly picked it up. "Boy," he breathed. "I sure hope it works."

He went to his desk, opened the flap with deliberation, drew out the three enclosures.

The over-all explanatory booklet, "Muscles for the Mighty," was biggest. It had a sky-blue cover, with a massive character aggressively displaying his musculature for the camera. Even Johnny was a bit appalled at the mammoth proportions of Thor Savage. "Oh well," he muttered. "Needn't go overboard." He turned to the slimmer pamphlets.

The first, with a picture of Hercules lopping off several heads of the Hydra, was entiled, "Titanic Torsos." The second, Hercules again, this time cleaning the stables of Augeas with something that looked like a snow shovel, was called, "The Pathway to Pectoral Power." Johnny, all but unconscious at the sight of the covers, hesitated actually to open any of them. He sat back, shifting his eyes from one to the next to the next. At length his hand stole warily out, selected the "Torso" material. I should think, he reasoned, that if I managed the torso, the rest would sort of follow. Thrusting the other two booklets under some papers in his desk, he opened "Titanic Torsos."

"Are you Frail, Feeble, and Infirm?" it demanded on the first page. "Do Girls Giggle and Guys Guffaw When You Go By?"

Johnny put the book down.

He picked it up again, skipped a couple of pages.

The text was thicker here, and chattier.

"Remember! Brawn's the Word! Here at Savage Studios, we specialize in building burly bodies. No punies, us. We don't care what sort of a wreck you are, we'll make a MAN of you, and no waiting in line. By following

120

this mail course carefully, in a few weeks you'll astound yourself and acquaintances. In a few months you'll be so power-padded you'll be using marline-spikes for toothpicks." Johnny whistled softly.

He sprang to his feet as Theo knocked on the door. "The bathroom's empty," she called.

"Oh. Oh, thanks, Theo," Johnny called, nervously rolling "Titanic Torsos" behind his back. He pushed it in with the others and sprinted for the shower before Anne could get there.

Before going downstairs, he took another look at the three books. It all seemed pretty formidable, and he was chewing his lip thoughtfully when he entered the kitchen. July, her breakfast over, was tidying up in a refined manner. She arched her head, licked the white bib of her chest, nibbled, licked again. Then with a small, square paw . . . very small for her size, as cat's paws are . . . explored behind her ears, abrading the fur with a wet pad.

"Atta girl," Johnny approved, "you get good and clean."

Mrs. Armacost eyed her son curiously. "What part does July play in your day's plans?"

"She's going to win a ribbon, if any of those lunks have eyes."

"Which lunks?"

"Over at Easy's. Didn't I tell anybody about this pet show?"

"It's the first I've heard of it."

"You have nice hair," Johnny commented suddenly.

His mother smiled with pleasure. "That's nice, that you think so," she replied softly.

"Well, about this pet show," Johnny continued after an unembarrassed pause. "You see, Easy Register's father has a small sort of barn that they're going to take down for lumber. . . . Golly," he added, furrowing his brow in thought, "there's going to be an awful lot of wood around

121

pretty soon. Not that Cooper and I could get the right time out of Easy. . . . Well, maybe Cooper could, but I couldn't. But maybe from the old Wellman place. They're starting to pull that down in a few days. . . ."

He sat down as his mother put breakfast on the table, waved July away, started some toast.

"Well?" his mother asked.

"Huh? Oh, very good. Could have had muffins, I suppose, but very good."

"Johnny, I'm not talking about the food. You haven't told me about the pet show yet."

"Oh, yeah. You see, they're gonna take down this little barn, so Easy figures to make a little use of it in the meantime. He's always figuring ways to make money, that guy, without doing any work, I mean," he added quickly. "So he's got up a pet show, dime a head. Winner gets a blue ribbon, six two-by-fours, and a box of tools Mr. Register doesn't want any more." Johnny studied July. "I sure could use those two-by-fours and tools. Don't you think July will win?"

"Well, darling, I don't know. She's a fine cat. But there might be Angoras or Persians." Johnny lifted an eyebrow. "What," his mother exclaimed, "about dogs? There are sure to be dogs."

"Dogs gotta look out for themselves. But I'll keep her on a leash so she won't run away."

"I think . . . that is, I meant that perhaps a dog might frighten July. . . ."

Johnny looked scornful. "Now, Mom. Look at her."

It seemed to be a clinching argument, the object of which had now disposed herself next to Johnny's chair. What she lacked in length of fur, she more than equaled in bulk. At that, Mrs. Armacost thought, it would take a brave dog to meddle with such an enemy.

"What sort of pet is Cooper taking?"

"That rooster of his," Johnny replied, shaking his head.

"Does Mr. Maloney approve of that?"

"Sure." Johnny laughed. "Mr. Maloney says it'll do the rooster good to get away from home and the hens for a while."

Mrs. Armacost nodded. "No doubt."

Johnny got up, patted his stomach luxuriously. "Like to see the leash I got for her?" he asked his mother, producing from his pocket a twisted red leather dog leash attached to a small red harness studded with brass. "Nice, huh?"

"Beautiful. Is it a . . . ?" Mrs. Armacost broke off, thinking better of mentioning dogs again.

"Uh-hunh. It was for a dog," Johnny said proudly. "Well, come on, July. Gotta brush you up for the contest."

"How are you boys getting over to Easy's? He lives on a farm, doesn't he? Outside of town?"

"Depends," Johnny said judiciously. "If you want to call a cow, three pigs, and a piece of cheesecloth a farm, then Easy lives on a farm. Anyway, he's moving away pretty soon. Won't make me cry."

"Oh, for goodness sake, Johnny, if you dislike him so much, why do you go over there?" his mother asked impatiently.

"Nothing else to do. Anyway, I want July to win a prize. That Easy's got delusions of grandeur, is all."

"You're hopeless. I happen to know that the Registers have a fair-sized farm, for being so close to the city."

"Okay," Johnny shrugged. "It's not my idea of a farm anyway. I suppose," he conceded grudgingly, "they'll have a bigger one upstate."

Mrs. Armacost shook her head, then smiled. "Well, have a good day, and I hope July or the rooster wins."

Johnny looked ominous at this coupling, so she hastily departed to make beds.

Half an hour later, she discovered the answer to her question—how they were going to get to the farm. Cooper

123

and Johnny set off on their bikes, with handlebar baskets bearing a strange cargo. In Cooper's a horrified rooster crouched, brilliant tail feathers streaming in the breeze, coxcomb bobbing crazily. Unbelievably, he too was harnessed and leashed to the basket wire. It must, Mrs. Armacost thought dazedly, watching from a bedroom window, have been intended for a cat. It would certainly not have fit July. July sat nobly erect, one paw resting on the edge of the basket, tail curled in an elegant sweep, pink nose sniffing fastidiously. She was gracious, proud, superbly caparisoned, and she rode like a Colonial dandy touring the countryside in a sedan chair.

Away they went, prepared to sweep all before them. Presently there was nothing left to show that such a company had ever been but two small feathers skimming idly over the walk.

In the late afternoon, Cooper trundled into his own back yard, released a permanently disorganized rooster, who did not appear to have enjoyed his vacation from the hens, then stood a moment pulling his ear after the manner of his father. Finally, with a shrug, he bounded up the rickety back stairs, entered the kitchen just as his father came in from the front of the house.

"Hi, Pop," he said. "You coming or going?"

"Just got back." Mr. Maloney walked to the sink, drank in quick succession three glasses of water. "Thirsty," he explained. "What sort of a day did you have, son?"

"Okay. Look, Pop . . . Suppose you could drop by the Register farm one of these days and pick up some two-by-fours and a tool box for Johnny . . . I mean, for me?"

"What're you getting stuff from . . . ? Oh, St. Patrick, don't tell me that loose-feathered chicken copped a prize." Mr. Maloney's mirthful shoulders began to shake.

"I don't know," Cooper confessed. "It did, or that cat of Johnny's did. Or maybe I did. Anyway, I'd sure like it if you'd pick up the stuff before that creep Easy gets to thinking things over. . . ."

"Sure, sure. I'll get it."

"Only be sure you say it's for me. Or don't say anything, maybe."

"Saaay, what's this all about?"

Cooper spread his hands. "So help me, I don't know."

"Well now, you better start knowing this minute. I'm not picking up anything till you tell me how you got it."

Cooper sighed. When his father spoke like that, you did what he said. "Honest, Pop, it's crazy. You see, this Easy character, he's plain awful. Nobody likes him. I guess he don't like anybody himself. Except," Cooper looked pained, "except *me*. I don't know why, unless it was because once I stopped a bunch of guys from grabbing his bike down at the school one day. I was on the Traffic Squad," he said defensively. "Anyway, you can't have guys like that getting away with the stunts they pull. . . ."

"Get on with it," Mr. Maloney said, after a pause.

"Yeah. Well, you see Johnny's real proud of this cat of his. . . ." He stopped again. How do you explain to a man like Pop, he wondered, that Johnny's sort of got to win out once in a while, because he's got such a buzz on about muscles that he's getting a . . . an inferiority complex or something. Cooper considered the unfamiliar words that had come to him in a moment of unusual insight. But just because I know about it, he thought, is no reason to tell everybody else. He frowned in an effort to explain his afternoon without explaining Johnny's troubles. "Look, Pop," he said carefully, "I told this goon Easy that Johnny and I had changed pets, just to see. . . . Well, I knew he'd give the old prize to me anyway, no matter what I took along, so I thought why not let old Johnny's cat seem like it was getting the prize. Any harm in that?" He eyed his father hopefully.

"You mean John don't know about this?"

"*No!* That's the point. I got Easy away and told him we'd changed pets because Johnny thought the rooster would win. Of course, Johnny's too honest to think of such a thing, but Easy's just naturally crooked, so he believed me. . . ."

"Coupla crooks together, huh?"

"Me and Easy? Heck, I was doing it for a reason. Anyway, what do I get out of it?" Cooper asked indignantly.

"Guess you meant well," his father agreed. "Easy give the prize to the cat?"

"Oh sure, I knew he would. So I said you'd pick the stuff up, and winked at Easy, like I was going to settle with Johnny later . . . get it back for myself, you know. Now Johnny thinks his cat won, and Easy thinks I'm going to beat Johnny up to get the tool box and two-by-fours back, and everyone's happy. . . ." He looked closely to see if this was true of his father.

Mr. Maloney nodded. "Okay, son. I don't think it was exactly honest, but you did it for a good cause. I'll get the stuff."

"And be sure you drop a hint to Easy, like you don't know anything about it, but everything's going to me. . . ."

"Well, I *don't* know anything about it," his father said. "Where's your ma?"

Cooper got up. "Guess she'll be back soon. I gotta feed the chickens. So long. And oh, Pop, thanks."

He went for the chicken feed, thinking it had all been easier than he could have hoped. Anyway, he thought, giving the rooster an extra dollop, anyway, I'll get to use the stuff with Johnny same as if I'd won it myself.

·

CHAPTER TWELVE

A LITTLE before eleven, when she was to go off duty, Theo went into the men's ward with a small flashlight which she directed at the floor. Its pale pencil beam threw a bleached light around the great room, and by its pallor she examined the restless sleepers, moving from bed to bed on silent feet.

She reached Mr. Warren before he died.

His eyes in the tiny light looked directly into hers, more clearly than they had for weeks. With inexpressible sadness Theo looked at the small still frame surrendering its life. There was no relative to send for. Mr. Warren had had a son, Dave. But Dave was killed during the war. There wasn't anyone else.

She drew the curtains on their oiled tracks, rang his bell, which would buzz at the desk, turned on the dim night light. He spoke for a while, whether to her she couldn't tell. Each word faltered out with supreme effort, shaped with care, produced with labor. Each word seemed to be the last. But for many minutes he summoned the strength for yet one more.

". . . my son, Dave, when he was . . . a little boy, we used to fish together. . . ." He watched as the light of a passing car crept in a luminous square over the ceiling, down the wall, away. ". . . 'Do you know what a genie is, Dad?' he asked me. . . . 'No, what's it, Dave?' 'It's a spirit sort of . . . comes out from a lamp. . . . It can be a giant or animal or anything it wants in Arabia—like build a palace or find the thieves.' And I said to him, 'You learn that in school?' 'Yuh, don't you wish you had one, Dad?' he said, the little boy while we fished. 'Well,' I said, 'I guess . . . it's all right. Don't you . . . learn sums and things?' 'Oh, sure, we learn that too.' 'Hope so,' . . . I said to him. 'Can't go to college on no jenny.' Then he got a bite . . . nice big pickerel." The eyes were clouding again, but the slow words formed and fell. "Wanted him to go to college . . . Dave. He got another sort of . . . education."

The rattle of the elevator down the hall came to Theo's ears, loud in the silence. Faintly a patient moaned in another bed. Theo didn't think that Mr. Warren heard. She didn't think he listened any more. Now, she thought, he doesn't really see.

"I only wonder . . . ," he mumbled, "at how . . . important . . . it all seemed."

His eyes closed. The air, for the last time, lifted his breast. And that, thought Theo, is that. A man's whole life . . . and he only wondered why it seemed important.

Judy Tracy, when she got there, said, "Oh, *no.*" She bit her lip. "Well, how do you like that," she said. "Just as we were going off . . ."

It was midnight when Theo, on her way out, got down to the hospital lobby. It was nearly deserted, dimly lit. A girl behind glass dreamed at the switchboard, a porter slumped in a chair. One cigarette-fumbling father-to-be looked up in harassment, saw the coat flung over her uniform, dropped his head to his hands.

A figure rose from a leather armchair, came toward her. "Hello, Theo."

Theo smiled. "Hello. What made you think to do this?" She was tired, her voice heavy, and she took it for granted that he was there for her. It seemed to please him.

"I was driving past a little before eleven, so I thought perhaps you'd like a ride home. The girl at the switchboard said you were still upstairs, so I waited."

"That was nice of you," she said, adding wearily, "A ride home would be wonderful."

They walked along the quiet street to his car. Most of the houses were darkened, with here and there a light, a moving figure. The hospital loomed like a great pile of dark blocks pasted with squares of orange light. Thin baby cries from the nursery reached her ears as they pulled away. She sighed, leaning her head back against the cushions.

"Do you have to go right home?" Paul Favor asked.

"Yes. No. I don't know." She smiled nervously. "Perhaps I'd better. I don't seem to be functioning very well."

"Would a short ride help? It's a nice night," Paul offered hopefully.

"Would it?" Theo's head turned idly against the car seat. She thought about Mr. Warren, wishing she wouldn't. "I'm tired," she said remotely.

"Of course you are. I'll take you home. Fannell Street, isn't it?"

"How did you know?"

He smiled a little. "I looked it up, Miss Armacost."

Theo sat up. "Please, don't call me Miss Armacost," she said ruefully. After a while, "If you'd like, a ride would be nice."

Paul said nothing, but accelerated a bit as they passed Fannell Street. The night summer wind streamed past them in a dusky rush. It lifted Theo's hair and, presently, her spirits. "I haven't been very polite," she said. "No 'thank you,' no proper surprise to find you waiting . . ."

"I'm glad you weren't surprised."

"That's good."

They were outside of town when Paul spoke again. "Are you hungry at all?" he inquired.

Theo considered. She nodded, reflecting that the stomach was surely a sturdy instrument.

"There's a diner up the road a bit. Would that be all right?"

"That would be fine." She wished she could put more animation in her voice, if nothing else. But Mr. Warren's lonely death stayed with her. Dr. Jordan had come, unsurprised, but with the stony sadness he accorded death, the victor. Oh, what does it matter, Theo thought restlessly, dead or alive, he was through living.

"Is something wrong?" Paul asked, not looking at her.

"It can't be helped," she said somberly. "I wish I weren't acting this way," she repeated.

Paul shook his head. "Don't say that again. You act the way you must. Are you one of those people who thinks emotions should be wrestled with in private and never betrayed to others?"

"I don't think so," she answered slowly. "I don't believe that you should burden . . ."

Paul interrupted. "I hope you aren't going to say 'strangers.'"

"You're not one?"

"Do you think so?"

"Well," Theo pondered. "I don't know how to answer that. I don't know you very well," she added carefully.

Paul, to her surprise, laughed. "What a cautious little thing you are," he said. "Let's have a hamburger and I'll dispel the mysteries that throng round me."

They pulled up to the diner, a slab of chrominum elegance, glaringly alight. A few trucks, one or two cars, stood in front of it. A neon sign blurted on and off. "EATS!" it cried in blinking red letters, then, "DICK'S DINER."

Inside, the counter was almost full. One couple sat at the farthest table, dreamily eying each other over cold coffee. The counter girl slouched up to Paul and Theo, pulling a stub of pencil from behind her ear.

"Evening, folks, what'll it be?" she asked without interest.

Theo, watching a fly cruise about the pastries, asked for coffee and hamburger, crossing her fingers. Paul nodded, and the girl ambled away to the icebox, extracted two wafer-thin slices of chopped meat, slapped them on the griddle, slit two rolls, shoved them on the griddle, then settled on one hip, back to the counter, and stared.

Their order given, Theo and Paul were accepted as familiars, and the conversation, which had quieted when they entered, gathered strength.

A thin man in a thin windbreaker slammed his fist on the counter, without force, for emphasis. "I said to her," he told his burly red-faced listener, "I said to her, there's too many Mick names in this family now, and never a bit of luck to go with them. I got a brother, I said, name of Vincent Conner O'Hara . . . he sells washrags and shoe-strings out of a suitcase. I got another brother, name of Edward Sean Thomas O'Hara. He hustles pool for a living. I got a sister, Mary Bridget O'Hara. Fine girl she is. . . ." The thin man brooded a moment. His friend chewed a chop, waiting for the climax. "So," said the small man ominously, "I said to her, we're gonna give this boy a name to make people sit up and take notice. Something to take off the Irish." He lapsed again into silence, seemingly permanent.

"Well?" said the big man, putting down the chop bone and wiping his fingers carefully on a paper napkin.

"Well what?" The thin man seemed suddenly cast down.

"Well, whatcha name your son?" the other demanded impatiently.

"Otto," came the sullen answer.

Paul gulped. The big man gaped. "Otto O'Hara?" he said unbelievingly.

"Otto O'Hara," the other repeated firmly. "Whatcha say to that?"

What the big man said to it was to burst into loud guffaws. Several other people at the counter eyed their food studiously, grinning.

"Salt to that name," the little man ruminated gloomily. "Name like O'Hara don't need any salt."

"Connie!" Mr. O'Hara yelled at the dreaming girl, who looked around indifferently. "Gimme my check." He stood up, looking frail and disheartened. "So long, Buck," he said to the big man without rancor. "See you in a coupla days." He went out quickly. Theo saw him climb into a huge trailer truck. It hardly seemed possible that so slight a man could maneuver so tremendous a machine, but the truck purred easily and rolled off without a jerk.

Connie thrust their food in front of them. Theo nibbled at hers apathetically. Men and their sons, she thought, remembering Mr. Warren, who had wanted to do something for his son, too. But what a strange way the little trucker picked . . . Otto O'Hara. Oh dear.

"Something wrong?" Paul asked.

"Don't you suppose he should have thrown in a Patrick between the Otto and the O'Hara?"

"It won't make any difference."

"I think it will. A name like that has to be reckoned with, one way or the other. . . ."

"Then he'll have accomplished his purpose."

Paul looked around the slightly soiled diner, sniffed the stale air, turned his eyes back to Theo: white face, small-boned, and weary; eyes darkly blue, and red curls that swirled carelessly. She's lovely, he thought. I wouldn't want to lose her.

Most of the truck drivers were paying their checks, with automatic compliments to the bored and skeptical Connie. "You know, Connie, I could go for you, if you wasn't so tall," one of them tossed over his shoulder as he left, picking his teeth. Connie's response was mechanically flirtatious, "Oh, I'll bend down for you any day," she said, and they laughed obediently.

"I'm not hungry any more," Theo said.

Paul agreed. In the car she felt a need to explain. "You see," she faltered, "I always expect places like that to be . . . gay. Drivers and pretty waitresses and jokes . . . That place was . . . so sodden."

Paul said nothing for a while. Then, "People won't fit into patterns, Theo." It didn't sound pompous—just an observation.

"Why not?" she asked rather pettishly.

"Because they just aren't bits of a puzzle. They won't stay still till you pick a place for them and then fit because you feel they belong there. They're alive. They move away while you're finding a niche to shove them in."

"I don't want to shove people in a niche. I want . . ."

"What?" he asked, after a long silence.

"I want people to be happy,"

"They are," Paul said seriously. "Or at least, nearly all people are, I think."

"I'd like to know what makes you think that."

"Perhaps," Paul was saying, " 'happy' isn't the right word. 'Happy' meaning joyous and wild with delight. Practically nobody has that all the time. Nobody, really. I imagine everybody has it once in a while. What I mean," he went on, turning into Fannell Street, "is 'happy' in the sense that a man accepts his own life and takes some pleasure in it, besides the disappointments, isn't that it? Do you know anyone who'd change places with someone else?"

Theo shook her head slowly. They drew up before the house, dark except for the hall light. Paul leaned over the wheel, chin on his hands.

"What you might learn, Theo, I mean to help you when you ache for someone else's sadness, is that most of us can bear our own problems when they come. It's other people's that seem unbearable."

She leaned closer, as though to catch the breath of his words in her ear. It seemed very natural that he should turn to face her in the dark, very natural that they should kiss. His cheek felt a little stubbly, the tip of his nose pressed against her cheek.

She leaned away from him, against the door. "You know," she remembered, "you haven't dispelled any of the mysteries."

"About me? They aren't very mysterious."

"Tell me anyway." She jumped from the car. "Let's sit on the glider, where Anne sits with her beaux," she said breathlessly.

"Your sister?"

She nodded.

"Where have you sat with your . . . beaux?"

The glider squeaked beneath them. The dark porch seemed vast, the house behind brooding, asleep.

"I don't remember," Theo said simply. "I don't remember anything about them. Not," she added frankly, "that there have been very many."

"That's good."

"Now tell me," Theo commanded.

Paul thought a minute. "You know Uncle," he said finally. "My father died a long time ago. Uncle has been my father." He pushed his feet against the floor, setting the glider in rocky motion. "My mother is his sister. Mother wanted me to study music. Uncle wanted me to go in the bank . . . his bank, that is." He smiled a little, a queer curve in the pale light from a street lamp.

"You like music?" Theo prompted softly.

"Oh, yes. . . ." His tone said more than the words. "I have a beautiful piano—a concert grand that fits in Uncle's drawing room like an end table. You have to

134

look twice to know it's there at all. I play . . . often. I played tonight, till I thought of going for you."

Theo remembered that he'd said he was driving past. Climbing a birch tree, she said to herself curiously. I'm finally climbing a birch tree. Only not alone. With a dark creature who loves music.

"What did you want?" she asked in a gossamer voice. "Music, or the bank?"

"Oh, I wanted to go in the bank."

Theo laughed. "Well," she explained, "it's certainly an original solution to a traditional problem."

"As a matter of fact," Paul said, "it's the other decision that's original, or unusual, I should say. I don't love music any less because I don't want to make my living from it. Possibly," he debated, "more. Anyway, don't you include bankers in your scheme for happifying the world?"

"Of course I do. Everybody. It's just that I expected . . . oh, you know," she concluded helplessly.

"You expected me to fling away the world for art. In my case," he added honestly, "it would have been a singularly easy struggle in a gold-lined garret. But, you see, something Mother overlooked . . . you too, though you have no way of judging yet . . . I'm not that good. At the music, I mean. Mother's dreams are apt to be a little . . . ready-made. That sounds unkind. I mean, she's confused between life and the rather genteel tradition of her novel reading, sheltered girlhood." He shook his head. "Does this make any sense?"

"Of course it does," Theo replied. "Only I'm afraid I get a little mixed up myself—between what is real and what is a rhymed couplet that I've read so often it seems real."

"Sometimes the poetry *is* the reality."

Earth's the best place for love, Theo thought. "Yes,

135

sometimes the poetry is the reality," she repeated softly.

Paul stood up. "I'll go now." Still he hesitated. "Thank you for letting me take you home, Theo."

Thank you for being Paul. "Thank you, too," she replied gravely.

"Friday *will* come, won't it?" he asked, one foot on the steps.

"I should think so. It might take longer than usual."

"Theo?"

"Yes, Paul?"

"You know how you looked in that diner?"

"How?"

"Like a rose in a garbage pail."

Theo, going up to bed, thought it was the nicest thing anyone had ever said to her.

CHAPTER THIRTEEN

MORNING TOSSED up through a welter of heat.

All the Armacosts arose early from drenched and sticky beds.

Johnny eyed his three booklets limply. Far from feeling any urge toward muscle-molding, he didn't even do his exercises. There's one thing, he thought, sitting in a sapless heap on the edge of his bed, about being thin, you don't feel the heat so much. He blinked at the floor. "Holy moly," he said aloud, "if this is not feeling it!"

Downstairs, white marquisette curtains hung in motionless, sculptured folds at the windows. A vase of flaring gladiolas seemed too bright to contemplate, and Johnny's daisies, a present to his mother, folded their white heads sadly toward the dark surface of the dining room table.

Mrs. Armacost thought that even the grandfather clock swung its pendulum languorously. In the kitchen, where sunlight streamed heavily, the air seemed to be full of sluggish fists beating at her as she turned from sink to stove.

Anne, hair piled high, wearing crisp shorts and silk shirt, appeared at the door. Little wisps of curl clung wetly to her forehead. She pushed at them aimlessly. "Why don't we just have some cornflakes in the dining room?" she asked. "It's cooler there."

"All right. It doesn't seem like much to eat."

"Who wants much to eat?" Anne took a basket from the kitchen closet. "I'll go pick some raspberries. Would that be nice?"

Mrs. Armacost said she thought it would. "Do you think a picnic would be nice?" she asked Anne, who shook her head and said it was too hot to go anywhere for one.

"Perhaps out at Price's Beach?"

Anne hesitated. Well, what do I say now, she wondered. Am I going to make the whole family suffer because I don't want to run the chance of seeing Doug with someone else or because I feel torn to pieces every time I even think of the place? She swung her basket, marking time. "Okay, Mom," she said after a pause. "If everyone wants to go, it's all right with me." She ducked out the door to the garden. I've made it, she thought, I've made the gesture. Now let the rest of them decide. She wandered slowly to the raspberry patch. The little globes of fruit hung thickly, clusters of dark red, warm and so loose to the touch that they fell at the merest brush of her fingers. The thick rich odor of them rose in the air, and birds at her approach winged off reluctantly. When the basket was full, she

137

plucked three ripely crimson tomatoes that drooped with tropic lushness from the vine. They snapped off in her hands with a weighty plumpness. Her fingers were stained with the sweet juice of the berries.

In the kitchen, she turned on the spray of the faucet, holding her hands beneath the cool splinters of water. She bent around and thrust her face under the tiny shower. It spattered on her hair, her shirt.

"What are you doing?" Johnny, at the door, stared in astonishment. "That's not sanitary, Anne," he objected.

"Sanitary nothing," Anne replied calmly. "I'm hot, and it looked good."

"Would you like to go swimming?" Johnny asked impulsively.

"I don't know, Johnny. Mom has some sort of plan about a picnic, I think."

"What's for breakfast?"

"Cornflakes and raspberries."

"What else?"

"Nothing else."

Johnny was incredulous. "What? You can't eat just cornflakes and berries. Where's the food?"

"Johnny, I don't care what you eat. But get it yourself. I'm too hot to eat or talk about eating." Anne sprayed the berries carefully, put them in a colander, wandered out of the room.

"Well, where's Mom?" he yelled after her. There was no answer.

Left alone, Johnny began to probe through the closets, stooping down to rummage toward the back of a low shelf. His fingers closed on a box, brought it forward. He sat back on his heels. "Crimers," he muttered. He put back the first box, took out several others. Muffo-Mix, Fasto-Krust, Kwickie-Kake. Johnny shook his head, remembering that his mother had never actually said she made the things herself. She had a way of just smiling when complimented on a cake. Come to think of it, Johnny recalled, I always *did* think it was a funny smile she got. He grinned, then, hearing a footstep, thrust the boxes back quickly, grabbed a can, shoved the closet door closed, and rushed toward the stove.

"What are you doing, darling?" his mother asked.

Johnny waved the can about. "Just trying to get something to eat. Anne says we're only getting cold cereal and berries. . . ."

Mrs. Armacost studied the tin in his hand. "Will you have your cat food heated," she asked, "or eat it out of the can?"

Johnny glanced down, up, at the ceiling, at his mother. He rubbed his chin with the tin of cat food. "Believe I'll just have an egg," he said finally.

His mother nodded. She took the can from his hand, returned it to the closet, bending over to peer in the back. "Well," she observed, straightening up, "I've always felt sneaky about it. I'm glad somebody knows. Do you think," she went on, "that I should have a family council and tell everyone else?"

"Why? Dad likes the stuff, and so do Theo and I. Anne doesn't care what she eats any more anyway. Tell you what," he said, "I'll trade you the toaster for the mixes, okay?"

Mrs. Armacost smiled. "It wouldn't be a fair trade. Theo already knows that Mr. Power fixed the toaster . . . finished fixing it, that is."

Johnny shrugged. "This is a wonderful age we live in, Mom," he said. "Airplanes, telephones, Muffo-Mixes. . . . You don't churn butter these days, do you? There's no reason to mix cakes either. Take advantage of what science gives you, that's the ticket. You don't want to be a scullery-wench, do you?"

139

His mother shook her head.

"Well then, it's up to you to avail yourself of modern methods. I think you're smart to use these things. Could I have some bacon and eggs besides cereal?"

His mother made a sound very like a giggle. "You may have anything you want, darling. Except," she added hastily, "muffins. It's too hot to bake. I mean, too hot to run the oven."

"Now don't get a complex about it," Johnny soothed her. "Just take it as a matter of course. We eating in the dining room?"

"It's cooler in there."

"Yuh. I'll put the toaster on the table."

When they sat down to eat, a large platter of scrambled eggs and bacon accompanied the cornflakes and raspberries. Also toast.

"I thought," Mrs. Armacost said, "that we might pack some food and go to Price's Beach for a picnic."

Theo shook her head. "I can't."

"Darling, doesn't your vacation start today?"

"Tomorrow," Theo corrected. Then added, "I have a dinner date tomorrow, I mean."

"That's nice, Theo," her mother said. "With Dr. Dolan?"

"No. With Paul Favor. He's the nephew of Mr. Coombes."

"That sounds like a French lesson," Anne spoke for the first time. " 'The pen of my aunt,' the 'nephew of Mr. Coombes.' "

"*C'est vrai*," Johnny agreed.

"Paul Favor, Paul Favor. . . ." Mr. Armacost mused, calling upon his fabulous memory. "I believe I had him in an English course a good many years ago. Yes, I remember him now. A dark lad . . . very fine boy."

"He wondered if you'd remember him. I think he likes you," Theo said. "One of your many students who

140

remember you after they've forgotten everyone else," she added proudly.

"You must have made quite a hit, Theo," Anne commented with interest. Her sister just smiled. "No, I mean it," Anne pursued, forgetting, for the moment, her own problems. "You just met him, didn't you?" Theo nodded.

"Well, that's what's known as making a hit."

"We . . . he . . . we seem to get along. He called for me at the hospital last night."

Anne was quite impressed. "Will we meet him?" she inquired.

"Naturally. He's coming for me tomorrow."

"The guy," Johnny announced abruptly, "is rolling in dough."

"What a peculiar way you have of talking, Johnny," Mrs. Armacost remarked. "I think perhaps you shouldn't go to the movies."

"Ah, Mom . . ."

"Well, is he, Theo?" Anne asked.

"I'm not sure. He lives with his uncle and works in the bank."

"Works in the bank!" Johnny hooted. "He's treasurer, or vice-president, or something like that."

"How do you know so much about him?" Theo asked curiously.

Johnny merely looked mysterious. "There's a word you can tell to the grapevine that the grapevine don't tell back," he quoted significantly.

"You do," Theo laughed.

"Do what?"

"Tell back."

"Not everything," John replied with portent.

"Where *do* you find out things like that?" Anne persisted.

But Johnny was not to be drawn. His source of information was simple, but as the cause of it was yet another scheme which he'd fostered and abandoned, he preferred to keep silent. Earlier in the year, he and Cooper had decided to start a newspaper. They had conceived the idea of interviewing prominent people in town, and in preparation had looked into the histories of a few likely prospects. Mr. Coombes being a very prominent person, they'd also encountered Paul Favor's name as they went through files in the library. However, Cooper, after a morning in the library stacks, decided that everything had already been written about everybody. That and the approach of the baseball season cut short their careers as journalists. From this sowing, Johnny reaped intermittent benefits in the form of astounding people with odd pieces of information. Now he succeeded in looking like a basilisk possessed of unending knowledge, though in fact he'd exhausted his supply concerning Paul Favor.

"I can't, at least not today," Mr. Armacost said reflectively. "Perhaps Sunday."

"Can't what on Sunday?" his wife asked.

"Go on a picnic. Isn't that what we were talking about? Oh, and of course, Paul Favor," he added, smiling at Theo in case she felt offended. She didn't. Mr. Armacost turned again to his wife.

"I didn't," she said, "ask to go on Sunday. It was today. Only now Theo can't."

"Neither can I."

"I thought you said you couldn't go Sunday?"

Mr. Armacost shook his head. "Today," he said resolutely. His wife looked confused and a little angry.

"What Dad meant, Mom," Johnny interposed quickly, "is that he can't go today, but perhaps he could Sunday."

Mr. Armacost nodded in a surprised way. "Isn't that what I said?"

Anne drifted away from the conversation. Anyway, they wouldn't go today. One day more safe in the house, where she wouldn't run the wretched risk of seeing . . . With a wrench, she steered her mind away from Doug. "Do you know," she said suddenly, and her voice was loud, "that if you have four children, your family is only twice as big as if you have one child?"

In the silence that followed, they all stared blankly at each other, then at Anne.

"Is *that* the kind of thing you think of when you sit in those dazes?" Johnny inquired.

"Well," she said defensively, "it's an interesting fact, isn't it? Did you ever think of it?"

"No," Johnny admitted. "Not that I wouldn't have led a perfectly happy life without knowing it."

Mrs. Armacost got up from the table. "I think it's astonishing," she murmured pacifically. "Would somebody help me with the dishes?"

The picnic plans having died a-borning, no one suggested alternatives. They debouched, one by one, to the shaded living room, fell, like a game of living statues into suspended attitudes, and prepared to endure the heat. Outside, the only sound was the keen of the katydids, an occasional bird note. Children were kept in, out of the brassy sunshine. Animals sought the shade beneath porches and bushes. July, careless of yesterday's honors, lay upstairs on the tile of the bathroom floor, back against the tub, tongue sticking pinkly through her open mouth.

Johnny alone pursued any activity. He lay on the floor, a large square of white cardboard before him, blocking it off in sections. Anne watched idly, thinking she might ask what it was all about, but putting off the words.

Theo spoke, her pleasantly harsh voice caressing in the way she had with poetry. "Not so much air as on a summer's day robs not one light seed from the feathered grass . . ."

"But where the dead leaf fell, there did it rest," her father concluded softly. They smiled at each other as though a message had passed between them.

Johnny looked up from his mysterious paper and pencil work. "I've about made up my mind," he declared, his voice scaling perilously upward. "I'm told I'll get over that," he interrupted himself grimly, "but it's sure taking an awful long time."

"Patience, son, patience," Anne advised.

"Gee, you really think that's the answer?" Johnny inquired acidly.

"What have you made up your mind about this time?" Anne asked.

"What I have decided, *Theo*," Johnny explained, "is that I'm going to be a cartoonist."

"Cartoonist?" Anne stared at him. "But you don't know how to draw, do you?"

"You don't have to. All you need is ideas. Then you just draw lines for the people. All the good cartoons are drawn like someone was scratching the paper with a pencil."

"I don't *think* so," Anne deliberated. "Some of them look like Hogarth to me. . . ."

"Those aren't any good, the ideas, I mean," Johnny said triumphantly. "They aren't art either," he added. "However, cartoonists with real humor, the kind I'm talking about, never draw well," he concluded unequivocally. "Now here," he said, getting up to show them, "is my first cartoon."

Obediently Anne, Theo, and Mr. Armacost fixed their attention on the paper. It had four squares drawn on it, with some scribbing in the first two, and the last one.

"What is it?" Anne inquired after a pause during which they all examined the squares closely.

"Oh, Anne!" Johnny sputtered impatiently. He sighed. "Well, this is how it is. One of these cartoons, with four blocks, you know how they go. In the first one, this guy is coming up to a girl. He's got a dog on a leash . . . that sort of blotty thing is the dog. Then, in the next one, she is holding up her hand, kind of stuck up, you get the idea?"

They nodded blankly.

"Well, now, something . . . you know . . . fills up the other block. And then in the last one, the guy bites her hand. See?"

Unspeaking, Anne, Theo, and Mr. Armacost shook their heads.

Johnny glared. "It's funny!" he bellowed. "She's stuck up and he bites her hand, instead of the dog. Surprise angle!"

"I still think you ought to be able to draw better," Anne commented mildly.

Johnny snatched away his humorous conception, stalked out of the room.

After a silence, Anne questioned her father. "Do you think he's quite bright?"

"Anne, stop saying things like that," Mr. Armacost answered sternly. "He's growing up." Johnny's father sighed, because Johnny was finding the road to maturity so serpentine and rocky; because Anne, stumbling on her own path, refused to see the hardships of her brother's; because, finally, it was hot and he was thinking about the fall semester. Sometimes, most of the time, he considered his students as willing, if not eager, explorers of the written thought, himself the guide, or, as Taine would have it, himself the leader

145

and they the scalers of the wall of truth. Unfortunately, as Taine would have said, they all too often scaled the wall only to find themselves at the bottom of a moat on the other side. He thought of his classroom, huge, old, many-windowed. It had an air, compounded of ancient books, golden oak, eraser dust, and steam heat, that was a pungent recollection of schoolrooms the country over. In September, when it was still warm, the students would have a freshness that he'd seize upon with delight. Sitting before him in their new fall clothes, opening their new books with the bright stiff covers and smooth pages, eying each other with anticipation—*each other*, Mr. Armacost repeated to himself. School seems to them, I think, a proving ground for their social success. Often enough, a field of adolescent failure. But where, and when, did learning lose its place? If it were only his own classes from which the freshness ebbed so quickly, then there would be the rather bitter satisfaction of admitting the disease was at least local. But he was not, he knew, a poor teacher. Not a brilliant one . . . but good enough to search for and fan any spark that ignited in his classrooms. Many people now grown remembered him. Some wrote. There was no greater reward for a teacher than this— that after leaving his sphere, a student should return to it now and then, because he wished to. No, he found that other teachers, better and worse than he, felt the enthusiasm ebb away, till only a face here and there seemed alight with any desire save a passionate one for the closing bell. Then the books, garlanded with pencil doodlings, snapped closed, the combs came out, and the young vessels, a good deal less than filled, streamed into the halls for the urgent business of date-making, date-breaking, shunning, contacting, hurting. The only really successful teachers, Mr. Armacost thought perplexedly, seem to be athletic coaches.

"What are you thinking, Dad?" Theo asked.

"What's that? Oh . . ." He cocked his head at her. "I was thinking that if the highroad to English literature were at 120 dash, more people would turn out for it."

Theo, usually so sensitive to his moods, just smiled at him encouragingly. Well, well, a girl has important matters to think on. . . . "That young man you spoke of, Theo. Paul Favor. I do remember him. A very interesting boy. I believe he was quite a musician?"

"Yes. He still is, I guess." Theo smiled, remembering their conversation. "But he's perfectly happy working in the bank."

"Music and money are not incompatible," said her father, who had never made much money himself and genuinely didn't regret it. He thought, you never see a hummingbird coming. It's as if a veil was lifted in the middle of air, and there he hangs, a jewel on spun glass wings. "Do you suppose that this heat would make the hummingbirds a little less cautious?"

"I suppose that if you went out in the garden and sat there waiting for one, you'd get sunstroke before you got the hummingbird," Mrs. Armacost said, coming in from the kitchen. She slumped into a chair like a wet towel. "Theo, would you like to come on a picnic Sunday?"

Theo said she would. "It would be fun."

"Perhaps Mr. Favor will like to go along."

"It wouldn't surprise me. I'll ask him." Theo was startled, a little, by the possessiveness that had already crept into her voice when she spoke of him.

"How old is he?" Mrs. Armacost inquired. And she was surprised, a little, by the speculation in her own voice. Perhaps, she thought, the instinct for husband-finding is stronger in mothers than we think these days. For their daughters, that is, she amended. I did think that sort of approach went out a good many years ago.

Theo said she thought Paul was about thirty. "A good age," Mrs. Armacost said, tapping her cheek.

"Good age for what?" Theo asked with amusement.

Her mother blinked. "Why, for . . . for anyone, really," she replied evasively. Her husband and daughter grinned. Even Anne responded with a remote smile. *Which brings me,* she thought, *to the problem of Anne again. A problem with one solution . . . time—a specific in which young people put no faith at all. But perhaps we could do something . . . a visit to some relative? My sister in Philadelphia?*

"Anne, would you like to go to Aunt Pat's?"

Anne looked up in surprise. "Aunt Pat's? What for?"

"For a visit, darling. I thought you might like a little trip."

Anne shook her head. "No, thanks, Mom." She stood up. "I do wish there was less publicity . . ." She turned as the phone rang, walked to it slowly. *I do not, of course,* she told herself, *expect this to be anyone special. It's been much too long now for it to be Doug. I expect nothing.* She reached for the phone.

"Hello, Anne?"

Well, why such a flap? I said it wouldn't be, didn't I? "Hello, Nora," she said flatly.

"What's the matter? Anything wrong?"

"Oh, no. Just the heat."

"Isn't it brutal? I was wondering, Anne . . ."

"Yes?"

"I thought maybe you could come over here and stay with me. I'm lonesome. Mother's going to be away tonight and the boarder's in Maine, so we'd have the house to ourselves, anyway."

"I'll ask my mother, Nora, but I think so. It would be fun."

"Well, maybe. The baby cries a lot. But then, you

shouldn't mind that. I don't think anyone ever minds other people's babies crying, do you?"

"I guess not," Anne answered, careful not to sound too indifferent. "Wait a minute, Nora, I'll ask now. . . ." She cupped her hand over the phone, called into the living room. "Mother? Would it be all right if I went over to Nora's today and stayed tonight?"

Mrs. Armacost was delighted and said as much.

"All right," Anne said into the phone. "I'll be along in a bit. Just get a few things together." She waved to the company in the living room, went up to put a nightdress, a toothbrush, the raspberry scuffs in a hatbox. As she started downstairs, she noticed Johnny's door open a crack. Knocking, she called, "What are you doing, Johnny?"

"Huh? Oh, nothing. Did you want something?"

"Just to say good-by. I'm going over to Nora Chapin's."

Johnny appeared at his door. "Come on in," he invited. "You going to spend the night over there?"

"Uh-huh." Anne looked around the room curiously. She was rarely in Johnny's room, and each time he'd done something startling in the way of decoration. This time, apparently, he'd been content simply to move the furniture around. Then she spied an anatomy chart on the wall, a big colored map of the human muscle structure. "Johnny!" she protested, wrinkling her nose, "what sort of pin-up is that?"

"Oh, I'm interested in musculature," her brother replied casually.

"You aren't angry about the cartoon?"

Johnny, beginning to feel as though he had constantly to disclaim anger, assured her he wasn't. "Just an idea. I'll still work on it."

"The only thing is, you shouldn't fly off like that every time people disagree with you." Anne swung her

149

hatbox, smiling at him. Johnny thought she looked extraordinarily pretty. It did not occur to him to say so. He said, "It's all right not to think it was good. But you didn't have to laugh at me. . . ."

"We didn't. I thought that was the point."

"Oh well." Johnny swallowed a yawn. "I don't think I know what the point was."

"I mean to congratulate you and July. That was very smart of her to win the prize, wasn't it?" Anne said, noticing July's blue ribbon pinned to the wall.

"A cat like that deserves prizes." He frowned. "The only thing is, I can't figure how that knuckle-head knew enough to give it to her. We don't get along so good, him and me. He and I."

"So I've gathered," Anne remarked dryly. "Well. Good-by. See you tomorrow."

"So long, Anne. Have fun."

Johnny closed his door as she left. He pulled the green ledger from the desk drawer, where he'd thrust it at her knock.

"I observe signs," he wrote, "of returning life in Anne. This may be temporary, because she's getting out for a while and probably she and her girl friend will talk themselves into a coma, which seems to be very good for girls. I hope so." He studied this, thinking it looked as though he hoped Anne would wind up in a coma, but didn't change it—since it's my book, he thought, and I hardly ever read back in it anyway. He went on, "This first cartoon is a flop from the family angle. I'll try it on Cooper. Haven't started on the muscle-building yet. It's too hot for one thing. For another, I have to decide whether I want to look like this guy on the cover. Muscles are one thing, but he looks like a float in the Macy parade. Will give this thought."

He tucked the Journal back in its accustomed place, pulled his clammy shirt away from his skin, ambled downstairs, trudged out the front door after his father's disappearing figure. "You gonna work in the garden?" he asked incredulously.

"Not yet. I'm driving Anne over to Harrison's. Want to come along?"

"Might as well."

The gravel was hot underfoot. The palpable white air pressed against them. Getting in the car was like plunging in a box of lava, and the motor boiled into action at the merest touch of the starter. As they backed from the garage into the swollen atmosphere, Mr. Armacost muttered with some truculence, "If this keeps up, I'm going to pipe for the Yukon."

"Me too," Johnny said cheerfully.

In the house Anne answered a question of her mother's. "Oh, I don't think she'd want to come over here, Mom. The baby cries, and I suppose it would make her nervous." She blinked at Mrs. Armacost's expression. "What's the matter?"

"Do you mean to tell me," her mother asked slowly, "that that child has a baby?"

"Oh, didn't you know?"

"I did not." She shook her head. "Her husband's in college, isn't he?"

"Yes." Through some impulse of loyalty, Anne didn't mention that Sam only went to college at night because he had to work in a garage during the day.

"How do they manage? Does her mother help?"

"My goodness, no. Mrs. Harrison is still angry about the whole thing. She says Nora did what she wanted to, so now she can take the consequences." Anne looked at her own mother curiously. "What do you think of that?"

"I don't think anything of it," Mrs. Armacost sighed. "It sounds pretty hard, but you can't tell how many things are behind it. Does the boy have any money?"

"He has something left over from the army. And he goes on the G.I. Bill. I suppose they have a difficult time. With one thing and another, I expect everyone does."

"Relatively. That makes a difference."

"But small comfort?"

"It depends on how much vision you have." She sighed again. "It does seem a pity . . . such very young people, with no time any more for youngness."

They have each other, Anne thought. She said, "There's Dad. See you in the morning, Mom. Say goodby to Theo for me. Where'd she go?"

Mrs. Armacost lifted her shoulders vaguely. She felt depressed and at least ninety years old. What do I know of their feelings, anyway, she wondered. I must sound like an old crank, and perhaps I am one. "Have a good time," she called as her daughter left.

CHAPTER FOURTEEN

"WOULD YOU have time to let me stop at the A.&P., Dad?" Anne asked as they drove. "I thought I could get some lemons and stuff for Nora and me. Iced tea."

Mr. Armacost said it would be all right. "Only for pity's sake, don't take long. That parking lot is blisterous." He thought a moment. "Blisterous . . . what a fine word."

"Could I have some money, too?" Anne went on.

"Oh. Well, all right. Lemons, did you say?"

"And maybe a little sliced ham and pickles and a melon."

"You're being sort of handy with my nest egg, Sister Anne." Mr. Armacost reached into his pocket, pulled out a rumpled five-dollar bill. "There you are," he said grandly, "my treat for you and the little bride."

Anne smiled. "If it weren't so hot, I think perhaps I'd kiss you."

"I think perhaps I'd accept . . . if it weren't too hot."

They turned into the A.&P. parking lot, indeed crowded and blisterous. "Want me to help, Anne?" Johnny asked, stretching his neck and pulling at his shirt.

"No, thanks, Johnny." Anne hopped out, flipped off toward the sprawling market.

"Girls are the darndest things," Johnny observed, watching her trim figure weave through outcoming shoppers laden with shopping bags, followed by aproned boys with boxes, all of them looking too hot, some resigned, some irritated . . . high prices, heat, everydayness. Anne looked like a pink sherbet trotting through a herd of baked potatoes.

"In what particular?" Mr. Armacost inquired.

"Well, take Anne. She's been glooming around for a week, acting like each breath would be the last. So here she is now, bouncing along to buy ham and pickles . . . not a worry in the world."

His father took out a handkerchief. "I wouldn't," he said, blotting his brow and neck, "be too sure. She puts up a pretty good defense even at home, where she probably feels free to let go a little, I hope. She'd be more careful in public. Girls are proud. What's the matter with her?"

"I think she's been jilted," Johnny said bluntly.

"Jilted. Such a pretty girl, don't you think? I shouldn't have thought . . ."

Johnny disagreed. "Oh, she's pretty," he admitted. "But that's not all that counts. Some guys," he added wisely, from instinct, not experience, "just don't want to be smothered."

"On the other hand, some think it's fine."

Johnny was tired of the conversation and a little embarrassed. "Not the one she picked," he said with finality.

Mr. Armacost recognized the dismissal, sighed, fell silent. But how unlike Anne, he thought, always so confident . . . how unlike her to smother anyone at all.

Anne, in the brightly lighted aisles of ketchup, cans, crackers, and condiments, considered the five dollars, selected a shopping wagon. Might as well get a bunch of fancy stuff. It would be fun to cook, though perhaps not too much fun to eat, since things had a way of tasting like wet cotton lately. Not, she thought, that I'm too good at it anyway. Once, she'd cooked a meal for Johnny, when through a series of misfortunes there had been no one else around to do it. He'd eaten it, then when they were clearing the dishes, asked how long it took to boil all the flavor out of everything. Anne smiled a little, remembering. She dropped a can of anchovies in the wire basket, followed it with a jar of olives, wandered on, her eye picking over the counters. A white-aproned boy trundled down the aisle, pushing a wide broom before him. As his pile of papers and dust collected before the brush and his collection of debris increased, a sprig of parsley maintained a saucy balance on top. Anne thought it looked cute. She smiled again, and the boy leaned on his broom for a second to ask what she was doing tonight.

"Nothing that would interest you," she said pleasantly. He moved on sulkily. Anne, going in the opposite direction, forgot him. She felt, concentrated on feeling, a numbness melting from her mind . . . distinct from the pain, still intact, in her heart. Why, she wondered, should this stupid dense feeling suddenly start to go? It's so strange, this feeling, and those others. Those others were unbidden waves of sensation which passed through her from time to time—brief, violent, unaccountable. Not always pleasant. At times, just standing in the dining room or bedroom, anywhere in the house, a sense of unutterable uneasiness would clutch at her . . . till she felt alien in her own home. Her family seemed some formidable company, hostile, unknown. When the impression passed, she'd feel rather sick. But much more often, for no more assignable reason, she had a ravishing sense of anticipation, a wheeling awareness that life would be startling, beautiful . . . that it held promise almost too wonderful to contemplate. These perceptions, coming as they did, for no reason that Anne could understand, left her as mysteriously. No way to summon, comprehend, or banish them.

Now she tried once more to know what caused them. What had been said or done today that the muzzy, torpid cloud which had filled her mind should melt away like mist before a drift of breeze? Pushing the wagon slowly, she frowned in deliberation, then shook her head and moved faster. Dad and Johnny would be broiling. She got some sliced boiled ham, some potato salad, a melon, lemons, and a bottle of ginger ale. While it was rung up at the cash desk, she decided the cooking wouldn't present such a problem after all. Merely a matter of getting some dishes out.

Then, walking into the glazed heat of the parking lot, she realized the effect, though not the cause, of her mind's sudden clarity. Something was in her thoughts beside Doug. Amazingly, she'd been thinking about Nora and about food. Even now, thinking that she'd not thought of Doug altogether, her heart cried out for him. But her mind steadily included other matters, as though weary of the languishing role. "Go ahead," it said to her heart, "break. But I've other things to do, and I'll be getting on with them."

Not, Anne realized, that I can depend on this . . . emancipation. It feels good, really, to be able for a little while to stand away from Doug. Oh, Doug, Doug, I wish I could meet you now, to show you how I don't mind not seeing you. I could be very gay, very nonchalant. I'd say, "Oh, hello there. . . ." Because there's nothing so casual as

155

saying, "Oh, hello there." It has the perfect note of indifference. A verbal shrug.

"Anne, for Pete's sake, are you talking to yourself?" Johnny hooted from the car. Several people glanced at her.

"Yes," she replied calmly, "but if you don't mind, darling, it was a secret." The starers looked away, smiling. Johnny reached out and took her bags, but said nothing more till they reached Harrison's. Then he said good-by.

"'By, Johnny," Anne said, wondering why she couldn't say, "Oh, good-by there." She giggled as she leaned over to kiss her father. "Thanks, Dad. I'll take the bus back tomorrow, so don't you bother about me."

"No bother at all," Mr. Armacost assured her, charmed by the giggle. "I'll miss you," he surprised himself by saying, and felt rather foolish. It was so unexpectedly nice to see her this way. "I hope it isn't just because you'll be away for a day or so," he added irrelevantly.

Anne understood. "It isn't," she said thoughtfully, "because anything. It just suddenly is. I wouldn't depend on it."

Her father smiled wistfully. "Well, make the most of it. 'By, Anne."

"And what," Johnny asked as they drove away, "was that all about?"

His father didn't answer for a while. When he did, he said, "Let's take some ice cream home, shall we?"

After she'd phoned Anne, Nora went into the living room with a vague idea of straightening up. Once there, she sank into a chair, lit a cigarette, and simply stared. It wasn't, as Sam thought, that the place was dirty. It just looked as if it were. The furniture seemed less arranged than shoved into the room and left there. Three dejected armchairs hunched uncomfortably close together, as though seeking to efface their individual ugliness in a collective one. Here and there assorted tables of dark wood bore their drab burdens of ashtrays, magazines, ecru doilies. The rug was Axminster, faded. The walls appeared to have been painted with clam chowder.

Then, of course, there were the elephants. Mrs. Harrison was one of those women who collects elephants. So far as Nora could tell, there was no real point—not beauty nor value nor rarity. If it's an elephant and will fit in the china closet, she thought gloomily, it's part of the collection. There'd been another added since she was last home —a present from the border, a plush Jumbo, with its head sort of pushed down to fit between the shelves. And, naturally, a couple of those sets of marching elephants getting smaller and smaller. At any rate, Nora thought, putting out her cigarette, you can tell by looking in the china closet, if you could bear it, that the house is actually clean. Every one of those things is dusted.

There were dishes in the kitchen sink. She put them out of mind. The baby was asleep. She hoped he wouldn't wake up too soon. She allowed herself ten minutes by her watch. In ten minutes it would be eleven o'clock. Then she'd get up, do the dishes, fix something nice for Anne's lunch, make some formulas. By then, the baby would be awake. Perhaps she and Anne could sit in the back yard, the baby in its carriage.

It didn't really matter too much. How nice, she thought, to be seeing Anne again. The last time was Christmas . . . when I'd just found out that I was pregnant. That was the worst time of my life, the very worst. And Anne looked so happy, so absolutely carefree. Oh, dear heaven, Nora cried inwardly, I'd have given anything to be like that again. To be able to walk out of a door without saying anything to anyone. To go to a beach or a movie or just simply walk out the door . . . free. She thought of the baby, the way he had of sleeping on his stomach, small rear in the air. She loved her baby and longed to be free of him. Once in a while, she thought wildly, just once in a while . . .

Her watch said a little past eleven. Nora put her hands on the arms of the chair, pushed up, and propelled herself to the kitchen. She started the dishes without giving notice to her drugged mind, so she was in the middle of the job before being aware that she'd actually started. Hot. Much too horribly hot. She wondered how the baby felt. When, a little while before, she'd gone to look, he'd been trickling all over with perspiration. He'd had a bath. He wore nothing but a diaper. There really wasn't anything else she could do for him, and anyway, he seemed to be sleeping very happily. How *can* he sleep in all this heat? Nora pushed at her hair, getting it wet. She wondered what Sam was doing. A little after eleven . . . thinking of him in a garage in New York on such a day made her a little faint. It seemed they could give him a few days' vacation, even if it was his first summer on the job. Oh well, she decided morosely, he doesn't care . . . or if he does, he'd just want to get off because of the heat—not to be with me. She bit her lower lip as the cold panic rose. Won't he ever want to be with me again? Is this how we're to spend our lives . . . apart, indifferent?

The bell rang, Anne's voice called, "Where are you, Nora?" The screen door slammed. Anne and Nora met in the hall, one precariously balancing hatbox and shopping bags, the other holding dish towel and baby bottle.

"Well," Anne said, "here I am."

Nora nodded, wriggled a hand, turned back in haste. "Come in here, will you, Anne? I'm in a ghastly thrash. . . ."

"What shall I do with this stuff?" Anne inquired, dumping it all on the kitchen table.

"What is it? Oh, Anne," Nora cried, "all this beautiful food!"

"I thought we could sort of eat cold things," Anne observed, storing her purchases in the icebox.

"That would be lovely." Nora put away the final dish. "It's good to see you again."

"You too." A pause. "Where's your son?"

"He's asleep."

"Oh, I wanted to see him."

"He's be awake soon. Let's just sit and talk. It's been so long since I've had anyone to talk to." Anne looked at her curiously, but all she said was, "I thought we'd make some iced tea. Then we could sit in back and chatter."

They carried the frostily beaded glass pitcher and two glasses on a tray into the backyard. Two faded canvas beach chairs faced each other, and into these they subsided cautiously.

"Guess they'll hold," Nora commented, pouring.

"Where's Sam?"

"Working. He has to work all summer."

"Oh, Nora, what a shame for you. . . ."

"Yes, isn't it?" Nora replied without expression.

Anne felt a little confused. She and Nora had never been stiff with each other before, but today the small talk was so labored that it seemed almost better not to talk at all. She drank the tea, pulled at a leafy whip of willow that drooped near her.

Nora took out a pack of cigarettes. "Want one?" she asked. Anne shook her head. "You don't smoke," Nora stated.

"No."

"It's very . . . soothing."

"I may try it sometime, in that case."

Nora lifted her brows. "What would you need to be soothed about?"

"Oh, I presume everyone must at one time or another," Anne replied carefully.

"I see." Nora stared at the ground. She lifted her head,

about to speak. At that moment the cry of the baby came from the upstairs room.

"Want to come up with me?" Nora asked, getting to her feet.

Anne followed, frowning. She had expected . . . well, she wasn't quite sure. But certainly not this. I expected, she defined for herself, to find a crisp little mother, a slightly lonesome wife . . . but full of eager talk and pride in all her possessions, a baby and a husband. Nora acts so . . . drained. It couldn't be all account of the heat. Anne was very puzzled. Nora, with everything she could want, behaving so empty. Perhaps, she thought, it's just that she can't find anything in common with me any more. She wanted to see me, but now doesn't know how to act. She's a wife and a mother, trying to talk to what she probably considers a child. Suddenly she felt annoyed. After all, I'm *not* a child. "Nora," she said abruptly, "I'm not a child, you know."

Nora turned from the crib, holding the baby. "Whoever said you were?"

"Well." Anne felt a bit embarrassed. "I'm sorry. But you act so odd with me, as if there were . . . unbridgeable worlds between us. . . ."

Nora shook her head. "There are, I guess. But I'm not thinking you're too young for me, if that's what you mean."

"Then what's wrong?" Anne cried.

They stared at each other steadily. Then Nora said, "Perhaps I'll try to tell you, after a while. Which really wouldn't be very fair of me," she added.

"Of course it's fair," Anne said harshly. "We used to . . . tell each other things."

"We did, didn't we?" Nora replied. "I have to feed the baby now. I thought you wanted to see him," she smiled, holding the infant up.

"I did. I do," Anne said quickly. "It's just that . . ."

160

"I know. Well, what do you think of him?"

Anne studied the little body held before her. Thin and hot it looked, sparse hair plastered to the pale pink head that drooped a bit, like a balloon on a peeled stick. The lower lip pouted out in an enchanting way, and big pansy eyes fixed uncertainly on her face. "I think he's perfectly marvelous," Anne said truthfully.

Nora smiled in a contented way, then made for the door as the pout progressed to a wail of hunger.

The day passed in such disorder that Anne, though she did little enough, had no time to feel anything but harassment and a nagging suspicion that Nora really didn't manage too well. Not, she added conscientiously, that I actually know a scrap about it, but you would think she and Sam would go mad in a little apartment if this is a sample of their days. She stopped at the thought. Well, that of course was it—the reason for Nora's strange resistance to speech or closeness, even though the invitation had been her own. Anne understood that Nora wouldn't want to discuss her failure. They'd have been happy enough to pore in detail over so young a marriage that had gloriously countered the Cassandra omens of the elders. But one that had failed, or possibly was so far merely in peril of failure, could not be easily spoken of. Nora had wanted her here for physical company in an empty house. But Nora, Anne decided, must lead the conversation because I don't know the danger places, what will hurt or what be safe to say. She leaned back in a drab armchair, eyes soberly regarding the china-closet elephants. She could almost hear Mrs. Harrison's plaintive voice in the mohair-stuffy room. She couldn't hear the words, but presumably they concerned a sick headache. This room is a headache, Anne thought, listening to the sounds of Nora putting her son to bed. Her son. That should be a proud expression. But then, she realized, Nora never did say "my son" or "our son." She said "the baby."

In a way, Anne meditated, "my son," would be a word of pride and accomplishment, whereas "the baby," said the way Nora says it, is loving but restrictive. "The baby" is a jailer, whose strength is weakness, whose mother is no more loved than his own fist, as each is a part of him. She'd watched Nora, in the space of fifteen minutes, move from mute adoration of the calm-eyed baby to almost furious rebellion. But, willing or unwilling, Nora had become an appendage.

Anne sighed. For a moment she wished it were tomorrow morning so she could run away to the peace of her own life and the sunny brightness of her own room. "What am I saying?" she exclaimed aloud, but Nora didn't hear. Peace of my own life? I haven't had peace for weeks . . . not since I first started going with Doug. But she knew she had. Her heart was breaking in lovely surroundings, among people who loved her. She didn't know what was happening to Nora's heart, but the comparison was not just. Nora had never had security, nor beauty, in her home—perhaps not in her marriage. Doug and I wouldn't be like that, Anne thought, and was immediately a bit bored with herself. I can't, she realized, seriously think of Doug around Nora. Even in my own eyes, it seems a rather insignificant disappointment. Doug got tired of me. There, she nearly sobbed, as simple as that. I've been making high tragedy of a commonplace matter. "It's *not* that simple," cried her heart. "It certainly is," Anne retorted coldly, feeling that it really was.

Nora came down at last, pushing her tangled, loosely hanging curls into further disorder. She felt Anne's eyes on her. Why does Anne look so tender, she wondered irritably. I must be as transparent as a piece of cellophane . . . and about as colorful. "How do you like my hair?" she asked airily. "I'm not wearing it this season." Anne got up, laughing. What heading does that come under, Nora debated. Indulgence? Or the sardonic smile? "Let's fix

162

something to eat," she said abruptly. Perhaps I shouldn't have asked her, she thought, and sighed remorsefully at the recollection of Anne's lovely presents, her obvious affection for the baby. But where shall we meet any more? It isn't the same, it just isn't the same. Anne, with her snug home, her lovely family . . . Anne, preparing for college and prom-trotting.

"I," Nora said, following up this idea, "could be properly called a pram-trotter."

But Anne didn't laugh this time. She leaned against the sink and said bluntly, "Well, why did you ask me to come?"

Nora lit another of her countless cigarettes. She studied its lacy glowing tip, the fingers that held it, the blue veins of her hand and wrist. Her other hand fell, suddenly lifeless, to her lap. "Because I'm lonesome, I guess. Because I thought if you were here it would feel as though I'd never . . . it would be like other times."

"Other times, we talked."

Nora's eyes were wide and lost. "Other times," she said slowly, "there seemed to be words. . . ." She shook her head. "This is dreadful, Anne. Please stay, and we'll try to be more cheerful. We can have a nice dinner, and then . . ."

"And then talk," smiled Anne. "I had no intention of leaving, you know."

Well, they could talk, surely. And if nothing got said, perhaps that was best.

After supper, Nora said, "Would you like a coke?"

Anne nodded.

Nora poured two glasses of coke, added some cracked ice and sprigs of mint. "They look pretty, don't they?" she asked, handing one to Anne.

"Mmm. Let's take it in back. Do you think it's gotten cooler?"

They sat in the canvas chairs, under the willow. It

163

wasn't dark yet, though the sun was gone. The clatter of dishware in neighboring kitchens, scraps of conversation, discordance of radio programs, mingled hazily with the throaty calls of birds giving up the day. Warmly the odor of leaves and moist earth thickened in the air, and the sharp sweetness of the iced drinks lay between.

"What are you doing these days, Anne?" Nora asked, her voice low with the peace of evening. "Who do you go out with? Peter?"

"Oh, Peter sometimes." Anne wondered if she could mention Douglas. She could. "I've been seeing a lot of Douglas Eamons." His name pressed at her throat, but she said it.

"Oh, Anne, he's divine. . . . You met him at Christmas, I remember."

"Yes. We walked in the snow." But this was going to be too hard, after all. Compared to Nora's loss of—what was it mother said? Youth? Well, that and more. Compared to her loss, mine is not important. But it hurts, even when I think it shouldn't, it hurts horribly. She remembered the poet's cry, "Pity me that the heart is slow to learn what the swift mind beholds at every turn." She probed at the pain deliberately, to punish her slow heart. "Oh, he's not mine exclusively. Dody Colman" (Oh, bitter taste!) "Dody Colman has a claim of some precedence."

"The ubiquitous Colmans," Nora said sympathetically.

"She's going to be a model in New York, Angie says her plan is to drive men mad with her moon-gold hair."

"She and her sister should go far, they're so utterly single-minded. They're also single," Nora added broodingly.

"Nora, are you going to explain any of these oblique remarks?"

"Not at all. And they're far from oblique. Could you go to New York with me?"

The question startled Anne. "When? What for?"

"Saturday. I have to look at an apartment. There's a

164

very nice, if lusty, woman we know, Ruby Cassidy, who's located some horror in uptown New York that maybe Sam and I can get. She's a friend of the superintendent. We can't stay where we've been, with the baby."

"Well, I guess I could."

"I'd like to have you," Nora said, unconsciously wistful. "Of course, we have to take the baby, so it won't be precisely a pleasure trip."

"Won't your mother be back tomorrow?"

Nora nodded. "Oh, she'll be back. But you see, ten minutes with the baby and Mother's crawling up the walls. She won't take him."

There was no answer to this so Anne said, "I think it would be fun to have him."

Nora acknowledged Anne's kindness, and her untruthfulness, with a smile.

Twilight nudged over the housetops and down, seeped through the grass and up. The two darks met, merged, till houses, trees, the girls sitting in canvas chairs lost their outlines, their color, becoming formless shapes in suspension. Then the street lights glowed alive, rectangles of yellow and orange sprang to being in the walls around them. The long-fingered sail of a bat skimmed past.

Nora and Anne fled for the house.

It was very late when they went to bed. At intervals through the still, hot night, Anne heard Nora's bare feet padding on errands for the baby, the tyrant.

CHAPTER FIFTEEN

ALTHOUGH NO peacock, Paul Favor took pains with his appearance. Tonight, the evening of his first formal dinner date with Theo, he took such pains that his mother, coming upstairs for a casual chat before he left, eyed him with sudden sharpness.

Mrs. Favor, tall, iced with blue hair and eyes, swathed in grape-toned linen of ruinously expensive cut, had an unexpectedly warm voice, a kindly heart that pumped along, comfortably aware that, in its own surroundings anyway, all that glittered was most assuredly gold. Her material scope was luxuriously narrow. Mentally, she was a good deal broader. If her ideas were, as Paul had claimed, rather ready-made, they were also widely inclusive. Furthermore, she at no time considered herself a suitable mentor of Paul's friends or future. The once discussed matter of whether Paul should enter the town bank or sail for the Left Bank had been her one sally into his privacy, and that took a completely unexpected turn that she was surer than ever the wisest course was one of passive and loving admiration. Both Paul and her brother mystified her completely, and that was very pleasant. Anyway, she would say to herself, every time I *do* interfere, things go awry. She had tried, with the best intentions, to let Paul finish his vacation in peace when her poor brother went to the hospital. . . . After all, what difference could a few days make? And Paul worked so hard. . . . Well, Paul had been very annoyed, and her brother had most vexingly refused to believe or understand her reasons.

She studied her son as he stood, shirt-sleeved and suspendered, scowling at a rack of plenty containing ties.

"Why not a bow tie, darling?" she suggested. "Always so nice with flannels." She too studied the ties. They looked amazingly similar, all dark-hued and sumptuous. The most dashing were navy blue with white polka dots or navy blue with thin red diagonal lines. "Your neckwear," she said pensively, "is terribly dull. Why don't you wear something gay? Your uncle has some lovely foulards. . . ."

Paul, who actually favored black ties but felt that they entailed the risk of appearing Grotonish, replied absently.

"My taste in ties has long since jelled." He selected a solid maroon four-in-hand, tied it expertly, slipped on his jacket, turned to his mother expectantly.

"You look lovely, darling," she said sincerely, invariably charmed by Paul's demand for approval of his appearance. She always expected him to revolve slowly before her. He didn't, so she compromised by walking around him.

"Inspection over?" he asked, as though it had been her idea.

"Over and successful."

They walked down the wide stairs together. "Would you have time for coffee?" she asked.

"That would be nice."

Mrs. Favor subsided on a sofa, before the coffee service. Paul drew up a chair, watched her long fingers manipulating tongs, cups, silver.

"That's one of the loveliest acts of women," he said.

"Pouring?"

"Yes. I'm taking a girl to dinner tonight."

His mother noticed the appositeness of the remark, but said merely, "Anyone I know?"

"Theo Armacost. Uncle knows her. She's a nurse at the hospital. Her father is Alec Armacost, the English teacher I had in high school. Remember the name?"

His mother did. She was, though, still thinking about Paul. He certainly had always made his own decisions. One very early one had been against a prep school. He wanted to go to high school in town, and he did. He had, she knew, enjoyed it very much. But then, that was one of the reasons she'd thought he'd rather study music than go in the bank. Well, well . . . "I think so," she said, sipping hot black coffee. "Will I meet her?"

"I guess so," he echoed. The pressure of a decision which had been forming itself for two days suddenly

167

erupted in speech. "In fact, I'm going to ask her to marry me," he said loudly.

To her own surprise, Mrs. Favor's reaction was instantly approving. For appearance's sake she demurred. "Darling, have you known her very long?"

"About three days." This seemed a rather slender acquaintance, so he added, "Uncle's known her longer than that."

Mrs. Favor let that pass. "Paul, I'm sure you always know what you're doing. At least, you always seem to, and that's about the same thing. Anyway," she added more firmly, "it's about time you got married, though I do think you and Miss Armacost should know each other better."

"I hadn't planned . . ." Paul hesitated. "I hadn't really planned anything at all. But I imagine a thing like this takes time. Maybe," he debated, "she won't want to marry me. . . ."

With the superb confidence of a mother whose son is about to propose that no sane girl could possibly refuse, Mrs. Favor disposed of that. "Don't be silly, dear. But I do rather hope you'll wait till your poor uncle is well."

Paul left almost immediately after that, kissing his mother fondly, if abstractedly, throwing her a final imploring glance from the doorway. She nodded encouragement, watched him go. Then she poured herself another cup of coffee, watching her hands critically, smiling a little. She thought perhaps a few tears. . . ? But she didn't really feel like crying. No man, she felt, should reach thirty without marrying. It makes them so peculiar. I wonder what she's like? She decided to run over and see her brother.

Paul, arriving at the Armacosts, raged at himself for turning a dinner date that he'd been looking forward to into something that made his throat dry and his back

168

prickle. He was decidedly nervous. Getting out of the car, he rubbed his chin thoughtfully, took a deep breath, strode to the porch. After all, he told himself, I don't *have* to propose. Even as he formed the thought, he realized it was nonsense. Of course he had to. It was as necessary to propose to Theo as it was to play the piano, or breathe, or hope for a better world, or do any of the things that made up life.

"How do you do, Mr. Favor," Theo's mother said.

"Hello, Paul," Mr. Armacost said warmly.

Paul put out his hand. "I'm glad to meet you, Mrs. Armacost," he said gravely. "How are you, Mr. Armacost? It's good to see you again."

"This is my son, Johnny," Mrs. Armacost said.

Johnny, who had, to his mother's pleased surprise, risen when Paul entered, now put out his hand, saying, "How do you do, sir?" His father shot him an astonished glance. Two such examples of courtesy in as many seconds made Mr. Armacost suspicious. But Johnny now decorously offered their guest a chair, inquired if he would like a beer, voluntarily turned down the volume of the ball game. Mr. Armacost gave up any attempt to follow the stream of hostly solicitude.

Silence fell.

They all started to speak at once.

Silence again.

Mrs. Armacost gestured to Paul, giving him the floor.

"I just wondered," he smiled, "whether you wouldn't like to go on watching the game."

"You like baseball, sir?" Johnny inquired.

Paul shook his head, wondering how far his stock would plummet at the admission. But Johnny was made of stern stuff. "Lot's of people don't," he admitted graciously. "Now, take my mother," he said, warming to the conversation, since apparently no one else wished to

169

speak. "She has the most peculiar attitude toward baseball I've ever known. . . ."

"Why, Johnny, I love baseball," his mother protested.

"I know you do. You see, Mr. Favor," Johnny pursued, quite forgetting that Paul didn't care for the game, "Last week, Mantle comes up to bat, bases loaded. So what happens? He strikes out. Mother nearly screamed, so naturally you'd think it was because the guy'd struck out with the bases loaded. But then Skowron comes up right after and hits a homer. There's Mom, still weeping over Mantle. 'What'll he feel like? The poor *boy*,' she says. She never even noticed Skowron's hit. Same with Hank Bauer. They bench him, and Mother spends the whole time wondering if he's unhappy, or what his wife says to him about it. . . ." Johnny's voice suddenly died down. Paul Favor was regarding him with interest, but his mother and father shared a look of concentrated astonishment. Johnny began to feel he was talking too much.

"Well," he said, getting to his feet, "maybe I'd better run up and jog Theo, huh?"

When he'd gone, Mr. Armacost smiled at Paul. "Theo tells me you still play the piano, Paul."

"Yes, it still seems to be one of my greatest pleasures." Paul wished they didn't all sound so polite. But then, he'd hardly earned the right to relax here yet. The fact was, Paul didn't relax easily with new people. And Mr. Armacost was here before him in a new role certainly. Mrs. Armacost was charming, and reserved. Paul smiled a little, remembering the way Theo had looked at him that day in the car. Quite obviously she'd thought his casually friendly approach was typical whereas it had been a revelation to him. Something in Theo, from the moment he'd bumped into her in the hospital corridor, had the effect of sweeping away his caution and stiffness. She seemed to startle him into unbelievable acts . . . as, for an incredible instance, the one he was about to speak of.

He cleared his throat slightly. "Mr. and Mrs. Armacost," he said, "I should like to ask you a question. . . ."

After Paul and Theo had driven off, Mrs. Armacost, unlike Mrs. Favor, dropped a few slow tears.

"She hasn't said yes," her husband mentioned gently.

"She will. I'm sure she will." Smiling moistly, she tried to explain. "I want her to, you know. Theo will be a wonderful wife, and I think she's already in love with him. It's just . . ." She stopped.

"It doesn't seem to me they've known each other long enough."

"You know, in this case, I don't think it matters. It's very odd," she brooded. "Both of them so . . . such reserved people, to get carried away like this. I think they're beautifully suited. To all appearances they're practical, almost phlegmatic. But there's Theo with her poetry and trees, and the boy with his piano." She mused a little longer, and said, "Oh, yes, I think she'll say yes."

There's so much love, she murmured to herself, her mind humming like a bee in the sun. Theo, she thought with dreamy sadness, and her practical Paul—money by day and music by night. Put that way it sounds a little shocking, she rebuked herself. But then, I suppose it's because all that money, with or without music, seems shocking to me. Her mind hummed idly, murmuring now Anne's name. "Anne and Nora," it reiterated, "Nora and Anne." So much alike. But I can forgive myself for hoping that Anne won't do as Nora did and offer her youth for love. A little time yet for Anne, the girl. Time enough for Anne, the woman.

A clumping sounded overhead. Mr. Armacost looked up, regarding the ceiling fixedly. "All that boy has to do," he said, "is stand still, and things start coming down around our heads."

"He certainly isn't standing still now."

171

"I'll wager he isn't doing anything more strenuous than writing in his Journal. The moving finger," Mr. Armacost said, with what his wife recognized as his epigram tone, "the moving finger, in Johnny's case, sounds more like the moving man." He smiled proudly at his wife, who returned the smile in a most stimulating manner.

"Dear?" she said.

He gave her his attention.

"Do you think I'm getting stout?" She regarded her nicely plump legs remorsefully.

"Not at all, not at all. You just flare nicely."

Once again they regarded each other with pleasure. Mr. Armacost returned to his paper, Mrs. Armacost to her reflections.

Now Johnny, she went on as though there had been no interruption, Johnny is in the preliminaries of life, and so of love, too. He says first, as a man will, "How shall I spend my life?" A woman, of course, asks, "With whom shall I spend it?" It comes to the same thing.

Theo, Theo . . .

Anne got home from Nora Chapin's just after Paul and Theo had gone. She was completely exasperated to have missed them, though until her mother mentioned it, she'd entirely forgotten that Paul was coming.

"What's he like?" she asked curiously.

"Very pleasant," her mother replied, wishing she could be more intense. I won't, she thought, say anything to Anne about his proposing. Theo would probably like to do that herself. Escapism, she realized clearly. But surely a mother is allowed a bit of that, or even desolation, when her first daughter marries—if, she supplied inwardly, she has also the grace to conceal it. . . . "Very nice," she added emphatically, and was not at all sure she'd improved her position. "How's Nora?" she asked quickly, to supply a distraction.

Anne frowned. "Well," she answered slowly, "I'm not really sure. We talked a lot, I guess. But nothing to tell me how she is."

"How does she act or look?" persisted Mrs. Armacost, who was very fond of Nora.

"She acts . . . spiritless. That's the way she looks, too." Anne's voice was perturbed. She still felt, obscurely, that Nora had betrayed her. She had taken a charming study of young love and turned it into something drab. Anne couldn't forget how wildly in love Nora and Sam had been, her own heart had beat fast at the wedding, seeing them so purely giving themselves to each other. Mrs. Harrison had sniffled, her eyes inky with protest. (Mrs. Armacost, who had been there too, had thought those eyes desolate, and sadly applauded the strength that restrained Nora's mother from weeping outright. . . . Many are watching, and each watches from his own angle.) But to Anne, the wedding had been a monument, not one for which she had any immediate use, being in high school, planning college, but a monument nevertheless, proclaiming beautifully the rights of the very young in love. How the elders wailed, "You can't," "You mustn't," "This is puppy love," "Madness," or worst of all, "This is ridiculous." But Nora and Sam withdrew so splendidly from the shrill cries. They knew what they wanted, and they took it. Well why, Anne demanded passionately, hadn't they kept it properly? How *could* they abuse such a trust, tarnish such a brilliance? *I* wouldn't, Anne cried to herself. But she didn't say, "Doug and I wouldn't," because she had no right. She wasn't, now, even sure of herself. She wished she'd never told Nora she'd go to New York with her. She wished she never had to see Nora again. "I wish it were time to go to college," she said shrilly, then flushed at her mother's stare. "Scuse me," she murmured. "The summer's too long, and too hot."

Mrs. Armacost said nothing. Her husband, however,

with his way of lifting phrases out of the air long after they'd been uttered, as though the words in some way still vibrated there for his inspection, said sharply, "She acts spiritless, does she?" He adjusted his glasses and went on in a lower tone, "Is she tired of marriage so soon?" He had never accustomed himself to Nora's married status. That little girl who used to play dolls around here? That moppet with the round chin who giggled in corners with Anne? Unthinkable. He'd said so when he learned of the marriage. He said so now. In addition, he frankly admitted to himself, a good part of his reaction concerned itself less with Nora than with Anne. Preposterous! Anne couldn't possibly . . .

Anne, not unaware of her father's attitude, made some attempt to lighten the figure of Nora, fast disappearing into shadow. "She's not tired of it. It's more that she's tired from it." But, of course, Anne mourned, that hasn't helped in the least. Now they'll think marriage has made her ill as well as unhappy. Oh, I don't want to think about it, she fretted. "I'm going to take a bath," she announced. Escape, via bath bubbles.

At the door, she remembered about New York, and wished she hadn't. Well, best to get it over with. "Mother, may I go to New York with Nora tomorrow? She has to look at an apartment," she said quickly, hoping to dispose of the matter one way or the other with as little conversation as possible.

Mrs. Armacost recognized symptoms of flaring impatience, and replied casually, "I should think so. You'd be back in the evening?"

"Oh, sure. We'll just go in and come right back."

"That's good. We've sort of planned a picnic at Price's Beach for Sunday."

Anne felt like screaming. Talk about occasion conspiring against people! I thought that wretched picnic had died a natural death. "We'll be back," she repeated sullenly. "It'll hardly be a joyous journey since we have to take the baby."

Mrs. Armacost frowned. "The baby . . . You're going to take a baby to New York in all this heat?"

"What else?" Anne shrugged. "Mrs. Harrison's stand is unequivocal. Nora had the baby, Nora can take care of it."

Mrs. Armacost made a decision. "You call Nora," she said, "and ask her if she'd trust the baby with me."

"Are you sure?" Anne asked doubtfully, intensely relieved, but feeling that some gesture of refusal was called for.

"Oh, of course I'm sure. I'd rather enjoy having a baby around. Just ask Nora to bring enough things, and I'll manage beautifully. Tell her not to forget diapers," she added. "You know, I once left one of you children with someone or other. I don't remember exactly, but I forgot diapers. It was really quite disastrous. I wonder who that was?" she mused. "She had nothing but linen guest towels to substitute. I had to replace them all. Dear me . . ."

Anne moved restlessly. "Well, if you're sure, I'll call her now." She started away, turned back. "It's very nice of you, Mom." She shifted about in the doorway, unable to leave.

"Well, go along, dear. Call her."

Anne went along.

"Really," Mr. Armacost murmured. "People who say that they'd like to be young again . . . What can they be thinking of?"

"You know something . . . ," Mrs. Armacost reflected. Her husband folded his book, keeping a finger in to mark the place, "Yes?"

"I've decided that it isn't the climate at all. It's me. I."

"What is?"

"The way I feel about spring," she explained.

"How is that?"

"Well," she said slowly, "for a long time now I've

175

thought that something was wrong with the weather. I mean, that there doesn't seem to be any spring any more." She paused, holding his attention by her solemnity "What I mean is . . . when I was young, the spring seemed so long, so exalting and budding, you know. But then, a few years ago, I began to think that something must have happened to the equinox or the gulf stream, because spring really became just a long cold in the head, sort of wet and prickly, and then all of a sudden it would be hot. Do you see at all what I mean?"

He nodded, and waited.

"I find," she went on broodingly, "that now autumn seems to be the . . . the season of beauty. That's significant, don't you think?"

"Well, I don't," he replied contemplatively. "But then, I've always preferred autumn. . . ."

"I suppose that's because you're a philosophical person," his wife decided.

Johnny wrote in his Journal, "Theo's new one (not that she's had so many, but Theo's a different sort of girl than Anne, although Anne's running a little low on men herself lately all because of that jerk Eamons) is a pretty nice guy. His uncle is a tycoon and could probably pave Main Street with doubloons. I wish there were still doubloons, pirates, remittance men, etc. Also wish that stuff from Easy's would get here. Still can't make out why that drip had to get out of character just before he leaves town. I like people to stay the way they are and as far as I'm concerned he's strictly rancid. If Theo marries this guy, and if she's ever going to marry anyone, she'd better get a move on, it will sure be funny to have her trailing around here in minks and so forth. 'Here,' says Theo, dropping in for afternoon tea (which we don't have but could probably rustle up a cup), 'here, Mom, have another diamond bracelet. . . .'"

Johnny leaned back in his chair, happily picturing his mother in furs and diamonds. Funny if Theo should wind up with a lot of dough, he thought. She never cares a bit about it, or buying things. Now Anne could *really* go through a bankroll. . . . She's positively inspired when it comes to spending money.

He reached into the desk drawer, shoved the Savage material aside with a nervous twinge of conscience, produced another notebook. On the cover a carefully inscribed title written in a mixture of Chinese lettering (as seen on Chop Suey cans) and Olde English (as conceived by Johnny) read, "A History of Cats." Below this was a subtitle, "A Short History of Cats." Nibbling on his pencil, Johnny read the last paragraph.

"Many urges and traditions form the Cat. A being complete, a cat is entire unto himself, an aristocrat whose family line traces back to where history becomes darkness and a few drawings on cave walls. Many of these drawings show cats. The CAT . . . privy to the broomstick rides, sleeper at the turf fire, mouser of the palace kitchen, marauder in the mosque shadow. . . ."

Johnny looked upon his work and found it good. Perhaps, after all, his best bet was to be a writer. The only thing he'd ever really stuck to was the Journal, and these occasional forays into creative literature. Even here, there was the matter of whether he was actually creative. He usually had his brightest inspirations just after reading a book, in this case, *The Master of Ballantrae*. After reading Stevenson, his mind was just naturally full of words like turf fire, marauder, tumbrils, and so forth. While the words flowed easily enough from his pencil, they were apt to sound a bit too much like what he was reading. So the question—was he sitting at the feet of the masters, or just plain cribbing?—was hard to answer. Still, the best bet so far.

"Where did your uncle ask us to go?" Theo inquired as they drove off. Her voice was brimming with pleasure.

"He said that, after all, he'd leave it to us. So I leave it to you."

Theo considered. "Do you know that houseboat that sells seafood?" she asked. "Carney's? Is that too far away?"

"Not at all. Carney's then."

"My vacation starts today," Theo announced as they purred along the black highway.

"Why, that's marvelous. Why didn't you tell me before?"

"I don't know why." She lifted her head, sniffing eagerly at the warm air rushing past. "Would you like to come on a picnic with us Sunday, or did Mother already ask you?"

"She didn't have a chance, I guess. I'd love it." Paul still felt a little tight in the throat. His hands on the wheel were slippery. How shall I ask, he wondered. What's the best way? Before dinner? After dinner? Heady with exhilaration, he glanced now and then at the slim girl beside him. She really wears the most amazing colors, he thought, forgetting that he'd never until tonight seen her in anything but a uniform. Theo, indeed, had a fairly wild color sense. Anne said that in anyone else, it would be design to wear an apricot dress and green shoes under that flaming hair. With Theo it was more a flight from white, and a haphazard attitude toward clothes in general. The effect she achieved couldn't have been more delightful to Paul of the sober neckwear.

"Did you see your uncle today?" she asked.

"Uh-huh. He thinks you're marvelous."

"That's good. I think he's marvelous."

"Lots of people can't stand him. I don't know whether it's the way he talks or . . . the money," he finished uncertainly, not sure how she would take the reference.

"My brother," she said calmly, "is terribly impressed by your uncle's money."

"And you?" Paul asked, after a pause.

Theo sighed. "You know, my reactions seem to come straight out of a novel . . . not a very good one, either." She gazed at the fields sliding past. "Well, no," she answered at length. "I'm not. I don't even think I like it much."

"Why not?" Paul asked, after several silent moments had passed.

Theo tried to put words to her feeling. "Perhaps it's the inequality, or maybe the responsibility. But that isn't it entirely. I wouldn't," she faltered, "ever want to have so much money that I could buy anything I wanted. I like to plot and plan for things. We all do, in my family. Even Anne, and she's something of a Sybarite. It's such a very real sense of possession, when you've waited and saved for . . . well, for a car . . . and then finally have the money to buy it. There are really a great many people like me," she assured him earnestly, "people who've never had lots of money, or been poor either for that matter, who just sort of like going along with small cars and little houses. We aren't built for the grand things, I guess." She looked at him hopefully, to see whether he understood.

Paul, however sincere he felt she was, and he didn't doubt for a moment that what she said she meant, felt no compunction about offering her a life on the grand scale. She'll adjust to it, he thought. And if she doesn't want it, he decided in a rush of passion, why then we'll move into a cottage and start saving for a car. Suddenly his constraint vanished. A wave of happiness swept through him with such force that he felt dizzy. Shall I ask her now, he wondered. Now? Or wait awhile? But the moments were giving him such delight, he took so much pleasure in the sound of her voice, that he relaxed, just listening.

Theo, not searching for topics, but happy because she was amusing him, suddenly produced the Bacon-Colman-Dolan triangle, the results of which were still undetermined. Paul laughed uproariously at the picture of Mrs. Bacon trapping her enemy with so novel a barricade as a walking frame, but he had a sneaking pity for Dolan, whom he considered a sort of shuttlecock driven between two expert rackets.

"Who'll win, do you think?" he asked curiously.

Theo pondered, decided in favor of Mrs. Bacon. "She's not young and beautiful," she conceded, "but Dr. Dolan's a bit afraid of Lydia, I think. And then, Mrs. Bacon isn't quite so good a flatterer as the Colman character, but she's a much better admirer, because she's sincere. She really thinks the man's a genius."

"What do you think of him?" Paul asked warily.

Without interest Theo observed that he was a good enough doctor and a nice enough man. Paul found this a highly satisfactory reply.

"Theo," he said, and his voice shook with intention, "do you, by any chance, like fishing?"

"I like fish. That's as far as I've ever gotten."

"It'll do, for a start." He laughed. Now? he wondered. Shall I ask her now?

But, after all, he waited till dinner was finished, and they were sitting over coffee, with a sharply briny odor in the air, and almost no one else in Carney's Seafood Boathouse.

"Do you like Chopin?" he asked, lighting her cigarette. She nodded, smiling like a sphinx.

"Ever been in the Adirondacks?"

Theo had. She was obviously enjoying his approach. But then, Paul thought, so am I.

"Do you," he said, solemnly foolish, "like Dalmatians?"

"The dogs, yes. The people I've never known, since I've never traveled further than Pennsylvania."

180

"That comes of not having money," Paul said quickly.

"So it does. However, I don't particularly want to visit Dalmatia."

"We could go somewhere else."

"What did you say?" Theo asked, so low he could barely hear.

Paul didn't reply for a moment. Then, quietly, he asked her. "What I said was, will you marry me, Theo?" She was silent so long that he grew alarmed. "Theo? I . . ." On a sudden inspiration he said, "Oh, I didn't . . . Theo, didn't I say . . . Theo," he cried desperately, "I *love* you."

She looked up at him then, and he sighed with relief. "I know," she said. "I wasn't waiting for you to say that. I was just . . . trying to memorize everything. Ask me again now."

"Theo, will you marry me?"

"Yes, Paul."

CHAPTER SIXTEEN

NORA BROUGHT the baby over early in the morning, in a battered canvas carriage, with an adequate supply of diapers and other necessaries. She thanked Mrs. Armacost fervently, then fled with Anne.

"Like a child released from school," Mrs. Armacost thought, watching them go in their town suits of cotton. She turned, somewhat hesitantly, to the baby. . . . It had been so long . . . and realized she'd never even asked its name. The little thing doesn't seem to have an identity at all, she was thinking—a small ghost whose only function so far seems to have been to haunt his mother with dreams of past freedom.

"What's your name, little one?" she asked in the soft voice women use for babies. The little one carefully shifted his attention from a revolving fist to the direction of the voice. He prepared to speak. His toes curled, his knees bent, he doubled his fists tightly, tilted his chin back. Then he drew a deep breath, opened his mouth roundly, and breathed out the softest of sounds. Then he smiled at her brightly, as though they were having a conversation.

Mrs. Armacost pulled up a chair, sat beside the carriage. He looks like a sparrow, she thought . . . little and plucked and boned in slender ridges. "I'll tell you," she crooned, "a little poem I know. . . ." Her voice seemed to have an extravagantly seductive effect on the baby, who arched his small back yearningly, dark eyes seeming almost to dive into hers. "A poem," she murmured, "by William Butler Yeats, who was a blossom of the branches, and the pride of Inis Fal. . . ." She strung out the words for this baby, who seemed to love them, who might possibly not have heard enough. For all babies love words. "I think there is more than I remember," she told him, "but I remember four lines and they make a poem. 'Cradle Song,' he called it, and wrote it for babies. . . .

> I sigh that kiss you,
> For I must own
> That I shall miss you,
> When you have grown."

Then, with her head on her arms, leaning on the edge of the carriage, she cried softly for three babies she missed very much. The baby like a sparrow didn't seem to mind. He mingled his soft sounds with hers.

Mrs. Armacost wasn't quite correct in her diagnosis of Nora's feelings. She felt more like a prisoner released from jail than a child released from school. That she would suffer for the joy of this freedom, she knew all too well. In the night, when her conscience burrowed like a mole, she would squirm with self-reproach, picture her baby ill or dead from neglect, promise herself with tears to love him more, never to leave him. But still, when the opportunity came, she would fly from him again on just such eager feet. Anyway, she reminded herself, today the baby was in wonderful hands, not like the times she left him with Ruby Cassidy. And, of course, Ruby is a darling, she hastened to assure herself. Only not exactly a motherly type.

Ruby Cassidy, assistant editor on a trade magazine, occasionally dropped, as she said, upstairs to see the Chapins, whom she considered chirpy little things in need of awakening. She had gotten nowhere with the awakening program, but still dropped upstairs because she liked them and they were nice to her. This was unusual in Ruby's experience, her friends (a word she used with an interrogation point) being natural backbiters who sometimes started snapping before the back in question was out of sight, or even turned. So the hospitality of the Chapins became the warm place in Ruby's chilly life. She had met Nora accidentally on Riverside Drive. Prompted by an impulse she never analyzed, Ruby had, for purposes of admiration, halted beside a baby carriage for the first time in her life. Possibly it was Nora's pinched and lonely face above the carriage that drew her, the young face with dreamy eyes gazing over the river. In a little while the two were talking together, and had discovered that Ruby had one and a half rooms just two floors below the Chapins. Having established this firm basis of common interest, a never-dry source of complaints about the landlord, the drains, the janitor, the lack of heat, Ruby offered Nora a cigarette. After a moment's hesitation, Nora took it, and having an ascendancy of four years over Cooper and Johnny, she liked smoking right away. So Ruby found someone to be nice to her. In turn, she was nice to the Chapins. She even, on occasion, played baby sitter while they saw a movie or went to Child's and danced. She grew so fond of them that when they were told to leave because of the baby, she rooted about through her wide acquaintance and came up with a superintendent who might rent them an apartment on One hundred eighty-second Street.

"And," said Ruby, "with every flat in New York sewed up tighter than the Merchants Bank, you'll be lucky to get it."

The train had a clacking, swaying movement as it eeled along the dusty, late-summer countryside. It had no air-conditioning. Soot swirled in through the open doors at either end. Looking through the window, Anne found it easier to see her own reflection than the sliding scenery beyond. She took a Kleenex, wiped a spot of glass, but made little improvement.

"Aren't you tired of the summer?" she asked Nora, who nodded a bit sleepily. "I am, this time every year," Anne went on. "I find myself perishing for one of those frosty fall evenings, and decent clothes. I don't like summer clothes." She thought of her new Scotch plaid suit with yearning.

"When do you leave for school?" Nora asked.

"September fifteenth." Annie felt Nora's wistfulness in the question. To change the subject, she asked Nora what her jobs had been like.

"Oh, they were sort of fun, while I was still feeling all right. That is, the second one was. I sold neckwear . . . scarves and dickies and such matters, in Lord and Taylor. The first was terrifying." But she smiled a little, being safely fired and in no danger of going back.

"What happened?"

"Do you really want to hear?"

"Well, of course. I've never had a job at all. I think I'd have died of fright."

"I nearly did. In fact, I couldn't believe it when Mr. Ward offered me the job. He'd given me some sort of shorthand test that I couldn't do at all."

"You mean to say you had to take shorthand?" Anne asked incredulously.

"I was supposed to."

"But . . . you weren't any better than I was, were you?"

"Not a bit."

Anne shook her head in awe. "How did you have the nerve to say you could?"

"I *told* him I wasn't very good at it. But I think he put it down to nervousness, or something. Anyway, he said I could have the job. It was with a textile firm, not a big one. They manufactured underwear."

"What a romantic job."

"Then, when I got there, the first morning," Nora went on firmly, having something now to speak of, "I got there so early I had to wait in the corridor for someone to unlock the office door. And along comes Mr. Ward. Honestly, Anne, he put up with an awful lot the few days I was there. He came along, saw me, and said, 'Ah, there, Miss . . . I'm sorry, I've got your name on a piece of paper somewhere.' Then when I told him it was Mrs. Chapin, and I really *had* told him the first time, he lifted his eyebrows, as though he'd accidentally hired one of those child-brides." Nora stopped at this. "Anyway," she resumed, "he whirled me into his office and started dictating letters that I couldn't possibly understand, and my hands were so cold that I probably couldn't have written it even if I had understood. He'd say things like, 'one lot of #204½ bals,' meaning a style of balbriggans, which is a kind of knit underwear, only nobody told me. So I ordered 'valves' instead." Nora seemed amused, but Anne thought it was horrifying.

"I thought people explained a job to you before they made you start writing letters."

Nora shrugged. "I did too. But they didn't. Anyway, I lost it, which was hardly unexpected.

185

"I should think you'd have been glad."

"Oh, I was. Neckwear is much easier. At least you can tell what's in front of you. And a department store is sort of fun." But her face settled again into the blankness that Anne had noticed so often since Nora had come home, as if, Anne thought, she telescoped into herself till nothing shows but glass and a shell.

"What's Ruby Cassidy like?" she asked, determined to keep Nora with her instead of closed in her hard shell.

"Oh, Ruby's very nice," Nora said with warmth. "Sort of hearty, and her language shocks Sam a little. But we like her a lot. She's been very nice to us."

"Be nice if you get this apartment. They're hard to find, aren't they?"

Nora turned and eyed Anne closely. Then she smiled. "Yes, Anne, they're very hard to find. In fact, they're just one degree removed from impossible. But of course we have to go somewhere," she said in a hard voice, "or I suppose we do."

They fell silent. Nora clasped her hands in her lap, squeezing them every now and then, till her entire body grew tense. Then she'd relax, shoulders drooping forward, eyes focused inward. Anne tried to stare at the passing country through the nearly opaque window. Hazily the fields waved past, bearing up their clumps of trees, herds of idling cattle. Then abruptly a jagged wall of rock, laced with water and sprouting weeds, would loom beside them as the train tunneled through a hillside. A few scattered houses appeared, and Anne strained for a glimpse of people . . . a woman hanging wash, a child pedaling a tricycle, a man climbing from a cleaner's truck with a coat held high on its hanger. Such fleeting pictures of people in the midst of their own lives gave her a sense of unimportance that was very comfortable. That woman hanging wash, who never glanced up when the train went by, what difference did it make to her if Anne's heart was broken, if Nora had made a mess of her life? What difference, indeed, did it make at all in the world? At this moment, right now, Anne thought, thousands of girls our age are thinking no one else has a problem equal to theirs. Theirs is the ultimate tragedy, the finalest humiliation . . . nobody else wakes with such dullness, goes to bed with such hurt. Fools! Anne cried within herself. All fools . . . they are, and we are.

Then the factories, outlying the towns, thrust their gloomy façades, their black smokestacks, their woven wire fences, upon the landscape. Ugliest of things, the factory now is hung with sweat along the brow. Oh goodness, Anne thought, Theo wouldn't like that.

"Theo is getting married," she said, turning from a squalid business area that would presently lead to a city.

"She is?" Nora replied, releasing her fingers from each other. "Is she happy about it?"

Anne stopped herself from saying, "Well, naturally," substituted, "I guess so."

"Who's she marrying?"

"Paul Favor."

"My word, she certainly did well for herself," Nora said, trying to keep the surprise out of her voice. But how in the world, she wondered, did that plain girl ever manage such a brilliant marriage? Theo Armacost had always seemed to Nora about as interesting as a cup custard, in spite of the red hair.

"I haven't even met him," Anne said. Knowing Nora's conception of Theo, she added, "Theo only met him herself about four days ago." She was amused to see that now Nora couldn't suppress her astonishment. It was immaterial to Anne what Nora thought of her sister. She like Theo's way of seeming uninteresting to people she didn't know well. It was rather like using the Hope diamond for a paperweight, and watching the people pass, saying, "Ah, a paperweight." But every now and then, of course, someone with sharp eyes would pause and study the innocent-appearing object. And then, Anne went on, pleased with her fancy, along comes Paul and simply pockets the thing. He must be pretty clever.

"When are they getting married?"

"During the Christmas vacation, so they'll have time to get acquainted."

"You mean they aren't sure?"

"Oh, Nora," Anne said irritably, "of course they're sure. They just like this first part, I guess."

"I'm sorry. I seem to be a little edgy lately."

"Well, you aren't alone in that," Anne replied, unpleasantly reminded of herself. But how dull we are, Nora and I, drooping around feeling sorry for ourselves.

The train snorted and dribbled into Jersey City, shuddered to a stop. Anne and Nora, brushing the soot from their clothes, walked to the Ferry, Nora protesting that the Tubes would get them into New York faster.

"I never take the Tubes," Anne said firmly. "I'm afraid to be under all that water."

Nora gave up. "But it really isn't water, you know. The Tubes don't run through the Hudson like a straw. They're in the mud underneath."

"All the more reason to take the Ferry."

The Ferry ran from Jersey City to Chambers Street. From its old, malodorous deck, they looked down to the Battery, where the Statue of Liberty rose in copper relief against the sky, and up the Hudson, to the piers, where the two red stacks of the *Queen Elizabeth* flared over gray docks. Below, the brown waters of the river rose, fell, and sloped away to the Bay.

Anne's New York was lovely, and limited. She liked Chambers Street, because she'd seen it so often, coming for a visit in the City. She liked its trucks and pawnshops and cheese stores, its exciting, tainted aura of Trade. She liked Seventh Avenue and Broadway, where her father took her to plays and the ballet. And the East Side, around Fifty-seventh Street, where the art galleries were, where sometimes, not often, her mother took her shopping. Anne's New York ended at Fifty-ninth Street.

Of Nora's she knew nothing—nothing of Riverside Drive, or the Lewisohn Stadium on hot summer nights, the Cloisters that Sam loved, or the Indian Museum that Nora had discovered.

The ride on the subway semed interminable to Anne. After One hundred sixteenth Street, the train roared into the open air. Looking down, she felt it was much too high for comfort. They teetered over this foreign part of Broadway and shot underground again.

"It's an awfully long ride, isn't it?" she inquired of Nora, who nodded nervously, dove into her bag for a slip of paper, consulted Ruby's sprawling directions for the fourth time since they'd started. She put the paper back, snapped the purse shut, gripped it tightly.

She looked imploringly at Anne. "Do you think it will be all right?" she asked urgently.

"Oh, I'm sure it will. After all, what can happen?"

"I might not get it!"

"Oh. Well, I suppose you will," Anne said without conviction, since she'd been thinking Nora was afraid she would. But how, Anne wondered, could anyone want to live so far away from everything? She felt so uncomfortable this far uptown that she'd assumed Nora did too.

"Here, we get out here," Nora said suddenly, leaping up, though the train hadn't stopped yet. Anne followed, preparing for unfamiliar streets.

At the apartment house they hesitated on the sidewalk, looking at a paper-blown, gritty court—a cavern of gray air. They moved through it reluctantly, to a stale vestibule. There was the button, with Super written under it, just as Ruby said in her note. Still, Nora's finger hesitated, hovering near the bell. Anne turned and looked out into the street, the alien sidewalks. She thought of Chambers Street. It, of course, was not very clean. But the dirt there was compressed and comfortable. Here it was scattered on wide streets, exposed and rather cold, even now in August. The buildings were too big, there were too many of these "courts."

Nora reached for the bell, pulled her hand away, turned uncertainly to the door again. "Oh, Anne," she wailed, "what shall I do?"

Anne, unsure of how to answer, shook her head blankly. All she wanted was to get home, to get away from here. But why Nora was hesitating she didn't know. Because she was frightened? Because she was afraid to be refused?

"Well, Nora . . .," she began.

"Lookin' for someone?"

They spun nervously at the sudden voice. Nora uttered a little cry of alarm.

"Sorry, thought you was lookin' for someone."

Nora took a breath. "I am," she replied. "You frightened us, coming up so suddenly."

"Sorry," he said again in a laconic tone. "I'm Fred Purvis, the Super."

Nora gave him an agitated smile. "I'm Mrs. Chapin. This is my friend, Miss Armacost. I think Ruby Cassidy told you that I might be up? To see an apartment."

Mr. Purvis agreed. He was delighted to see Mrs. Chapin. He said as much.

"Thank you," Nora said unhappily. How did I ever *get* here, she wondered. With Anne so nobly pretending it's all perfectly normal . . . this place, this man. Do you see what you've done to me, Sam, she cried silently. Do you see? "May we see it?" she asked, trying to sound eager and pleased. Perhaps he'd get angry if she acted cool, perhaps he wouldn't give it to her. She wished with all her heart she hadn't asked Anne to come.

190

"Sure, sure," said Mr. Purvis. "Just step into the elevator here, and we'll look the place over." He guided them into a perilous cage that rattled uncertainly up its shaft. Anne said nothing, and Nora was aware of her every second. Poor Anne, she thought suddenly, how very unpleasant this must be for her, how she must want to get out of here and go home.

"Place's just been redone. You'll find it very nice," Mr. Purvis was saying around a wad of gum. "Not at all, not at all," he went on, waving off thanks that Nora hadn't offered.

They went down a grimy, tiled floor, to apartment 5E. Mr. Purvis fitted a key into the lock, swung the door in, stepped aside with a courtly gesture. "There you are," he informed them. "Bright as a button."

The walls were newly done, to be sure. Painted green from the ceiling to the floor. The painter had covered every inch of wall space, baseboards, wall sockets, doors, and window frames with bright emerald paint. Then he had flowed off into the kitchen, brush dripping, and covered everything but the sink and stove with the same brave hue.

Mr. Purvis clucked at the splatters on the brassily varnished floor. "Bit of turpentine," he nodded, "be bright as a bug."

"Only one bedroom?" Nora asked.

Mr. Purvis shrugged, looked at her sideways. "Forty bucks a month?" he said meaningfully.

Nora sighed. She wandered to the kitchen door, ran a surprisingly practiced eye over the pipes and cupboards. "Roaches," she said drearily.

Mr. Purvis blew out a breath.

They went through the living room to the small bedroom, with which the painter had dealt in his same overall fashion, using blue.

"Tell you what, Mrs. Chapin, you're a fortunate wom

191

. . . girl, gettin' a snug little nest like this in these times. There's folks would give me plenty for a chance at this place. Oh, don't get me wrong," he said, raising his voice at Nora's expression. "You're a friend of Ruby's and that goes a long way with me." He winked, rubbed a finger under his chin. "You can tell her I said so, too. Bright as a button, that Ruby." He examined his nails, flicked his fingers, looked over at Nora, who was staring out the window, at Anne, who was studying the floor. Again he shrugged a little, reached in his pocket for a cigarette, which he lit with his head tilted back, one eye closed. He blew out a ribbon of smoke, started to speak, then took another drag and leaned against the wall.

Nora looked out of the window as far as she could . . . about fifteen feet, to the back of another apartment building. She looked down in the alley. Some boys were rolling dice down there. A few drab washings flopped on their lines. She looked up. A small strip of sky was visible over the edge of the building opposite.

"Well?" said Mr. Purvis, a patient man.

Nora thought of Sam, coming home to this in the evening. But then, she reminded herself, what he was going home to now was no better, except for the green walls. It's just that it's empty, and smells of paint, she thought. When we have some furniture in it, some curtains, maybe it will be all right then.

"When could I have it?" she asked tonelessly, not turning around.

"Sign the lease, move right in." He walked into the kitchen, butted his cigarette in the sink.

"Lease?"

"Sure. Protection all around. Two-year lease."

"When do I have to sign it?" Nora felt a little frightened now, committing herself to this alien place. But what else can I do, she wondered distractedly. Two years . . . surely Sam and I will be together that long. She'd

192

been running her finger along the window sill, but at this thought she stopped, her nail burrowing in a little groove. Oh, Sam, Sam, she cried silently, you couldn't leave me? The barrenness of the little apartment, the wakeful nights, the quarrels and coldness and dust seemed now to point to one end, which she hadn't seen before—that Sam might leave her. Beside that loss the rest was insignificant. She didn't care about anything else at all—not her mother's tears, Anne's friendship, not anything, if only Sam would be with her.

"I'll have to phone my husband," she said, turning from the window. Sam didn't want her to phone the garage, but she couldn't be bothered with that now.

Mr. Purvis rubbed a hand over his face. "Look, Mrs. Chapin," he said slowly, "I'm doin' you a favor, on Ruby's account. But you sign that lease today or you don't sign it. That's all there is to it." He let each word out very distinctly. He's been perfectly pleasant so far, but Anne felt it would be no trick at all for this man to turn nasty. Ruby, she thought, had better watch her step with this one. By now, Anne had disassociated herself from the whole matter. She'd stay with Nora so long as Nora wanted her, but she wouldn't think about this place or look at it one second longer than she had to.

"I'll phone my husband," Nora repeated with unaccustomed firmness. "Then I'll come back and see you." She walked to the door.

"Okay," Mr. Purvis said, "but don't take too long."

Nora didn't reply.

She and Anne walked, wordlessly, to a drugstore. "Get a coke or something, will you, Anne?" Nora asked. "I'll phone Sam." She went into a booth, closed the door, stared for a moment at the black instrument. Her finger shook a little as she dialed.

"Yeah?" said a bored voice.

"Is this . . . is this McAvoy's Garage?" Nora asked, taking a deep breath.

"Yeah."

"Is Sam Chapin there?"

"Yeah."

Annoyance helped her shaky voice. "Well, would you please get him for me?" she asked with narrow politeness.

"Yeah."

There was silence. Then Sam's voice, "Hello?" Nora smiled a little at the sound of him. The smile faded as she wondered what he'd say.

"Sam?"

"Nora!" His shout rammed in her ear, and she leaned against the back of the booth, a little giddy with relief. Sam was very glad to hear from her.

"Sam, I'm sorry to bother you. . . ." She could say that now. She knew she wasn't bothering him.

"Oh, Nora, you . . . of course not. Gee, it's good to hear you."

"Sam, I just saw this apartment Ruby told us about. It's horrible. Painted green from end to end . . ."

"Great. I love green," Sam interrupted. His words seemed to come rather thickly.

"What's the matter?" Nora asked. "You sound sort of funny."

"Oh." Sam paused. "Well, I got in a little argument last night. My mouth's sort of swollen."

"You mean . . . a fight?" Nora shrieked.

"Well. I was really fighting for your honor. Guy insulted you so I socked him."

Nora shook her head with bewilderment. "Insulted me?" she quavered. "Who in the world . . . ? I mean, I don't know anyone. . . . Who was it?"

"I don't know. This guy said anyone who'd marry me was a dope. So I'm not going to let anyone call you a dope, am I? I had to sock him." Sam was laughing now.

194

Nora blinked incredulously at the phone, shaking it a little. "Sam," she said sternly, her heart leaping at the sound of her own voice, so possessively had she spoken, so like the old days. "Sam, were you drinking?"

"Two beers, honey. But two beers on an empty life sort of went to my head."

"Empty . . . life?"

"Oh, Nora, you know . . . without you. And the boy. When do we get this apartment so we can all go home?"

"Sam," she said, laughing a little, "I . . . well, we can get it right away. Only I have to sign a two-year lease."

"Sign a twenty-year lease, only get it. Nora?"

"Yes, darling . . ."

"Is the baby with you?"

"No. Mrs. Armacost has him."

"Oh."

"What was it?"

"I just thought perhaps . . . I'll be off at five. If you could wait till then and if it was all right with your mother I'd go up with you for Sunday. Only I guess you better not leave the baby that long."

Nora thought rapidly. Then, "I don't think Mrs. Armacost would mind keeping him a little longer, Sam. I'll ask Anne, but I'm sure it will be all right."

"Anne's with you?"

"Yes. We came down together. I don't think she likes our apartment," she added, feeling very safe.

"Well, we probably won't either," Sam replied easily. "I suppose Anne will wait and go back with us?"

"I . . . don't know," Nora said. "I'll call you back."

"Soon?"

"Very soon. 'By, Sam. . . ."

"So long, honey."

Nora hung up, sat for a second with her eyes closed. Then she sailed back to Anne, sitting dismally before two flat cokes.

195

"Good," said Nora, swinging onto a stool. "I'm dying of thirst."

Anne studied her closely.

"Things work out all right, I take it?"

"Oh, fine, fine. Sam says to go back and sign the lease right away. . . ."

Anne couldn't think of anything to say. Nora reminded her of those mummers' masks, drooping one time, grinning the next. That's all it takes, Anne thought dully, just a word from a man. I'd do the same thing, if Doug should call me. Maybe, when I get home . . . maybe today . . .

"That's wonderful, Nora," she said brightly. "Really wonderful."

Nora finished her coke. "Anne, do you suppose, that is, do you think your mother would mind . . . keeping the baby a little longer?" she finished in a rush.

Anne shook her head. "Probably not. Why?"

"Well, Sam gets off at five ,so he wants to come up for tomorrow, and we thought I could . . . I mean, we could . . . you and I, wait for him and ride back together."

Anne smiled. "Mother won't mind, I'm sure. But I think I'll go back now. If it's all right with you," she added. I want to go home, she thought. I want to get away from here and never come back. She shuddered away from the thought of the apartment, Mr. Purvis, everything about this day.

Nora tried not to agree too quickly, but the chance to ride alone with Sam was so wonderful. Now they'd have so much to talk about. Or now, really, it wouldn't matter if they talked or not. They'd be together. From now on, they'd be together. No doubt the dust, and the quarrels, and the moments of longing for freedom would be with them too, from time to time, because she was Nora, who didn't like to keep house, and he was Sam, who was young and overworked. But that didn't matter. What did matter was that Sam wanted her with him, and she wanted that too. Sam, and the baby, and me, she thought, and the thought was warm, like something to hold. "That's all right, Anne," she said. "I know you don't like it up here very much."

"Oh, it isn't that . . ." The words were lumpy. Better, Anne thought, just to say good-by and leave.

"I'd better run," she said, picking up her purse. "The cokes are my treat."

For a moment they stared at each other, remembering the many times they'd said those words, "The cokes are my treat."

"Oh, Anne," Nora cried, "what is . . . ?" She stopped helplessly, knowing there was nothing that could be said.

Anne nodded her head slowly. "I know," she said. "Isn't it strange? Well, so long, Nora."

"So long, Anne. And thanks."

What they were saying, of course, was good-by.

CHAPTER SEVENTEEN

SHORTLY AFTER Anne and Nora left for New York, Mrs. Armacost received a note in the morning mail. Written in a hand only to be described as elegant, it read: "My dear Mrs. Armacost, May Paul and I hope for the pleasure of your company, and that of your family, at dinner this coming Tuesday? I had hoped perhaps we could make this arrangement for Sunday, but Paul tells me you plan a picnic. I am sorry to say that his own experience with picnics has been limited to, I believe, none. That is, family picnics. He is so delighted with the prospect of this one that even were you so kind as to offer a rearrangement of plans, I should not feel justified in accepting. Paul tells me that he hopes to bring your daughter Theo to see me Saturday evening. I look forward eagerly to meeting her, and am already completely prejudiced in her behalf. Paul has spoken in the past with such deep admiration for Mr. Armacost, and my faith in Paul's own judgment is so settled, that I have no hesitation in predicting beforehand that I shall recognize in her all the amiable qualities which Paul and my poor brother have described. Please do not trouble to reply. Theo and Paul will be able to give me my answer on Saturday evening, I am sure. Cordially, Jane Favor."

Mrs. Armacost blinked at this message, read it over again, handed it to her husband, who glanced at it idly, then began again and read it through with the keenest enjoyment.

"I'll bet that woman hasn't read a book written after the close of the nineteenth century."

"I should think, if she writes that way, she'd think that way, and she certainly doesn't."

"How's that?"

"Well, Paul's proposal was certainly not in the best Edwardian tradition. When the gentry, of the last century, I mean, decided on so rash and precipitous an alliance, it was generally effected by an elopement. Certainly there should be strong feelings between the families . . . an undowered girl and a young man so richly blessed. . . ."

Mr. Armacost cut her short. "There seems to be something contagious about Mr. Coombes. He influences the speech of people he hasn't even met. I, for one, shall be a hardened anti-semanticist before this wedding is over."

Johnny, strolling in, stopped thunderstruck at the sight of the baby carriage. He leaned over and peered intently at the occupant. "What's this? A baby? How'd it get here?"

"Nora brought him over. It's hers," Mrs. Armacost added as an afterthought.

Johnny, always rather fond of Nora, frowned. "That baby's too young to have a baby." He prodded the tiny figure with his fist.

"I don't suppose you'd take him for a walk."

"Nope. Don't suppose I would." The baby burbled at his finger. "Tell you what I will do. I'll take him out in the garden for a while. Looks as if he could use a little sun."

"Not too much. He probably isn't used to it."

"What's his name?"

"I don't know."

"Humph. Probably it's Sam. Okay, Sam," he said, releasing his thumb from a clinging fist. "I'll grab a bite and we'll go out for a while."

"How old is he?" Mr. Armacost wanted to know.

"About two months, I'd say."

"Not very big, is he?" her husband criticized.

"Oh, I don't know about that," Johnny said. "He's not so small, for a baby."

Mrs. Armacost decided it was going to be a fairly easy day. "We're invited to Mrs. Favor's for dinner Tuesday," she told her son.

"Over at Coombes'?" he said cheerfully. "That's great. I hear the bathrooms are tiled with mother-of-pearl, and they use solid gold dustpans."

"Oh, darling . . .," his mother protested.

"Not only that," Johnny continued, "but once a month they throw everything in the place out and get new. . . ."

That evening Theo and Paul drove through the gateposts of Mr. Coombes' home, proceeded a few hundred feet through a colonnade of gray beeches, rounded a sweep of driveway, and pulled up beneath a side portico. The house, aged red brick with traditional fluted columns gracefully soaring the height of the façade, was surrounded by flowers, riotous in color, restrained in scope, and the greenest, thickest, trimmest grass Theo had ever seen. She thought of her father seeing this, which was undoubtedly not the garden proper at all, and sighed.

With quiet rapture she gazed at the many trees, tall, full-crowned, seeming in some way more serene than other trees, protected as they were in this still park. It was, indeed, a park. She could see hothouses a good distance away. It seemed she could hear the rippling flow of water over stones.

"Is there water?" she asked curiously.

"A little brook, back in there. I'll take you in a while."

Theo, determined not to be awed by grandeur in the house, lost her heart to its beauty. The wide, low steps, the great white door with its delicate fanlight, the first glimpse of the lighted hall and the arching stairway. . . .

They went into a great room, carpeted with Orientals, deep colors winking in the lamplight. At the far end was Paul's Bechstein. Theo knew if she ran her finger across the open lid the dark mahogany would slip beneath her touch like silk.

As Mrs. Favor crossed the room, Paul murmured his introductions with nervousness and pride, grew silent.

Mrs. Favor, much taller than Theo, looked deeply into the lifted eyes of the girl Paul had fallen in love with so quickly. What she saw seemed to reassure her. No matter that she knew the right and proper course—losing first place with Paul would hurt. But this Theo, with her placid, pensive eyes, was a sharer, not a hoarder. There would be some part of Paul left for his mother. So Mrs. Favor thought.

"Hello, Theo."

"Hello, Mrs. Favor," Theo replied huskily, wondering whether it hurt very much to meet the woman your son loves.

"Come and sit with me, will you?" Mrs. Favor asked, gesturing to a scarlet chair. "Oh dear, perhaps you'd prefer a different chair . . . the color, you see."

Theo laughed. "I don't think I'd improve matters much anywhere else," she said, eying her crimson dress with its yellow sash. "My sister says I have a very odd color sense." And indeed, she looked a little wild, with hair like a jack-o'-lantern burning over the reds and yellows. Mrs. Favor and her son thought it was magnificent. They smiled at each other, at the splash of color in the scarlet chair.

So easily the restraint slipped away. They sat, three people rather sure of being friends, in a satisfied silence.

"Well," said Paul, rising, "anyone like a cocktail?"

Mrs. Favor and Theo nodded.

"I'll make them," Paul said. He lingered, gave them a slow smile of pleasure, strode away.

"He's leaving us alone, I presume," Mrs. Favor said.

"Has this . . . is this . . . ?" Theo began, and regarded Paul's mother with entreaty, not sure how to continue.

"You mean . . . sudden?"

"Yes," said the girl gratefully.

Mrs. Favor deliberated. "Well," she answered thoughtfully, "I certainly could not deny its suddenness, could I? As to whether I think it rash . . . I'm pretty sure that it will be safe now for me to say no. And then, Paul is almost thirty." She stared at the rug, lifted her eyes to Theo. "Don't you think a man should be married by the time he's thirty? It's a theory of mine."

Theo thought a man should, if by the time he was thirty he'd found someone he wished to marry.

"If he hasn't, the probability is that he never will. That's why I'm so pleased about Paul and you." Briefly, Mrs. Favor looked shy. "He's rather wonderful, isn't he?" she said, almost reluctantly.

Theo laughed. "I thought men like Paul occurred only in Jane Austen."

Mrs. Favor properly took this as a beautiful compliment.

"I'm glad you've come, my dear," she said warmly. "Will your family be able to come on Tuesday?"

"Nothing could keep them away."

"Isn't that nice . . . ? We'll see a good deal of each other, I hope."

"I hope so," Theo answered gravely.

"My poor brother, how he *would* love to get home. Will you and Paul be seeing him soon?"

"We thought after we'd had dinner tonight."

"That's very considerate of you, Theo."

Theo shook her head. "It's not at all. I like Mr. Coombes enormously."

He's certainly much taken by you," Mrs. Favor allowed. "I think you'll be good for us. Sometimes," she continued pensively, "this family strikes me as a little rarefied. . . ."

Paul came in with the cocktails in a silver shaker and the conversation slipped to generalities.

Theo, nestled in the brilliant chair, watching these two handsome people against their beautiful background, sipped her cocktail reflectively. Perhaps I'm making it all up, she thought. It really seems quite impossible that I should actually be in such a home, with these graceful drawing-room characters. Neither of them seemed quite real now—Mrs. Favor in her beautiful gray gown, Paul in his faultless flannels. It's all so . . . Quality. Her eyes drifted around the room to the piano again. That cost as much as all our furniture together, she thought wonderingly. And, as with Mrs. Bacon, she demanded, "Why?"

Why do these people have more than they could ever need or want, when Mrs. Bacon has nothing? Because, she thought, Mr. Coombes had a father who had a father who founded a bank. Mrs. Bacon had not. If it wasn't as simple as that, it was close. Mr. Armacost had a saying, "You can be comfortable by your own endeavor. You can only be wealthy by taking from someone else." Well, Paul was wealthy. He hadn't taken from someone else . . . yet. But he took what was taken. And what did she propose to do about it? Demand that he give it away? She couldn't help smiling. Refuse to marry him? Oh, nonsense . . .

"Paul," Mrs. Favor said, "play something, won't you? Theo is staring the piano out of countenance."

"Would you like that, Theo?" Paul asked gently.

How ridiculous I am, she thought. I can't do anything but marry him, because I love him. It wouldn't be easy to marry a man who was too poor, and it won't be easy to marry one who has too much. Only, since it's Paul, what else could I possibly do?

"Oh, please," she said, realizing they were waiting for her to speak. "Please, play. . . ."

Not easy, she repeated to herself, half listening to his somber music, half to her own sober thoughts. But surely every marriage is a risk to the weaker person. Between Paul and her, the strength was his. He was quiet, his attitudes were gentle, and he didn't array his thoughts for every eye. But in these few days Theo had encountered the stillest strength of will she'd ever known. Someday, she thought now with a slight smile, I'll call it bull-headedness. Then she thought, I'm being terribly prescient tonight, and it isn't intelligent of me.

The dreamy etude . . . splendid dark instrument, strong fingers on the glistening keys, vibrant in the luxuriant dusk.

Chopin, she mused, had many ideals, but Chopin drifted into society, fell in love, and died of one or both. What arrogance we have in our thoughts. . . . Here am I, comparing myself with Chopin. Here am I, too, sitting with Paul and his lovely mother, condemning them, wondering whether to marry Paul or not. How frightening it would be to know another's thoughts. Even those of the people you love . . . especially those. She remembered Emily Dickinson's prayerful relief that the mind was silent.

"Thank God the loudest place he made is licensed to be still. . . ."

I love you, Paul, she thought. There, you can listen to that, or I'll tell you so myself. I believe I'll love your mother. Theo lined her mind with tender thoughts, listening to the music of the lost and lonely Pole.

CHAPTER EIGHTEEN

COOPER ARRIVED at eight-thirty Sunday morning. He set a basket on the table in front of Mrs. Armacost, who had been wondering about sandwiches. Peanut butter and jelly, she'd been thinking. After all, no one wants to eat too much when it's hot. This wasn't very convincing reasoning, since Johnny's appetite remained at all times unimpaired by weather. Well, then, she went on, they'll just have to be satisfied. I'll make a lot of sandwiches and we'll take fruit and buy soda pop from Mr. Price. I don't see why a picnic shouldn't be fun for me too, she frowned. Then Cooper entered with the basket. Mrs. Armacost brightened. "What is that?" she asked hopefully, and was not disappointed.

"Ma thought you'd like a little extra food," Cooper explained.

Mrs. Armacost studied the proportions of the basket, hefted it, and smiled. "Oh, yes, a little extra is always welcome," she said, opening the lid.

Mrs. Maloney had apparently cooked for a Sunday school picnic, then sent it all along with Cooper. Or perhaps, Johnny's mother checked herself, she just meant for Cooper and John to eat it. However, she decided, this picnic is really going to be fun for me, because I'm not going to add a single thing except fruit. There was a huge thermos jug full of chicken salad, two dozen cinnamon buns, still warm, eighteen carefully wrapped thick sandwiches, a dozen boiled eggs. Also the always forgotten pepper and salt. Mrs. Armacost beamed at the basket, turned to Cooper.

"Really," she murmured, "your mother is the most amazing woman. I'll write her a little note and you can take it home this evening."

"Forget it, Mrs. Armacost," Cooper said, waving his hand. "Ma likes to do things like that."

"Wouldn't your mother and father like to come on the picnic?"

Cooper laughed. "Heck no. They don't like to do anything Sundays but sit on the side porch and rock. Pa reads the paper, and Ma fans herself, and every half hour they say something."

"Sounds very sensible to me," Mr. Armacost said, entering the kitchen, a little self-conscious in his duck trousers and white shirt open at the neck.

"You look nice," his wife said admiringly.

Mr. Armacost said, "Hmm." He was versatile with this sound, able to give it endless significance, whether or not there was any. This "hmm" didn't seem to mean anything in particular, but his wife, still thinking about the basket of food, smiled at him in a way so exhilarating that he decided to wear white ducks every Sunday.

"Cooper," Mrs. Armacost said, "run up for Johnny, will you, and ask him to help you pick some fruit from the garden. There's a good boy."

As Cooper went out, Anne came in, trying to look festive. "Morning, everybody," she greeted.

"See what Mrs. Maloney sent over," her mother invited.

Anne peered into the basket. "Good heavens, who's supposed to eat all that?" July jumped on the table, thrust a pink nose toward the provisions. Anne, looking around to be sure Johnny was absent, shoved her off. "Go climb a tree, July." She studied the cat lazily, adding, "Or have you already?" July lashed an expressive tail, turned lightly away.

"I'll get this stuff into the car," Mr. Armacost decided. "Where's Theo?"

"Last time I saw her, she was reading."

"That's a deplorable habit she has," Mr. Armacost disapproved. "Nobody should read anything except a newspaper in the morning."

"You do," his wife reminded him. "In school," she explained.

"Different world altogether." Her husband picked up the basket, looked around for more. "Isn't there anything else?"

"The boys are going to get some fruit. I am quite sure we won't need anything else," Mrs. Armacost emphasized.

"Has anybody got any rope?" Johnny inquired, coming in with Cooper.

"Not me," Anne said. "I reached the end of mine long ago."

"What do you want rope for?" Mrs. Armacost asked. Not waiting for a reply, she said, "If you'd rather not come, Anne, we'll understand."

Anne flushed. "Sorry, Mom. Sure I want to come." She walked around restlessly. "I'll get the fruit," she offered, taking the basket.

Mrs. Armacost sighed. How long, oh Lord, how long, she implored, looking after Anne. She turned to Johnny. "Rope for what, darling?"

"Well, you know that little island there, in the middle of the lake? Cooper and I figure we can tie a rope to the big tree, then walk up the bank and swing out over the water. If we had a rope."

"Is that safe?" Mrs. Armacost demanded of her husband.

"Sounds splendid," he replied enthusiastically. "Ought to be some in the basement, boys." The three of them rushed off to see, leaving Mrs. Armacost's question unanswered.

Paul offered to take the boys in his convertible with Theo, an offer accepted immediately by Cooper and Johnny, vetoed by Mrs. Armacost.

"For Pete's sake," Johnny grumbled, "it's only a ride in a car. They were alone last night, weren't they?"

"Johnny!" his mother warned.

"Well, I mean it," Johnny insisted. "Just because people are getting married, does it mean they have to skulk around avoiding people all the time? It's no wonder there're so many bachelors," he concluded cryptically.

Theo laughed. "Oh, let them come with us, Mom. Johnny might get a complex and wind up a bachelor himself, and that would be terrible."

Johnny, who privately considered any marriage (except that of his parents) an act of lunacy on the man's part, reserved comment, but allowed what he hoped was the expression of an incipient complex to contort his face.

Mr. Armacost shuddered. "Go, by all means," he surrendered.

Johnny's face smoothed. "Might as well get started right away, Paul," he said. "You can help Cooper and me get the rope tied." He herded the three others out, waving a hand of good-will toward his parents.

"What," demanded Mr. Armacost, "happened to all those 'sirs' he was lavishing on Theo's intended the other night?"

Mrs. Armacost's eyes wrinkled with amusement. "I do believe he was trying to help her. Now that the matter's settled he sees no reason for further formality. Is that rope thing going to be safe?"

"Of course. I think it'll be fun."

He watched Anne coming through the garden. Her hair was plaited in two thick braids, tied with blue ribbons. She walked beautifully. I believe, her father thought, that if she put that basket on her head it would balance perfectly . . . she has just the right gliding carriage for it. "Eve, with her dish of sweet berries and plums to eat . . . ," he murmured. Then, "Any young squirt who would hurt that girl ought to have his end paddled." He gave his glasses an angry shove, so that they slid down his nose. Righting them, he glared at his wife.

"Anne isn't without faults," Mrs. Armacost said gently.

"Of course not. No one is. But Anne's faults are charming. Just charming."

His wife turned away to hide her smile. She was sorry for Anne, and for Anne's father. She was also sorry for Doug Eamons. Children have such awkward feelings . . . all thrust and grab. I suppose it takes years, learning to advance easily, to retreat without leaving a mess behind. Some people never learn at all. But then, of course, when an adult behaves gauchely, he calls it candour. "Shall we go, dear?" she asked.

Anne sat in back with the baskets as they drove. This picnic was a hurdle, an ordeal . . . the final ordeal, Anne hoped. She hadn't been to Price's since Doug last took her, nor passed the Wellman house. For no reason that she could seize on, the idea persisted that if she could get through this day without crumpling under the weight of memories, she'd start to be all right again. Perhaps her mother's remark about youngness, or Nora's dismal life . . . or, perhaps her mind, less patient with wounds than a heart, had simply grown weary of wondering, waiting, hoping. She still drove her thoughts away from Doug, turned sickly from the memory of places they had shared, fled from the remembered sound of his voice saying, "Anne, I love you." She could herd her thoughts to other matters, to college, to Theo's marriage, but maintained the most tenuous safety from the reminders of her slow-to-learn heart. But now, she mused, I *want* to forget. Before, I was just torturing myself, always thinking back.

She sat straighter. Far down the road was the Wellman house, barely visible through the trees. They drew near. . . . Ivy over the Captain's Walk, birds nesting in eaves and crevices. As they passed, she saw a great yellow-winged butterfly fan through a broken window into the sunshine. She imagined the still, hot rooms, murky from curtains of leaves, dust-covered floors confusedly patterned by the feet of small marauders. She thought of the dark stairwell, with folded-winged bats hanging high. Johnny said the Wellman house would be delivered to the wreckers tomorrow. Anne felt it was an omen. Tear down the house, tear down the memory, tear down her love. She did not think how much more of memory, of age and ashed lives, of love and its fulfillment or loss, would go with those walls than her own brief structure of pleasure and pain.

Today, Price's was thickly strewn with bathers, loungers, picnickers. The Armacost family cleared, with difficulty, a space of sand for themselves, laid their old beach blanket, sun glasses, towels, down, left their basket in care of Mr. Price, who leaned on a calloused elbow cheerfully surveying his swarming beach, and prepared themselves for gaiety.

Paul, Johnny, and Cooper were already on the little island, which lay some five hundred feet from the shore. Though minuscule, it was dignified with a name: Tent Island. This because of its shape—fifty feet long, the banks on either side sloping up to a ridge at the top, it did look rather like a long, low pup tent. One tree grew on this island, so large that the requirements of its roots prevented any other tree from taking hold. Johnny, nonchalantly perched on a thick branch, was tying the rope as Mr. and Mrs. Armacost sat down on the sand with Anne. He looked, from this distance, amazingly agile, a bit simian, long legs wrapped around the bough, thin arms moving busily among the leaves.

As Mrs. Armacost had suspected, the branch to which Johnny was tying his rope stretched over the farther side of the island, so that she would have no way, other than swimming out, which she did not propose to do, of checking his activities.

Once again she inquired of her husband whether the rope would be safe. Once again he assured her it would, his enthusiasm, however, somewhat tempered by proximity. In the closeness of his kitchen, the picture of himself sailing Tarzan-like through the air at the end of a rope had had a wild appeal. During the ride he'd rather cooled toward the idea. Now it seemed preposterous. A dignified crawl to the island, a leisurely return . . . this was quite sufficient. No need to hurl myself about like Tom Sawyer, or that fun-loving Rover boy, whichever one it was. Thus he argued with himself, to such good effect that he never even got as far as the island that day.

The pleasant spectacle of people bathing was enough to occupy his time and attention. There is something about water, he decided, that evolves the common denominator. Possibly because it's difficult to have pretensions with so few clothes on. Of course, there is the danger of forgetting not only pretense but dignity, he observed, watching a few young couples more or less entwined on the sand. His eye moved on to more comely subjects. By the water's edge small children paddled, splashed, screamed, and laughed. A very absorbed little boy carefully constructed a series of canals and roads, toting pails of water to fill his waterways that immediately drained, crumbling walls which he painstakingly rebuilt. A father carried his wildly protesting small daughter into the lake, dunking her determinedly in spite of her anguished tears.

Mrs. Armacost frowned. "There is always a man like

that behind drownings," she said in a vexed tone. "She'll never like the water, just because of him, and someday she'll drown, and that will be because of him."

Mr. Armacost agreed in principle, but thought possibly she might escape drowning.

"You just wait and see," his wife replied ominously.

"All right," he agreed, continuing his study.

A short way out an old man bobbed through the water, employing a stately breast stroke. So old that he no longer fit his skin, which floated as he moved, he advanced in a placid manner through the wavelets, a smile of content- ment on his face, a hat, most amazingly, settled firmly on his head—a white canvas hat, with green inset eyeshade and an elastic band beneath the ancient chin to ensure its position. The back of the hat, Mr. Armacost observed with fascination, was wet in a ring that went halfway up the crown from the water sloshing over the swimmer's back. The front was quite dry, except for a few drops splashed on the eyeshade. Mr. Armacost, not removing his eyes from the sight, put a groping hand out to tap his wife's arm.

"Look," he murmured, "just look at that."

But Mrs. Armacost was watching the children. Reluc- tantly, Mr. Armacost transferred his attention. He gave a start of disapproval. "Say, what's the little wretch going to do?" he demanded, as a boy, perhaps a year older than the young canal digger, ran straight for the elaborate sand construction into which had gone so much loving labor. The running boy never hesitated. He crashed with destructive feet through the entire development of roads and gullies. As the smaller boy sat back in stunned dis- belief, the destroyer . . . laughed. The next move was so quick that only the Armacosts, who had been watching, caught it. The little boy hurled himself at his tormentor, throwing them both off balance. They rolled furiously in the sand, kicking and crying, sand shooting around them.

Abruptly, with the arrival of two enraged mothers, the battle ended. The older boy was dragged bellowing away. The small one, ignoring his mother, picked up a handful of wet sand, flung it squarely on the retreating back of his enemy. "Yah, ya dopey fat-head!" he screamed. The mothers exchanged narrow-eyed glares. For a moment Mr. Armacost thought *they'd* start rolling about in the sand, kicking each other. But they contented themselves with murderous stares. The little engineer was borne off to the comfort of ice cream, the other to some fate in which Mr. Armacost now lost interest.

"If it is true," he said thoughtfully, "that our characters are formed by the age of six, then it's no wonder the world is always at war." He returned to the more pleasant contemplation of the old gentleman swimming with his hat on.

Paul, coming toward them from Tent Island, crossed the path of the ancient paddler, who gave him a decorous nod. For a moment Paul simply blinked, then grinned broadly, bobbing his head in return. He ran up the beach, shaking water from his black hair and laughing. "This is really marvelous," he shouted, dropping beside Theo. "Did you see that old boy?" he went on in a lower tone, rubbing his head with a towel.

"I'm trying not to see anything else," Mr. Armacost replied.

"Paul, did you try that rope?" Mrs. Armacost asked anxiously.

"Oh sure, I took a swing on it. Perfectly safe, Mrs. Armacost. Those two are having a whale of a time."

They all looked toward the island, from which loud yells of heady delight rang over the water. Mrs. Armacost could see the white rope lift tautly and slowly up the farther slope, then snake swiftly out and up. Now and then she got a glimpse of flying arms or legs as Johnny or Cooper loosed his hold and hurtled lakeward.

"You're *sure*?" she insisted.

Paul nodded patiently. "Very sure. Aren't you going to try it?" he asked Mr. Armacost.

Theo's father shook his head. "On sober contemplation I've decided against it."

Paul grinned. "You're missing the opportunity of a lifetime." But Mr. Armacost was adamant. "Come on, Theo, you're due for a swim," Paul decided.

They waved and ran for the water. Theo, brilliantly trim and small in a flamingo bathing suit, streaked into the lake like a salmon. She and Paul swam side by side down to a grassy bank, where they pulled themselves out and sat, legs dangling, saying little, reflecting in their eyes and attitudes the words they didn't speak.

With incredulous surprise, Cooper and Johnny had watched Paul leave. One swing on the rope and off he went! They couldn't believe it.

"What's the matter with the guy?" Cooper asked, staring after the strong swimmer heading rapidly for the beach.

"Beats me," Johnny said, "unless he wants to get back to Theo."

"But she'll be there all the time." Cooper shook his head, abandoning hope for people who got engaged. "It sure takes the fun out of things," he said to Johnny, who nodded with understanding. "Well, come on. . . ." He grasped the end of the rope, backed up the slope as far as he could, ran down a few steps, and with a tremendous leap flung himself into the air. Unlike Johnny, he made no attempt to turn a sprawling projection into a dive. He waved through space like a starfish, seized his nose, plummeted into the water. A geyser rose where he fell.

Johnny, with instinctive precision of movement, released the rope on his upward arc at just the moment which would allow him to curve over into a dive. He cut into the water soundlessly.

"Oh, boy!" Cooper exulted. "Boy, was this a swell idea."

"Too bad we didn't think of it sooner," Johnny said regretfully.

"Yeah. Oh well, we can do it the rest of the summer and then start early next year."

Johnny soared away. Returning, he yelled to Cooper, "Hey, did that stuff from Easy's get to you yet?"

Cooper smote his forehead. "Holy cow. Forgot to tell you. Yeah, Pa picked it up on his way back from Wellman's. They start tearing down Wellman's tomorrow. Want to go watch?"

"Sure. Did . . . is the tool box good?"

"You oughta see it. One screwdriver's broke, and the keyhole saw needs blades. But it's good all right. I'll get it over to you tonight."

"No. Don't do that," Johnny said, sitting down. "Keep it at your place, huh? We'll work on it over there."

"Work on what?"

"Whatever we decide to make. Two-by-fours, okay?"

"Swell. What *are* we going to make?"

"Think we can get any more lumber from Wellman's?"

"Pa says he'll find us a few sticks . . . so I guess we can count on a bit of pretty good stuff. Got anything in mind?"

"Nothing special yet. I just think I'd like it better if we keep the tools at your house and worked on things over there. Think your folks would mind?"

"Heck no, why should they?"

Johnny, remembering his spurned cartoon, didn't reply. It isn't that they mean to be mean, he thought, his mind on his family. They just don't understand that you have to poke around before you decide what to do. I guess, he decided honestly, I poke around more than most.

"Cooper, do you ever give any thought to the future?"

"Whose future?"

"Your own, of course. What you'll be, or anything?"

"Nope. I let you do all that figuring, Johnny. The way I look at it, the future'll come along and then I'll take care of it."

Johnny shook his head. "You're wrong," he said earnestly. "Now's when you have to plan. You mean you aren't taking anything special in school?"

"Not a bit of it. Are you?"

Johnny had to admit he wasn't really specializing yet. "But this year I'm going to start. Darn it all, Cooper, you can't just drift. You gotta know where you're going."

"Tell you what, John my boy, whatever you take, I'll take." Cooper considered this a handsome offer which should end the subject, but Johnny persisted.

"Now look here, you can't take what I take. You give it thought, then decide what's best for your sort of personality, don't you see?"

Cooper didn't. "What's good enough for your personality's good enough for mine," he said. "You decide for both of us." He looked absently at a large log drifting along near the shore. "Come to think of it," he said, "I'd sort of like to be a logger, up around Hudson Bay, or wherever it is." He watched the log with growing interest. If it comes near enough, he decided, I'm going to get on and try a little log-rolling. The brown log swung in, turning gently, closer and closer. Then it nudged the shore, right in front of Cooper, who leaped to his feet and carefully stepped aboard. He didn't dare speak to Johnny. It took all his breath to balance at all. The pressure given by his touch sent the log slowly bobbing away from shore, and, at first, all went well as boy and boat set sail. In a moment however, feeling the log tip slightly beneath him, Cooper took a short step forward. The log rolled a bit, Cooper took another, quicker step. The log turned faster, Cooper moved quickly to keep his balance. Finally he was tearing along at breakneck speed, trying to keep up with the log, pitching and spinning beneath him.

Suddenly the log dipped under the surface, upended till it stood nearly straight, and fell, hitting Cooper on the side of his head.

Johnny, who'd been watching with delight, waited for Cooper to reappear. He thought perhaps they'd go after the log and try again. He waited. Then he sat up apprehensively, staring at the water. One second more and he plunged into the water, deep down. Cooper seemed to be lying at the bottom, not moving at all. With pumping heart, Johnny propelled himself through the resisting water. He hadn't taken a good breath before he dove and he felt like crying, or screaming. In his mind he shouted Cooper's name over and over. Still, his body urged forward, and then had a grip of Cooper's trunks. The pull to the surface was too long. Johnny knew he couldn't make it holding Cooper's limp and heavy body, trying to pump upward with just one arm. Everything in him seemed to be tearing apart, and the water moved like molten lead around them. Burst, burst! he shrieked in his mind and he thought the water flowed into it. Then, in a moment of final agony, Cooper's body lightened, moved, and together they sobbed into the air. Huge, broken gulps of air rushed into their lungs as they stumbled into the shallow water and fell trembling on the grass. Cooper got very very sick, leaning over the water, retching in spasms that shook his body.

After a while they lay back, shaking with fright and fatigue. And after many minutes had passed, they looked at each other. Johnny was crying a little, from nervousness. Cooper's eyes were still stunned, and one of them was rapidly turning color. Both were filled with the inexpressible love that comes from the knowledge of how great a loss can be.

"Johnny?"

"Yeah, Cooper. Don't . . ." Johnny swallowed, not knowing how to go on.

"Okay."

They stared over the lake, to the other shore.

"Cooper," Johnny said at length, his breath still coming gustily, "I don't think we better say anything about this. Might make people nervous."

"Yeah, but . . ."

"What?"

"Well," Cooper said slowly, trying to pick the words, "it sort of . . . sort of shows you're, ah, pretty strong, you know. And that's important to anybody," he hurried on. "Be something to . . . say, you know. Hauling a dead weight like me around." He grew silent, hoping he'd put it right.

Johnny smiled. He took a deep breath and blew it out. "Cooper," he said, rather dramatically, since it was a mental farewell to Thor Savage, "there's more than one way of being strong." He pumped up. The tension was more than either could stand. "Think you're ready to swim back?"

"Sure, if we take it easy."

"Well, let's go get something to eat, huh?"

"Okay."

Johnny was struck with a sudden thought. "How're we gonna explain that mouse?" he asked, indicating Cooper's eye. "It's turning color."

"Tell them a fish hung it on me," Cooper said. "Let's go."

When they got to Price's, Anne trailed her mother to the bathhouse, to the beach, saying nothing. She settled in the sand, a little in back of her parents and stared at the water. She didn't feel like staying, or going. She didn't feel like anything at all. I feel, she defined for herself, as if everything has lasted too long. The children's

217

scrap at the edge of the water escaped her notice. The old man swam slowly past in his canvas hat. Anne didn't see him. Her parents spoke unheard. But I'm going to have to do something about this, she told herself numbly. It simply can't go on forever. I have a life to live, and it just can't become meaningless when I'm seventeen. What will I do for the rest of it? Once again she felt a tremor of hostility. What right has he, what *right*, to mix up my life this way?

She rolled over on her stomach, scooped at the sand with one finger. Her mind moved restlessly, flicking at Doug. Doug testing the cellar stairs, turning his bright face up to her . . . Doug dancing with Dody . . . Doug kissing Anne in his car, late at night, and laughing . . .

If there was only some way to push through time, to shred it aside and get further away, get on with it . . . If I were in college now, she thought. If I were there, with a nice wool skirt, and some strange girl to talk to, a girl I'd like because I wouldn't know her . . . trotting down a corridor to someone's room, where we could sit and talk about things . . . filling up the time. Studying . . . things like anthropology. Oh dear heaven, if time would only move along. This summer has lasted forever. She dropped her head to her hands. Her breath flurried the sand in little cyclones.

Then, at a voice, she lifted her eyes. And saw Doug, with Dody.

Her hands and toes burrowed into the sand like little frantic animals clawing for escape. If her body could have followed, she'd have burrowed after, down and down. With bitterness and longing she stared at Dody beside him, privileged to stand where Anne no longer had a right to be.

He turned. Over the beach, over the people, over his long silence, their eyes met and held. Anne could see his throat move as he swallowed tightly, his mouth move, as though to speak. For this brief moment of communication there was a plea in his glance toward which she leaned as to an outstretched hand.

Then he swung away, and ran with Dody into the water.

Anne stared after them for a long time. Then she got up uncertainly, and without a word walked toward the rapids.

The rapids were above the beach. Leaving the sand, she stepped on a stretch of grass that led into a lane of trees. It wound lazily at the lake's edge, thickening till she could no longer see or hear the people on the beach. Here in the summer-drugged trees it was silent, except for the flicker of birds, their swift calls in the massed leaves, and the purl of water over stones.

She walked slowly, now and then putting out her hand to sweep aside a branch, till she reached a bit of grass beside the path of steppingstones that led to the center of the rapids. Huddled to the ground, without thought, she swayed to a pain that was part remembrance, part release. Her eyes were stinging, her throat ached, and, at length, there were no tears left to fall. Drained of emotion, she lay back and looked up the spiring slim trees to the leafy branches and the further blue, feeling oddly peaceful, almost slumbrous.

Well, this is the way it happens. You don't believe it, but it does. All this time, underneath all the ache, I've been thinking there'd be a day that he'd come back, a day when he'd explain, and it would be all right again. He isn't going to explain. He's never going to tell me one word of a reason. And he doesn't have to . . . because I know. He's afraid of me. He's worked too hard, he and his father, for him to go to college, and that's all he wants right now. So Dody was smarter than I was. I loved him too much, and he didn't love me enough, and neither of us knew what to say. . . .

So, she thought, getting up, walking carelessly over the steppingstones to the swirl of the rapids, I just go on from here, that's all. She sat down, holding tight to a great stone, letting the water's cool current pull at her body.

I wonder if there really is anyone named Finlay Arden Todhunter, who would dance with me, while I wore a white dress, close and sparkly and cloud-like. . . .

She thought perhaps there would be. Or someone like enough. Only it won't be Doug, she thought, listening as if to a faraway voice. It won't be Doug. And she knew there would never, anywhere in the world, anywhere in her life, never be anyone again like Doug.

With a little sigh, she released her hold and slid with the rapid waters down to the lake.

That evening, a hummingbird mistook Mr. Armacost for a trellis. Paul had gone home, driving Cooper. Mr. Armacost had gone into the garden. His wife, passing the window with a fruit-stained basket, glanced out. Then she called softly to the other three.

"Come here," she whispered, gesturing toward the garden. "Look . . ."

A concerted sigh of triumph rose as they watched Mr. Armacost crouched immobile among the blossoms, while the hummingbird, gleaming and darting, suspended in air, drank from the flower in his outstretched hand.